MW01242897

Ronald J Blunt

Nov. 23, 1998

The Smoking Gun

Ronald L. Blunt

The Smoking Gun

LEATHERS   PUBLISHING
4500 College Blvd., Leawood, KS 66211 — 1 / 888 / 888-7696

PUBLISHED BY LEATHERS PUBLISHING
4500 College Blvd.
Leawood, KS 66211
Phone: 1 / 888 / 888-7696

ISBN: 1-890622-36-2

Library of Congress Catalog No. 98-066617

The Smoking Gun

Dedication

To my wife,
who is part of everything I do.

One

BEN WINN could see his breath as he stepped out of the van. He looked at what was supposed to be the edge of Main Street to ensure he found the best footing on the ice covered surface. Each side of the wide street was piled high with snow.

In February every four years this was the most important town in the country, even though fewer than 20,000 people lived here. In the decades that the national media had been coming, the town never changed. All of the principal business establishments were lined up on each side of Main Street. Except for those using the parking lot to the side of McDaniels

Grocery—and if they were not in the grocery store spending money, McDaniels' grandson, who now ran the store, would see to it that they were towed—everyone doing business here parked at an angle on Main Street. There were no sidewalks to maintain. Each establishment was responsible for its own store front. Some had poured concrete, others had let the usually frozen tundra between their building and the asphalt of the street fuse together from the constant walking traffic. If they were around when the highway department, who maintained the city streets by contract, came through, they might even get some extra asphalt thrown their way to make a sidewalk of sorts from the street to their door. This town knew little of zoning ordinances. There was a wide array of signs. The TrueValue Hardware store had the largest neon display, although the light bulbs were now out on both the "T" and the "V" and had been for as long as anyone could remember. Harry's Barber Shop had a candy-striped pole of red and white that the children in the town had long since learned was deceiving. And the Diner had its famous wooden Indian, called "Tonto" by the locals, that had been either photographed or filmed by every major news organization in the world.

Accompanied by his entourage of four people who were getting their marching papers from Jack Savage, Winn pulled the gray wool overcoat together, not buttoning it, but holding it with his hands as he followed the youngest of the group, Bill Stevens, a young Harvard graduate, into the Diner.

As he approached the counter covered in green formica, the short old man wearing a greasy cook's apron that was once white came towards him. Sticking out his hand and letting the overcoat fall open, he spoke the words that everyone in the Diner knew, including George Washington Jones who wiped his hands on the apron, a ritual he repeated countless times every day.

"Mr. Jones, I'm Ben Winn, and I'm running for President." The television cameras that had been waiting for him at the Diner were crowding in for better shots, as Winn's entourage shuffled to find that happy medium between room for their candidate to work and the most free media coverage possible.

George Washington Jones had turned 73 years old in December. He had been running the Diner in Bellville, New Hampshire, for as long as anyone alive could remember. There were two maxims written about and discussed repeatedly in this town and, for one month every four years, all across the United States. No Republican had won the party's nomination for President of the United States since Tom Dewey in 1944 who did not carry the Bellville Township in the New Hampshire Primary, and no Republican had won the Bellville Township as far as anyone could remember who did not start his campaign effort by introducing himself to George Washington Jones and his customers.

"So why do ya want to be President?" asked Jones, smiling for the cameras as he exposed the absence of two more teeth than he had missing four years ago. Jones had intended to get false teeth before the onslaught of politicians and newsmen this year, but time got away from him. The question he posed to Winn was the one the news people came to expect as the first out of his mouth every four years.

"Because I need a steady job," said Andrew Benjamin Winn, the Senator from Texas, smiling.

"We got a lot of people up here with the same problem, Senator," responded Jones with his homespun wit.

"We've got that problem all over this country, Mr. Jones. I intend to put this economy back in business, and business is what puts people back to work." Winn smiled for the cameras as he and Jones let loose of their handshake for the first time.

Winn began moving down the row of stools on the customer side of the counter shaking hands with the all white male crowd, mostly over 50 years of age, who came to the Diner for coffee and breakfast every morning during the Primary; some came frequently during the remainder of every four years as well. "I hope I can count on your vote," said Winn to each, alternating his line occasionally with different words that accomplished the same purpose. New Hampshire was the only part of the country where you did not vote for a presidential candidate unless you had personally shaken his hand. Usually the local folks ended up shaking hands with just about every candidate and then, by whatever standards they used, picked one from whichever party primary they voted in.

It made no sense to anyone why New Hampshire got to play this important role in the presidential selection process. Polling information showed that they did not have much in common with most of America—they were more religious, less educated, more eccentric, less worldly and, simply, more or less different than most other Americans. Lying on the Canadian border between Maine and Vermont, New Hampshire did not even represent the people of New England. Its one million people, which comprise less than one-half percent of the United States population, live in largely rural surroundings in a state where over three-fourths of its territory is covered with forests. New Hampshire is the only state in the Union that has neither an income tax nor a sales tax. Yet every four years the voters of New Hampshire speak for the entire nation.

Skirmishes had always existed at the national party committee meetings led by states desiring an earlier election contest than the New Hampshire Primary. The rules were bent enough that a few states were allowed caucuses, a vote of electors chosen by the state party, or "straw polls," a vote of residents and non-residents alike who are interested. But no one had been approved for a vote of the general populous prior to the New Hampshire Primary. In spite of all the complaining about how unrepresentative it was, the event worked well for the parties, the candidates, and the media. It allowed them to focus their efforts and resources in a small concentrated area until the field could be reduced to a more manageable number. Thus, like most traditions, it had more practical than philosophical roots.

"So, Senator, do you think you've earned the job, or do you think you're just the sentimental favorite because you're a national hero and all?"

Winn turned and saw the face of Henry Rothstein emerging

from the bright hand-held lights being used by the camera crews. Winn questioned why Rothstein was the best that CNN had to put on his campaign. His cynicism and quest for the sensational had, however, made him a household name, one of the "media celebrities," and from the news director's point of view his assignment of Rothstein to the Winn campaign was a statement that CNN believed Winn would be there at the finish line; the finish line was where CNN wanted its ace political reporter to be.

Jack Savage, as campaign manager, had drilled them all on this question. It would come because it was one of the few places Winn could be attacked. It was the place where Savage would attack if he were on the other side. Winn had all the right credentials, had paid his dues, and except for an occasional personal indiscretion, he was a dream candidate for the White House. He was also a hero, made so by the media over his efforts in defeating the now infamous "Red Surprise." What the media built, however, the media had to tear apart. This approach sold papers and attracted viewers. It was the way of the world, and nothing new to anyone who had been in the business as long as either Winn or Savage. Savage intended, however, to use "Red Surprise" for the strength that it was, not to let the media turn it into a flaw. It was, after all, the wave they had ridden to this point.

"Henry, so you got the short end of the stick, huh?" asked Winn, teasing him about his assignment. This was the first day Winn had hit the trail as an announced candidate. Savage had orchestrated the victory in the Iowa caucus with Winn still maintaining the public posture that he was not interested in the job. Two days ago in San Antonio, his home town, Winn announced he was answering the call from the voters of the Iowa caucus, a sentiment that seemed, according to the polls, to be shared throughout America. Savage had a package for each reporter of data from several pollsters supporting this conclusion; the package also contained prepared background materials, including black and white glossy photos that Savage preferred over anything in the media files, and an official media release on the announcement. Winn entered the race eight days before the New Hampshire Primary, even though Savage had ensured months ago that Winn's name would be on the ballot in New Hampshire.

"You should take that as a compliment, Senator," said Rothstein without modesty. "Do you think you should be elected because of your role in defeating the Russians?"

"What kind of question is that, Henry?" Winn tried to keep his composure, smiling, not wanting his annoyance to come through. As soon as he said the words, however, he wanted to take them back. There was no need to offend a major network correspondent when this guy was going to be in his face, reporting his campaign to the public, for the next ten months. "I know it's not your question, Henry, but one that you are repeating from the opposition camp."

Winn stepped forward, next to one of the several metal tables covered with plastic tablecloths that were crammed into the Diner. There were people sitting at each table, all of whom had come for the free show and to shake the hand of the next President of the United States. The camera crews pushed in, with each camera bobbing and weaving to make sure it had an unobstructed view for a close-up of Winn. A crewman holding an electric spotlight for NBC knocked over a cup of coffee on one of the tables. He glared for a moment at the local man who was wiping coffee off of his overalls. The crewman's look was one of inconvenience, irritated that the man having breakfast was in his way.

"Henry, over the next ten months you will never hear me talk about 'Red Surprise,' " said Winn, looking into the camera rather than at the reporter. This statement was farther than Savage would be happy with; never say never in politics—Savage wondered why politicians could not learn this lesson. But Winn felt it a safe overstatement to emphasize his point. "I'm running for President because I'm tired of inept government intrusion on our lives; I'm tired of paying taxes so that one more government agency can be created to attack hard working Americans trying to make a living and raise a family; I'm tired of a government bureaucracy that grows like some uncontrollable virus ..."

"Senator, haven't you spent the last 15 years as a part of that system?" Rothstein was like a bulldog. He would take any side of an argument and pursue his premises with indignation and righteousness. "For example, didn't you sponsor the bill to create the ...."

This time Winn politely cut him off, before Rothstein could talk about the Department of Domestic Welfare. This spiraling bureaucracy had seemed like such an enlightened goal when Winn was still an unabashed liberal trying to do for the people what they could not be trusted to do for themselves.

"Henry, I helped create some of these problems, yes. And, I am proud of the goals we were trying to accomplish. But, like many Americans I learned from the tragic 'liberal experiment.' Spending more tax dollars is not always a solution. More often than not, the best way to fix something is to get the government completely out of it. Look at how cheap gasoline is at the service station; thank Reagan for deregulation in the 1980s. Look at how much you pay in taxes for health care—care that usually isn't worth paying anything for—thank, or maybe I should say blame, Clinton for nationalizing health care in the 1990s. In this learning process, I discovered that the Democratic Party and their solutions were more often than not only good intentions that would create new problems. I served as a Democratic Congressman for 12 years. But when I ran for the Senate two years ago, I did so as a Republican. I am now running for President as a Republican. I want to fix problems, by giving people a chance to fix them themselves. I believe this is what the Republican Party stands for." Winn smiled into the camera, but then in a pause that he knew would end up on the cutting room floor, he let his "politician's gaze" wander around the crowd to see which local Bellville Republican dignitaries might be in the Diner. Bill Stevens had given him a list of whom to be prepared for, and Stevens would ensure that Winn shook all the right hands before leaving.

"So how about the question, Senator?" Rothstein was like a shark, momentarily distracted by the smell of blood in another direction, but after charging in and exhausting that source, he was back on the original scent. Rothstein was one of the new breed of media celebrities that went to the highest bidder. He had started with CBS as a reporter for its famed *60 Minutes*. Too good to play a bit part there, but not good enough to unseat his predecessors, he had accepted an offer by NBC to become their chief White House correspondent. He was now in his second contract with CNN as their chief political correspondent. This was the final year of his contract, and he intended to stay at CNN only if a new record offer was put on the table. He knew that to get a record offer he had to make news, not simply report it.

"Henry," started Winn, looking into the camera to create the intimacy with the viewer that is required for political success, "I am certainly not going to act ashamed of my involvement in defending this country from a nuclear attack by unchecked totalitarian power. I'm proud of it. To some, maybe my role in that crisis alone doesn't qualify me to be President—but my record of public service is longer than most running in this election. God knows I grew a great deal during the Russian ordeal and learned much about how governmental power operates and what motivates it. I learned what too much centralized power can lead to, and I learned that this country should never forget that its number one obligation is to defend this democracy from forces without." Winn paused, then continued. "But I'm no hero. I did what any other American would have done in my shoes." To the contrary, Winn knew he was a national hero and, while he was running for his life, he had done what few Americans could have done during the Russian challenge.

Winn paused briefly, still looking into the camera as if he were talking to a dear friend who wanted advice on some personal tragedy. After giving the film enough footage to end with sincerity, Winn briefly turned his eyes to Stevens, a movement that only the politically astute would comprehend.

"Thank you, ladies and gentlemen," said Stevens as he stepped between Winn and the cameras, raising his arms as if to signal a touchdown, but in reality blocking the view so that the cameramen would disengage. "The Senator is on a tight schedule here and we must keep him moving. Please feel free to film him, but we will need you to hold all questions until the media conference we are having at the Holiday Inn in Manchester at 3 p.m. It's on your schedules." Savage planned on holding a mid-afternoon media conference every day until the New Hampshire Primary. The local television stations from Manchester and Dover, as well as the nearby stations in Albany and Boston, would follow the campaign around the state and eat up anything the campaign put out. Media releases would be issued later on most days so the print media would not be offended; they would be given their own stories that first came to the attention of the public in their morning headlines. The polls showed that voters were still influenced tremendously by what they read in the newspapers and by whom the newspapers endorsed. The Manchester Union remained as influential as ever throughout the Merrimack Valley.

Rothstein made some notes in the 3 x 5-inch spiral pad he carried. He was used to being cut off, but he knew he would get plenty of access over the next few months. They needed him as much as he needed them. He would raise the general theme in his background voice-over on the news tonight. He intended to push the theme until the whole country doubted what the pundits considered a sure thing at the moment. Once Rothstein had Winn bleeding, he would help create the miracle bandage, because it was in both of their interest for Winn to cross the finish line first. Rothstein was 54 years old, an age where most reporters are moved to the side or into the off-camera jobs at the studio. With a constitution that thrived on one-niters with cheeseburgers and bourbon for dinner, the tall, lanky Lincolnesqe man was in his prime. In spite of the obvious contradiction in positions he sometimes pursued, his intensity appealed to the viewers as sincerity. Having been divorced twice, leaving with no emotional ties to the children of either marriage, this is what Rothstein lived for. If he was not covering politics with a camera behind him and a deadline ahead, then he would not be living.

As Stevens talked to the press, Arnie Walker lightly touched Winn on the arm, guiding him toward one of the tables, whispering the name "John Ferguson" into his ear. Arnie was a young lawyer—Winn liked to hire young lawyers even though he had an MBA—who had worked for almost a year in the Senate for Winn. At Savage's invitation, Walker had left the security of the government payroll for the excitement of a presidential campaign. He was a gofer, often a driver, someone who remembered the little things so Winn did not have to be bothered by them—but he thought he was working for the next President of the United States. He could not fathom what job he would end up with in the White House, but any job in the White House would do.

"John," said Winn with a broad smile as he extended his hand to the man now getting up from one of the tables. "Don't stand up. I'm really glad you could make it." Winn shook Ferguson's hand solidly, an important political tenant, and then gripped Ferguson's hand with both of his own, holding the pose steady as he made solid eye contact with the Chairman of the Bellville Township Republican Party. He reserved the double handshake for pronounced sincerity; it had an impact on the media who accepted that pictures of such handshakes underscored particularly important events. Everyone watching the news in Bellville that night would be certain that Ferguson was an early and strong Winn supporter. Many people in the Township did not need a better reason to swing their support to a candidate.

"I would not miss it, Senator," said Ferguson, "or should I get used to 'Mr. President.' "

"You better call me 'Ben' like you always have, John." Winn

had only met Ferguson once, when he worked the Republican National Committee meeting last fall. The people sitting at the table with Ferguson and others looking on would never guess that, however, and they certainly would never be told. Ferguson was sure that Winn was going to be the next President of the United States. It served both of their interests for it to appear they were old friends.

"We will not have a problem in Bellville, Ben. Not next Tuesday, not in November. Hardy is no friend of the working man, and the folks around here are astute enough to have figured that out." Randall Hardy was the favorite for the Democratic nomination. Ferguson did not think the competition in the Republican Primary significant enough to talk about.

"I know you can do it, John. But, let's don't look past the next game. Daily and Lorenzen are not going to just lay down and concede," said Winn reminding the group of the Republicans in the contest.

"They would if they knew what was good for them," said Ferguson laughing. Winn smiled as he patted Ferguson on the shoulder; it was a sign that Savage had told Arnie Walker to watch for. The others laughed with Winn and Ferguson, wanting to be insiders.

"Senator, I'm sorry, but we are getting behind schedule," said Walker quietly, but so those nearby could overhear.

"OK, Arnie," responded Winn with a look and tone of disappointment. Looking back to Ferguson and his group, he continued, "There is just not enough time. Stick with us; we can only do this with your help." Winn shook Ferguson's hand again and then the others around the table. He would have his hands and feet massaged frequently; they would still begin to look swollen and reddish before this campaign was over.

Finishing his instructions to the media about where Winn was heading and where they could get the best shots—it was all written down but you could not rely on these guys to do their homework—Stevens returned to Winn's side and began to usher him toward the front door of the Diner. Winn exchanged smiles and handshakes with other occupants of the Diner as they headed towards the exit, giving Stevens an occasional look of annoyance and exasperation. Stevens knew he was doing exactly what Winn wanted, but it was important to leave the voters with the impression that Winn did not want to leave them, that he was being forced out the door by these young men in suits and ties.

Savage had personally selected Stevens to be the Media Director who would travel with the candidate throughout the campaign. An Assistant Media Director would be at the "War Room" with Savage in Alexandria, Virginia. Stevens was not a likely candidate for the job, but Winn did not question Savage. Winn knew that a good candidate, a winning candidate, would pick a good campaign manager and then do what the campaign manager told him to do. He was sure he had picked the best campaign manager in the business.

Stevens was a youthful 26-year-old with longish, but politically acceptable, dark hair that covered the tops of his ears and often hung down into his eyes; Stevens was constantly pushing his hair back. It would become a joke on the campaign, and he would be continuously offered by the other campaign workers everything from axle grease to bee's wax to slick his hair back. Stevens was almost short at five feet, eight inches, with a trim build of 150 pounds. His boyish looks and large dark eyes conveyed sincerity, giving him almost instant credibility with the media. A graduate of Harvard law school, Stevens had worked as the communications director for a small congressional campaign in Connecticut that used Savage as a consultant. Savage was good at spotting talent that carried little or no political baggage from their campaign trails. Stevens was perfect.

As the entourage walked back into the cold, Winn blew "smoke" into the air as he pulled his overcoat back together in front and joked to the media people about the weather. The camera lights were now obscured by the bright sunlight that glistened on the snow, but Winn knew the cameras were still rolling. He would be "on the air" all day and would remember not to let his guard down. Andrew Benjamin Winn was 43 years old, a political star, and the darling of the media. While they did not like his new conservative politics, the media was enchanted with his humor and wit. He was fun to be around and always made good copy. The Senator from Texas was smart, clever, and handsome—any two of which would usually ensure some political success. He was now rich, and money, wisely used, was the ingredient that could overcome all negatives in politics.

Winn reached out his hand to "Tonto," saying, "My name is Kemosabe and I'm running for President." The media laughed. No one would use these bits of entertainment inappropriately unless they were willing to be cut off from access. Lack of access was death to any media person. As Stevens pointed to the door being opened by Arnie Walker, Winn walked into the barber shop next door to the Diner where he would have another "spontaneous" encounter with the voters that had been prearranged right down to the furniture being moved around so the media could fit in the area that usually contained chairs where the locals sat while waiting for Harry, who cut all of the male heads of hair over age ten in the town.

HE STOPPED CHANNEL SURFING when he hit CNN and saw the face of Winn on the screen. He turned up the sound that had been muted while they made love and heard the recognizable voice of Henry Rothstein in the background.

"There is your man, babe," he said to the woman lying next to him clothed only by the black sheet from his king-sized bed.

"Change the channel," she said, rolling her eyes away from the television. "Find something interesting like Geraldo," she added sarcastically.

Anthony Baroni looked at his lover and smiled. She was physically attractive, but not beautiful. She was a bit too tall at five feet, nine, and a bit too big at 145 pounds. But she carried herself with the pomp and circumstance of the rich powerful heiress she was, and money and power make intensely sensual and wildly attractive what would otherwise be an average-looking person. With her short brown hair and one facelift, she tried to hide her age of 39 years. She hated it that Winn looked younger than she, even though he was four years older.

"So where are we going to fuck when you're the First Lady?" asked Baroni, while laughing and turning up the sound on CNN so it could not be avoided. Baroni was a lawyer who worked in a small firm that did more lobbying than legal work. He was successful even by Washington, D.C. standards, earning over $500,000 a year. He had some of the biggest industrial clients in the country. He got them laid when they were in Washington and made them think he was getting legislation affecting them in the best possible condition to protect their interest. At 35, Baroni lived life to the fullest. He was fond of the ladies and liked to romance them in exotic places. He would never tie himself down to one relationship, nor would he ever have a relationship that was based on much more than sex and pleasure. He had met Andria Hamilton Winn at a cocktail party with her husband. She had given him the "look," and he brashly called her on the telephone the next day to say he had roses and champagne that had been inadvertently delivered for her at his DuPont Circle condo. She laughed at his boldness and agreed to meet him for lunch. She had met him frequently during the six months since, often spending the night. Her husband was always traveling and did not care enough to be concerned anyway. He almost never called at night and, if he did, readily accepted her excuses for not being home.

"Turn it off, Tony. I hate that son of a bitch and I don't want to deal with him here." She was spoiled and used to being the center of attention; Daddy had taught her no other way. Winn's profession required that she fit into his life, a life where the spotlight stayed on him. She liked the power and notoriety, but she could get both with her money; it did not require politics. She was enchanted with the idea of being First Lady, but she could not conceive of living much longer with Winn. She was in love with Baroni. He liked to have fun and he gave her constant attention. Who needed the White House? She could buy Baroni any house in the world.

"OK, baby," Baroni said affectionately as he clicked off the television. He did not love her any more than he loved any woman, but her money and her marriage to a U.S. Senator made her a great conquest. Her husband might be the next President of the United States. The thought of "fucking" the President's wife caused a thickness to return to his groin, even though they just had sex. He would always see other women too, but this was a special victory, and he was willing to put in the extra time required.

"Why does he make you so unhappy?" Baroni asked as he snuggled his naked body up against hers, separated only by the sheet. He stroked her hair affectionately. "You must leave him, baby. This is too special to keep it a secret." He meant nothing that he said. It was a game. He wanted her to say yes to his constant proposals, but he did not want them to be fulfilled. He wanted to be "fucking" the President's wife and have the First Lady blindly in love with him.

She thought he was so sweet. At first she had wondered why Winn could not love her the way Baroni did. Now she only thought of Baroni and was tired of the inconvenience that Winn was imposing on her life.

"I love you, Tony," she said as she bent her head down and kissed his cheek. "Life is so complex." She paused, then added, "But I want to live it with you."

He smiled.

Two

"**W**HAT ARE THE NUMBERS, Jerry?" asked Jack Savage as he leaned back in the out-of-style arm chair in the Manchester Holiday Inn. This would be the field headquarters until the election next Tuesday. Savage would spend the rest of the campaign away from the candidate in the War Room in the upstairs suite of offices on King Street in Alexandria. He was determined to be here during this week, however. New Hampshire was like no other State. There were two campaigns to mount in New Hampshire. One was for the national media. Savage would be setting the stage, the framework within which the media would report the campaign over the next eight months. Once this framework was established, the campaign would plow through the other States with its paid media campaign and the candidate hitting the high spots for photo-opportunities aimed at the free media.

There was, however, a second campaign in New Hampshire. It was the same whether you were running a presidential campaign or a race for one of the 424 seats in the state legislature. This campaign required constant personal attention by the candidate to the local voters. They joked about how many more hands Winn had to shake before he had shaken the hand of every registered Republican in the State. Savage would be in New Hampshire to direct both campaigns.

"It's incredible, Jack. Before he announced, 'Our Man' led in the New Hampshire polls with 35%. Daily had 29% and Lorenzen brought in 15%; 21% were undecided. I never worked on a campaign that was won before the candidate entered the race. Yesterday, the undecided rocketed to 'Our Man,' who now has 57%. He has picked up five points off Daily and six points off Lorenzen. If the election were today, Daily would get 23% of the vote and Lorenzen would get less than 10%. Only 10% of the people are still undecided." Savage usually did not allow long-winded explanations. There was not time for patience in a political campaign. Jerry Swords lived and breathed the numbers, however, and Savage knew he had to let the pollster wallow in the results a little. It's what kept Swords motivated. Savage did not believe Swords had a clue about how to move the numbers, but he was an expert at reading them.

As Savage turned to another campaign worker in the room, Swords knew he was dismissed. Savage operated with a brisk style that was accepted only because all recognized his brilliance and knew he would deliver them to the promised land. Swords would be doing tracking polls in New Hampshire each day until the election was over. During the week he would also run a national poll and a poll in the 16 southern states that would vote on Super Tuesday, where the campaign would move next.

"Mary, call Hoffman and tell him I want the Down Home Spot running right after the news tonight." All of their paid media would be focused on New Hampshire this week; all of the time slots had already been booked and paid for. Savage decided the campaign would lose its "reluctant spontaneity" if they were running anywhere else until the New Hampshire voters had spoken with the loud voice they were given by the national media. The "Down Home Spot" was a 90-second commercial canned months ago on location in New Hampshire, with Winn walking the countryside, contemplating the fate of the world, with locals spliced in expressing their support. It was hokey, with inspirational John Philip Sousa music in the background. It was perfect. It was designed to fit in with Winn's first day of campaigning in New Hampshire. Viewers would accept the footage and voter praise as being contemporaneous with Winn's announcement and arrival in New Hampshire. Only a close observer would notice that no snow was on the ground. No one could tell that Winn was burning up in his overcoat when they filmed the commercial. Besides, there was neither the time nor, in the early days of the campaign, the desire for the media to bash Winn. There would always be oddballs, like Rothstein for CNN, but Savage figured the honeymoon would last at least through Super Tuesday.

The hotel was a dump, which Savage continued to point out to everyone and to no one. It seldom was more than a third occupied, although in February every four years you need not stop if you had not made reservations months in advance. Savage had directed the reservation of several rooms. The headquarters was a room adjoining the bedroom where Savage would go for privacy and, occasionally, a few minutes of sleep. The two rooms were identical with wallpaper that would almost qualify for art deco, but was simply old and out of date. Savage's bedroom had two Early American double beds and a matching chest of drawers. The beds had been removed from the other room and replaced with two long tables and folding chairs, and a collection of three unmatched overstuffed chairs grouped around a coffee table where Savage held court. Both tables were lined with phones, each operated by one of the young volunteers that had been bused in from Washington, D.C. Local young Republicans were being used at Savage's insistence, but they were not involved in this operation. Most were on the street handing out campaign literature.

Savage held up his styrofoam cup, which was dutifully taken by one of the volunteers, filled with hot, black coffee and returned to the field general. Savage sipped the coffee, then made an ugly face as the bitter, strong taste registered with his taste buds.

"How the hell can we win a campaign, if we can't make coffee?" he bellowed to no one in particular. The young volunteer who had brewed the pot blushed; she had never made coffee before, but thought she had followed the instructions on the Folgers can correctly.

Jack Savage was 38 years old, young to be running a presidential campaign, particularly one that might succeed. He was an enigma. He was tall and dark, if not handsome, built like an athlete except for the slight middle-age bulge around his waist. He ate and drank whatever he liked, which was anything fried or with sugar, washing it down with lots of coffee and Pepsi. He slept little, and if he complained, he then was reminded of the quantity of caffeine he consumed on a daily basis. Savage could clean up well, but unless he was doing one of his rare appearances at a formal political event or a network interview, he wore blue jeans, a pair of old brown Bally loafers, and a long-sleeve shirt with the sleeves rolled up.

Jack Savage graduated first in his class from the University of Missouri law school. During his third year, he ran a successful campaign for a young candidate for Lieutenant Governor. He achieved some national recognition two years later, when he put the young Lieutenant Governor in the U.S. Senate. He had worked on one election every two years since; each campaign was a winner. He had sought out Winn and offered his services in Texas, if Winn would run for the Senate. Neither talked about the possibility of a presidential campaign to follow, but both were thinking about it at the time. For over a year, most of the pundits predicted that Winn would run for President; many used as one of their reasons the fact that Savage had refused to sign up with any of the announced presidential contenders. A presidential race was about all Savage had not accomplished in his brief but dramatic political career. The onlookers predicted early that Savage would not set out this presidential race and that he had already picked Winn as his candidate.

Winn and Savage worked well together. Both were extremely intelligent and, thus, each recognized that quality in the other. They let each other do their jobs, and they had confidence that each would do it well.

"Where is Daily's itinerary?" barked Savage as he picked up Lorenzen's schedule. He had people on the inside at each campaign that funneled out information; it was good politics and if you did not do it, you were not doing your job.

"Here," said Mary Ellen Barker as she handed him the one-page sheet that had been faxed directly from the Daily campaign office. "Floyd should have given it to you." Mary Ellen Barker was a 23-year-old shapely blond who wanted to emerge as Savage's right hand. She did not mind if she reached that spot by stepping on someone else—in fact, she would probably enjoy her ascension more if it were accompanied by someone else's downfall. She would be happy to have sex with Savage as part of her career move, but so far he had ignored all of her advances.

Savage perused each itinerary to see if he had missed anything while he contemplated the opposition's strategy. There was a candidate's forum at noon at the Concord Rotary. All three candidates would be there; Savage had no problem in arranging the last-minute appearance of Winn at the forum. Both of the opposition candidates were still running the conventional campaigns that would have been expected without Winn in the race; that is, lots of main street stumping. Savage had given a great deal of thought to what he would do if he were running against Winn. Good politics was like any other competition; you had to anticipate your opponent's strategy. Good defense won as many elections as good offense.

"It's Nina Steinberg of NPR," said Barker as she held up the receiver of a phone with the hold button flashing. "She says it's important and she will talk only to you."

Savage reached out his hand without saying anything, and Barker walked from the table carrying one of the phones with a long wall cord. He usually would not let the media control him, seldom taking a reporter's call the first time around. That was what he paid Bill Stevens for. This day was different, however; both Daily and Lorenzen had to be prepared for Winn to enter the race, and both had to be ready to take their best shot. The election was only one week away.

"Nina, are you up here freezing your ass off?" asked Savage as he picked up the phone. He despised Steinberg; she despised him. She was the quintessential liberal reporter, slanting everything she did with her liberal political bias that assumed that people could do nothing for themselves, and the government's job was to take from the rich and give to the poor. Steinberg was, of course, rich, all money made by her father in the publishing business, and she made no efforts to turn her inheritance over to the public. A common double standard according to Savage's way of thinking. Second and third generation rich kids always were the worst, wearing their elitism on their sleeve, while protesting that they were merely identifying and protecting the less fortunate.

Steinberg ignored Savage's question. "Look, Jack, I'm going on the air at noon with a New Hampshire summary, and I'm getting hit everywhere about Winn's affair with some young black female lawyer in Washington."

"That's odd, Nina, since you're the first person I know to come up with this fiction." Savage had expected this to be an early salvo, probably pushed by the Daily people. Daily was from the bowels of the Detroit political machine, and mud slinging, with hints of racial innuendo where possible, was a mainstay of Michigan politics.

"I'm going to have to go with this, Jack. So if you've got something more intelligent to say, don't protest later that I didn't give you a chance." Savage knew she would like nothing better than to report her story and end it with the damning "the Winn campaign was contacted but refused to comment."

"What's your point, Nina?" It was classic, but Savage never got used to it, never allowed it to pass without his veins swelling up and his blood pressure rising. These type liberals were the biggest bigots of all; she would push her agenda by trying to smear Winn with the white voters.

"Winn is big on family values ...."

"Winn never says shit about family values," shouted Savage, cutting her off. "Are you going to report this mystery woman's height and hair color, or just the color of her skin?" The sarcasm was dripping off his voice. There was silence, during which Steinberg considered whether she was being recorded.

"I just report the news, Savage," she said, using his last name for the first time, one she felt aptly described this conservative Neanderthal.

"For the record, Steinberg," said Savage in a condescending voice, "Ben Winn has never had an affair, i.e., he has slept with no one but his wife since his engagement." He and Winn had covered this point. "I dare you to report something to the contrary." Savage was now standing, as a silenced room looked on. His tirades were well known, but had not been viewed by some of the new campaign workers.

He let his threat hang in the air. Steinberg considered its implications. If she used this, Savage probably had some grand scheme to get the NAACP on his side for the election. He was also known for filing lawsuits during a campaign; he got an injunction against CBS Radio in a Senate campaign in Missouri; an unheard-of legal result that had cost a reporter his job.

"So what do you expect me to do, ignore this story?" she asked, as she considered the corner Savage was working her into.

"I'd like you to do the decent thing, but I can't say that I expect it," said Savage, still very close to the line between backing her off and making her so angry that she went forward without weighing the long-term implications.

"Fuck you, Savage," said Steinberg, having lost all the thunder she stormed in with, ready to destroy the Winn candidacy.

"Fuck you, too, Nina." Savage hung up the phone. Everyone in the room looked on. Barker was the first to speak.

"You pissed her off, Jack. She'll run the story just to get back at you." Most of the campaign workers had heard of the black woman, a model, or maybe lawyer, but attractive. They all assumed that Winn was having an affair; they had come to expect it in politics. Barker had figured out what Steinberg was ready to report.

Savage looked at her briefly. Her comment was not worth a response; she did not know how to play the game. Steinberg would not run the story, at least not today. It would take more pressure from the Daily people than this. Reporters were aggressive and confrontational, but they did not react well to people who had the balls to stand up to them. It was not expected. They were the media, First Amendment and all that stuff. Everyone should bow when they passed.

Going through the open door to the adjoining room for privacy, Savage ordered: "Get me Guy Williams on the phone; he should be at his office in D.C." Guy Williams was the political consultant for Wilbur Daily.

Three

"GENTLEMEN, the next President of the United States, Andrew Benjamin Winn," shouted the speaker in his baritone voice. The moderator for the Concord Rotary Club was supposed to be neutral, a position he had maintained during the introductions of Daily and Lorenzen, but he proudly bellowed his support on the introduction of Winn. Savage had it arranged; the old man was proud to be an "insider" and would relish the story for the few years he had left. His introduction began the "spontaneous" demonstration that Savage had also planned, where Winn Rotarians stood up applauding and yelling, many pulling out red, white, and blue "Win with Winn"

signs that the campaign had discreetly put under the tables be-
forehand. In seconds, virtually the entire crowd was standing
in its ovation of Winn.

Daily and Lorenzen each sat at the head table with scowls
on their faces, exchanging looks with their campaign people,
giving each worker a look of disapproval. Daily would give
hell to somebody for allowing this in front of the Rotarians, the
national news cameras, God, and everyone.

Winn stood up from his plate of barely touched chicken breast
and broccoli and gripped the hand of his introducer with the
two-handed handshake for the cameras, smiling broadly. In
the center of the speaker's table sat a podium equipped with its
own microphone, but littered with microphones taped on by
the media. The large room was filled with tables, ten seats
apiece, where the reported crowd of 600 people had eaten their
chicken breast and broccoli. Waiters stood in the rear of the
room holding coffee pots and plates of pecan pie, puzzled as
to how to serve the standing, applauding crowd.

"Thank you," said Winn, leaning into the microphone and
then pulling back to let the crowd continue its ovation. It was
the only face-to-face of the candidates today, and the film footage would be broadcast by all the networks and local television
stations. After three "thank yous," during which Winn did not
intend the crowd to stop its cheering, he now began the obligatory raising of the hands and asking the crowd to "Please take
your seats." At first the crowd only responded more vigorously,
now chanting, "Winn, Winn, Winn."

Winn analyzed the crowd with his appreciative looks. Health
willing, all of these men would vote, and most had wives and
children that would also vote. In two days he was the front-
runner for the Republican nomination for President; he had not
seen any results, but suspected the polls would also show him
soundly defeating any of the potential Democratic nominees,
including Randall Hardy. Being the front-runner was far better
than the alternative, but when you are on top, you have nowhere to go except down. The least amount of activity re-

quired to maintain is the best strategy. No debates; keep the media under control. Luckily Winn did not have any siblings, which had been the Achilles heel of many recent Presidents. His wife was somewhat irresponsible, shopped and drank a little too excessively—but she was on balance a political plus, not a liability.

"Thank you." The ovation had lasted for almost ten minutes. "Please take a seat." Winn had given Stevens the look, and Stevens began signaling their people to take their seats. Within moments the "spontaneous" ovation was ended as planned. There was enough film; the point had been more than adequately made.

"You are too kind." Another 30 seconds was lost in applause and cheering. Then, Winn continued. "Thank you, Jim, for that most gracious introduction," Winn said as he turned to recognize the President of the Concord Rotary who had introduced him. "You know, in San Antonio I have for years been part of the Big Brothers program, which I know Rotarians support generously." Winn did not really regret not having kids, but because he was not a parent, he had to use the second-hand Big Brothers stuff for his folksy humor. "I was at an event with a seven-year-old Hispanic boy named Jorge, that I had taken several places. We were at a ceremony commemorating a new part to the zoo, and while I knew Jorge would hate the ceremony, it would be short and I thought he'd like to see the new exhibits to the zoo. After an introduction of me similar to that given by Jim, Jorge turned to me as the crowd cheered and said, 'Hey, Ben, David Robinson must be here or something.' " The crowd laughed. People in the campaign smiled. They had no idea whether this or any of the other hokey Big Brother stories were true. Winn probably did not even know any more. "So every time I hear an introduction like that followed by cheers and applause, I begin to look around for David Robinson." The old men in the crowd laughed again, delighted to have a man running for President who did not take himself too seriously. Not since John Kennedy had anyone pulled this off effectively.

A smattering of applause broke out again.

"They tell me that I only have five minutes to speak. You know putting a short time limit on a politician is like putting a plate of BBQ ribs in front of a hungry farm hand and telling him to only eat one." The crowd again roared in laughter, many patting their large guts.

"Gentlemen," said Winn, letting his smile slowly turn into a pleasant, but more serious expression, "what I have to say is simple. I am here to apply for a job. I want you to hire me to be your President. It's a job that anyone of you, all successful businessmen of Concord, could do as well as me, but like any employer, you don't have the time and you have to pick someone else for the job. Someone that will run the company the way you want it run, even when you're not there, even when you don't have time to pay attention." Winn paused, then continued.

"But for years now, this company hasn't been run the way you want. You and I know that getting the government involved is seldom a good solution; it is only a cause of more problems—expensive problems. The best solutions usually involve getting the government out and letting people do things for themselves without the interference of government regulation and without charging you more taxes to pay for the regulatory bureaucracy. Look at the low price of gasoline at your service station—you can thank Ronald Reagan for deregulating the oil industry in the 1980s. Look at the increasing taxes dedicated to what is loosely called health care—you can thank Bill and Hillary Clinton for nationalizing medical services in the 1990s. I like the Reagan way. How about you?" The crowd erupted in cheers and applause.

It was no accident that Winn was last. After a few half-hearted attempts to calm the crowd back down, Winn spoke into the microphone, barely audible in the crowd noise, saying "Thank you, I'd like to be your next President," and after waiving his arms triumphantly, he shook hands with everyone at the head table except his opponents and then stepped into the sea of greeting Rotarians. He was quickly picked up by his staff, who, 15 minutes and hundreds of handshakes later, would usher him out the front door and into the campaign van.

"IT REALLY PISSES ME OFF, Gus. We've been in this race two days and you're already using racism and that crap to damage us. It will backfire." Savage had been up against the Washington firm that Gus Williams worked for twice and he beat them soundly both times. They were an old established organization, still propelled by the fame of their founders, but left with little creativity or enthusiasm. They had not had a new idea for a decade.

"Everything pisses you off, Jack. What do you expect us to do, lay down and let your pretty boy run over us just because the Russians made a name for him?" Williams spoke with a gravely voice, damaged by years of cigar smoking. Williams thought the voice and the cigars were fitting for a man of his stature and occupation.

"I expect you to do what's right."

"Don't bullshit me with that 'what's right' shit, Jack. This is politics. Grow up. Your boy likes the dark ladies. How should I put it; he made the bed, he can now lie in it." Williams laughed, amused by his rude humor.

Savage was furious with the frivolity with which Williams spoke about such serious issues. These were issues that had ripped up the country, ripped up people's lives for decades. As long as the Gus Williams of the world were there to fan the fire, these prejudices would continue to destroy.

"Whatever," said Savage as he hung up the phone. Williams did not expect the great Jack Savage to lie down so easily. He wondered what Savage had in mind. Like a chessmaster, Savage had the reputation for always having his next move planned. Williams figured he would put out a media blitz on "Winn the family man" and "racism issues are out of bounds." The latter was standard, and it only reinforced the racism that the story was planted to feed in the first place.

Savage dialed the next number himself, an uncommon act. People often joked that Savage would know how to take over the board of directors at the phone company, but did not know how to dial a telephone.

The cellular phone rang three times before it was answered.

"Yeah," said Walter Dunn.

"It's me. Send them the file," said Savage.

"Done."

There were no hellos and no good-byes. Walter Dunn laid the private cellular line back down on his office desk. He got up and went to the old but effective safe setting beside the door. He turned the combination lock the appropriate directions and then pulled out a brown envelope that contained one set of pictures. He had the negatives and another set in a safety deposit box at the Bank of Virginia. He opened the envelope and slid out the pictures to either make sure or revel in his accomplishment one more time. Dunn smiled. How could a guy be stupid enough to do this if he wanted to be President? Dunn also inspected the copies of birth certificates in the envelope. They confirmed that all of the boys were teenagers, minors—a legal as well as a moral crime.

AS THEY CLOSED THE DOOR and left him standing alone in the room, Winn grimaced and asked himself if he really wanted to be President this bad. The Manchester Holiday Inn did not have such a thing as a presidential suite. This was the best they could offer, one of the rooms done in the last remodeling, which had occurred eight years ago. The carpet was a then-trendy gray. The walls were covered with salmon-colored printed paper. The room was furnished with larger, newer Early American pieces. The manager had delivered roses to the room from a supporter and had sent a bottle of champagne to the room, "compliments of the management." Any way he sized it up, Winn saw this as a small, shabby hotel room, where he would spend the next few nights.

Winn opened the closet to ensure that one of the staffers

had delivered and unpacked his hanging bag and suitcase. He then tossed his blue suit coat on the bedspread and opened the chest of drawers until he found his running shorts and white socks. It was 8 p.m., and he had one more meeting scheduled, at 9 p.m. The next meeting was with Savage and some of the campaign workers. It was not typical for him to meet with Savage, but this was probably more to boost the morale of the workers than anything else. There was not time to jog, nor had he made the arrangements for the privacy and security needed outdoors. There was time, however, to do some push-ups and ab work before a hot shower.

Winn took off his tie and shirt and looked at himself in the mirror over the chest of drawers. Not bad for 43, he thought, but only because he worked at it. It was nights like this, when he was exhausted and would like to lay back and veg out with a cheeseburger and coke, that he always found the motivation to work out. Call it guilt, or vanity, or whatever, but if he gave in now, he would miss a work-out when he needed it the most.

Winn slipped out of his black loafers and socks, then pulled off his suit trousers. He instinctively unbuttoned the suspenders from the pants and tossed them separately on the bed. He pulled his running shorts over his boxers, then put on his socks and running shoes. Winn pushed the table and its two chairs farther into the corner to give himself some more room on the floor. He then sat down and began his stretching ritual. He rolled over on his stomach, feeling the carpet uncomfortably against his bare chest. He then clipped off his first set of 15 push-ups. Winn hopped to his feet and paced the room for a couple of minutes to let his muscles recover, then hit the floor for his second set of push-ups.

If anything, Winn had lost a couple of pounds. He wanted to ensure that he could say the same thing at the end of this campaign. At six feet, two inches and 170 pounds, he was lean and muscular. His upper body was more built up than his lean legs, since he left it to running to keep his lower body in shape instead of weights. He was not, however, out of proportion, a concept he kept focused on; he had done this routine long enough to know what the results would be.

After completing five sets of push-ups, Winn rotated to his back and began the first of three different types of crunches. With his feet on the floor, knees up, and hands behind his head, he did 25 crunches forward. Then, lying flat on his back, he raised his legs in the air 25 times to work on his lower abs. He then did a set of rotation work for his obliques, with 15 reps to the right, then 15 to the left. He jumped up and paced the room for a few minutes, then returned to the floor for the next three uninterrupted sets of ab work. He did this two more times, then patted his flat stomach as he looked in the mirror. Satisfied that he had done all he could, he walked into the bathroom and turned on the shower.

His shower was long, by campaign trail standards, and hot. Winn pulled on a long-sleeve navy polo shirt and a gray ski sweater. He wore dark blue slacks and a pair of gray Reebok after-ski boots. He was a candidate 24 hours a day, but he liked to give a youthful, casual appearance where appropriate. He would never give up the suit and tie for daytime activities and had frowned on politicians, such as former President Clinton, who became known for such poor taste.

As Winn was combing his short blow-dried brown hair, the phone rang. It was 9 p.m. Winn picked up the phone from the bathroom wall and heard Stevens' voice before he could say hello.

"Senator, are you ready for the meeting?"

"Sure, Bill, if this is really necessary." Winn was a good candidate, which meant he almost always went where he was told and almost always did as instructed. He had, however, earlier protested the necessity of a meeting with campaign workers. These people were already going to vote for him, assuming they were registered voters in New Hampshire and not volunteers bused in from Washington, D.C.

"Jack thinks we need to do this, Senator. I believe he has a few things to talk over with you as well," said Stevens, resisting the protest as he was expected to do. "I'll be right down to get you."

Winn hung up the phone, and before he could sit down to glance over the *Washington Post* he had requested, there was a knock at the door.

"Senator, it's me, Bill."

Winn opened the door and saw Stevens still dressed in the conservative business suit he had worn all day.

"Either you're overdressed, or I'm a little too casual," joked Winn.

"You look comfortable, Senator, yet presidential." It did not need to be said that Stevens had not had the time to change clothes, working the media in the bar of the hotel from the time they arrived an hour ago until now.

"It's hard to get used to those guys," said Winn, referring the Secret Service agents standing near the elevator.

"Get used to it," said Stevens. He was in charge of the advance work for all of Winn's appearances, and for two days had spent precious time getting coordinated with these goons so they could check for bombs or whatever where Winn was going. Savage instructed Stevens to use these guys as a showing of Winn's importance to the public. Stevens needed to spend more time thinking about how to pursue that strategy. Savage worked every angle.

They walked down the hall into another wing of the hotel, where Stevens opened the door into a room that was structurally like Winn's, but not as recently remodeled. As Winn walked through the door, there was applause from the crowd that moved forward to shake his hand.

After a few minutes of pandemonium, the sound stopped abruptly, except for a few more words being uttered by Winn to one of the cute female workers, as a standing Jack Savage pounded the table with the palm of his hand.

"OK, let's get going, people. The Senator still has places to go tonight." Savage knew that he did not, but it was always important to make people believe that every moment of the candidate's time is precious and demanded elsewhere.

"Senator, you looked real good today." The crowd of about 30 people had slid into folding chairs or onto the floor. Winn took the only open seat, which was at the end of the table where Savage stood. The table was covered with phones and information copied on fax paper. He smiled at the group in recognition of the compliment Savage had bestowed.

"Jerry, give the Senator a rundown on the numbers." This event was largely staged for the benefit of the workers and so Stevens could report to the media that Winn had been involved in a campaign strategy session. Savage wanted him to look like a hands-on guy. People do not like presidents who take orders, even though that is what any smart president does during a campaign.

Swords went through the numbers he had given Savage earlier in the day. He apologized for not having anything more recent, but explained they were doing evening polling and would have fresh numbers by midnight. Neither Winn nor Savage was concerned. They knew they were ahead. Their mission was to stay there.

There was a brief silence when Swords finished. Winn broke the silence.

"Looks like 'so far so good,' " he said, grinning at his understatement. "So what can go wrong from here, Jack?"

"Nothing," said Savage, who then paused before adding with a smile, "unless they find the smoking gun." Winn laughed, then the others cackled and hooted like they did anytime a candidate made an attempt at humor.

"All right, people," said Savage, back to business as usual. "Everything is planned for tomorrow. Jim, you are ready for the statewide door-to-door literature drop, right?" A young college man, state chairman of the New Hampshire Young Republicans, nodded affirmatively. "And you will use the same people for a second paper blitz on Monday?" Savage asked, as the young man nodded again.

"I want bumper stickers put on every car you see. Have

your people ask, but put them on while asking. Don't piss anybody off, but don't give room for 'no.' I want the same approach with the yard signs. We have pre-designated locations for strategic signs, but I want to go door to door. Shame them into it. Tell them their neighbors are having a sign, and you don't want them to feel left out. I want to see red, white and blue 'Win with Winn' shit everywhere I go." The regional campaign directors for the state all nodded proudly in response to Savage's instructions, peeking looks to see if the candidate knew they were responsible for all of this coordinated activity.

"We will have TV and radio saturated," said Savage, beginning to pace as he rallied the troops. "You are backing the front-runner. The next President of the United States. Be proud. Tell your people that the candidate sent you out tonight, told you personally that he was counting on you." They would all be happy to blow their encounter with Winn way out of proportion and needed little encouragement to do so. Savage knew that the longer you reach the personal touch of the candidate the more you could motivate.

"Bill has some stuff set up somewhere so you can preview the ads and know what people are seeing," said Savage, as Stevens nodded in agreement, shouting out the room number where the equipment was located. Nothing made people feel more on the inside than seeing the television spots before they aired.

"I want you to make these people think they have known Ben Winn his whole life; he is the boy next door, grown up, smarter than ever. Everyone's all-American boy." Savage paused again, then continued. "You'll hear dirt and criticism. No matter what it is, say 'that's old news; the Daily and Lorenzen campaigns made it up in desperation; the media laughed at it, and if I were you I'd be careful about repeating it. I know you're up to date on politics,' or some shit like that. Anything you hear, phone it in to Sarah Riley. She will be the keeper of the trash." Mary Ellen Barker gave Riley a jealous look, covetous of her verbally acknowledged position of importance.

"Senator, anything you want to add?" That was the set-up line. Winn would come through.

"We cannot do this without you," said Winn, still sitting, but leaning forward with a commanding presence. "You will always remember being a part of this, but more importantly, I will always remember each and every one of you for the part you played in making this happen." Winn paused, and then stood up.

"The American people want us to do this. At first, I had second thoughts. You all know the sacrifices that must be made in public life. But the people spoke loudly in Iowa and we decided to go for it. It's time the American people had folks just like them in Washington, people just like you. If you do your job, I promise that I'll do mine." At that moment everyone in the room was convinced they would be working in the White House for the next President of the United States. "I cannot tell you how much I appreciate your help. You are a vital part of history in the making."

Applause seemed to erupt spontaneously when, in fact, Savage had started it. Then, only ten minutes after the meeting had started, this job was done. Winn held his hand up in appreciation, then started walking to the door shaking hands and repeating the standard lines of gratitude and encouragement. Halfway across the room, Savage put a hand on his shoulder and told the group the Senator had to go. Everyone reluctantly backed away as Savage ushered Winn out the door.

"Good job, Jack," said Winn as the door closed and they walked down the hallway toward Winn's room.

"It's easy to sell this kind of product," stated Savage as much to himself as to Winn.

"Is that what I am, a product?" asked Winn laughing.

"A damn good one," said Savage with a wide grin, now tuned back in to the present.

One of the Secret Service guys had come forward to the door and inserted a key to let Winn in. Savage followed.

"Coke?" asked Winn.

"No, I never touch the stuff. Strictly a Pepsi man," said Savage.

"Well, we don't have to agree on everything."

"We don't have to agree on anything, Ben," said Savage, grinning as the pure political strategist that he was. "It is pleasant, however, that we do agree on most things I consider important."

Winn wondered if Savage would really take a campaign where he did not believe in the candidate. Savage was a different breed. Winn knew Savage could win with such a candidate, but he did not think Savage was put together that way. In spite of his cynicism, he detected something else in Savage, some purpose. Winn knew that Savage had selected him for this campaign, just as much as he had picked Savage.

Winn sat down in one of the overstuffed armed chairs and popped the top on a can of Coke. Savage stayed standing. He was not going to intrude on the candidate's private time any more than necessary. Such private moments were few and far between, but critical to keeping the candidate fresh and focused.

"Things look great, Ben. Nothing unexpected." Savage paused, as Winn waited for the anticipated "but."

"I got a call this afternoon from Nina Steinberg. She was poking around about an affair with a 'black female lawyer' in D.C. I don't think she will go very far with it unless pushed hard by Daily or Lorenzen. My guess is Daily's people gave her the lead, but I think they will back off." Walter Dunn would see to that, thought Savage. "But, you might want to call Dorothy."

Winn smiled. "That's easy for you to say; you don't have to talk to her." Savage had met Dorothy Wallace; she could be a hellcat. He smiled at Winn.

"Anyway, she knows it's coming," said Savage, "so do whatever you think is best."

This was nothing unexpected. Winn and Wallace had talked it over. She accepted that it would be an issue, but it irritated her. She had given Winn up so that he could have politics; the media should leave her and Winn alone. She told Winn he needed some real skeletons in his closet so that they would not be chasing after this "crap."

"This story will dog us the whole way because they don't have anything any better," said Savage. "One picture of Dorothy on television, and every male will know that any red-blooded American would give up his right arm to be in bed with her. If anything, the story will help you with men. It will shake a few female voters; they will burn with jealousy when they see Dorothy. When the story goes, people will believe it. But, in the end, it won't mean shit, other than we have no serious problems. We may even pick up a few black votes from the deal."

Winn said nothing. He was now picturing the dark perfect naked body of the 5' 3", 110-pound woman that he would always love. He wondered if Savage believed him when he said he was not sleeping with her.

"Good night," said Savage, as Winn noticed for the first time that Savage was opening the door to leave.

"Keep it up, Jack."

"All the way, Mr. President."

Four

"BABY, I want to take you out dancing. You deserve better than this," begged Baroni, as he rolled over on his stomach facing her with his big pouting brown eyes. She thought he was so adorable, and he knew it.

"Come on, Tony. It was risky enough to go out before. But, now, I have media people chasing me everywhere I go. I was afraid they would follow me here." She wondered if they had. She had driven around the streets of Washington like a criminal trying to detect and lose a tail.

"Oh, baby, they keep you all cooped up." He knew they would be a "hot" item if they went out; that was why he wanted to go more than ever. As a Senator's wife, she was known. But, as the wife of the future President of the United States, she was now famous. It made him erect just to think about it. He knew, however, she would not go. He was teasing her, and enjoying it.

"OK, baby," he responded, almost whining. "So where did you tell his Majesty that you would be tonight?" he asked as he lightly squeezed her bare nipple.

"He has not called since we did the happy couple thing in San Antonio. I suppose he thinks I'm at Sally's. He knows I don't like to stay by myself any more." Sally MacArthur was one of her several friends whom she had confided in; she was part of the group of "girls" that had lunch at the Club every week before bridge.

"And does he know why you don't like to stay alone?" he asked as he walked his fingers from her breast down her silky smooth legs.

"Tony!" she exclaimed, as he gently pushed a finger inside her. She moved her body slightly as she softly moaned. They had just had sex, but she could not get enough of him. She and her husband had nothing but sex as a formality any more, had not for months. With Tony, she made love. She forgot everything else, thinking only of his hard, olive-colored body, loving the way he explored her and let her explore him.

"Oh, baby, I love you," he said lying. Then, he began a path down her body with his tongue. She moaned loudly as she put both of her hands on his head and pushed him closer.

WHEN THE PHONE RANG, Dorothy Wallace was sitting on the couch in her contemporary Georgetown condo. Sitting with her legs beneath her, wearing a Hard Rock Cafe tee-shirt, she could pass for 17. Fresh and beautiful, she had the look of a model or actress. Almost as a contradiction, she pushed the long black hair out of her face and then leaned over to make notes on her legal pad with all of the focus and concentration of a rocket scientist. The couch and coffee table were littered with stacks of documents, originally stuffed into the oversized brief case that waited nearby. She intended to do less work when they had started their own firm. She was hopelessly, however, a hands-on person. She was the reason her practice was so successful; the fact that she never let go of any of the important pieces is what kept her clients coming back, willing to pay more than she ever charged, although that was plenty.

Dorothy Wallace was 31 years old and a senior partner in a firm of 30 lawyers she co-founded three years ago. At first, it was just her and Gary Heitzman. Heitzman was 52 and had been on the management committee at Jones & Day. He was a brilliant thinker, connected to Wallace by their common bond of graduating first in their law class at Yale, although 20 years apart. Heitzman had been the head of the corporate department at Jones & Day, where Wallace had been its most promising young partner through her work in the real estate department.

She needed a change after seeing her life flash in front of her during the Russian crisis. Heitzman had suggested over lunch, almost jokingly, that they should get out of the big-firm rat race—the same big-firm environment they had both yearned for during law school—and start their own practice. Wallace was hooked immediately and ultimately persuaded Heitzman that he had already made enough money, salted away in various investments, that he did not need to worry about any financial risk to his wife or four college-age children. You only live once, and you never know when that chance will be taken away. Besides, they were the horses that pulled the cart, the doers, not the moochers of *Atlas Shrugged.* They could do everything they enjoyed and do it better, if they were unshackled by the people that went through life clinging to the more capable.

They started the firm with two associates, two secretaries, and one paralegal. Now Heitzman & Wallace had 28 associates, 15 paralegals, and an administrative staff of 23 people. They had moved offices once already and were now expanded beyond capacity at their luxurious offices on Connecticut Street. Wallace had two major clients and many more knocking at the door. She could literally pick and choose her work, and she could bring in enough business to keep a hundred lawyers busy. Her main clients were Twenty-First Century Properties, Inc., whom she had represented at Jones & Day, and Monroe Enterprises. Between the two, they owned commercial real estate throughout the world.

She was working now on the documents to be used as exhibits in a case where she was suing the FDIC to force the sale of an office building in San Diego to Twenty-First Century Properties. She had negotiated the contract with the owners of a Southern California S & L, before the FDIC took over. The FDIC wanted to sell the building, but felt that Twenty-First Century had committed enough assets to the project that the FDIC could get a higher price. She was suing them in federal court, claiming an intentional fraud by the FDIC, and thus neither the government nor its employees were exempt from damages under the Federal Tort Claims Act. She was also suing for enforcement of the contract, but had less standing on that issue under the financial institution regulations, which allowed the regulators to void contracts at will when they took an institution into receivership. She figured the FDIC would settle by following through on the contract; they were bureaucrats and did not want to risk personal embarrassment, let alone their personal finances, in fighting one of the few companies that could afford to take on the federal government. The lawyers for the government, which included a private firm in Washington brought in as outside counsel, were intimidated by Wallace and were finding fewer and fewer theories to fend off her legal arguments. The FDIC was, in fact, blackmailing her client. She had made a clever legal argument in her complaint filed in federal district court, and it probably would win in front of a jury, particularly with the pretty, vulnerable-looking Wallace making the case against Big Brother.

Wallace was not a litigator, but she and Heitzman agreed

that law firms were mistaken in setting up departments just to handle court cases. Seldom could a dispute be separated so neatly. A dispute arose out of a transaction, and more than likely the transaction lawyers—the experts in some field of law— would settle the dispute before or during any litigation. If not, she and Heitzman agreed that the transaction lawyers were the best equipped to try the cases, not some lawyer who knew nothing more than the rules of procedure and the personal habits of all the local judges.

She reached over and picked up the ringing cordless Sony telephone from the coffee table and pressed a button instinctively as she raised it to her face.

"Who's calling me this late?" she asked with mocked irritation, having no idea who was on the phone. She often answered the phone with even more unusual responses, knowing it was one of her friends or family. Few clients or business acquaintances had her home phone number. Everyone who wanted her—even most of those calling for her infrequently agreed-to dates—could leave a message at the office. This was her private turf and respected as such by anyone who wanted to stay in her good graces.

"Pleasant, as usual, huh," he said. She instantly recognized his voice, and her shapely thin shoulders slumped with the weight of the anxiety it brought on.

"Ben, what's up?" she said, upbeat, trying to disguise the impact his call had on her.

"Not much, Dot. Just your usual presidential campaign stuff. You know, kissing babies and ...."

"Kissing ass," she said, recovering to form.

"Yeah, that too."

"You calling for the black vote?" she asked, joking, but again tense over the impact race had on their relationship. She thought it was "bullshit" and it made her angry; yet she knew it was reality. As much as she wanted to blame Winn, she knew it was her choice.

"Your vote is not what I want from you." He could not

resist teasing her. He became excited, sexually, intellectually, in every way, just from the sound of her voice. He imagined her in her condo, could see her petite black legs stretching out of the tee-shirts she wore to bed.

She usually participated in such bantering, but it rubbed her the wrong way tonight. He sensed it immediately and regretted saying anything.

"So you're getting tarred and feathered for sleeping with a black girl, huh?" she asked in an even, if not intemperate, tone. She never missed a thing. She was his kindred spirit, his soul mate in so many ways. She was one of a kind, and he knew he could never love anyone else after admitting that he was in love with her.

"Nina Steinberg of NPR called Jack this morning. I figured someone would contact you." He paused awkwardly, then continued. "So I thought I'd give you some warning."

"It was only a matter of time," she said. "I won't show them the pictures," she added sarcastically. It was her nature to take it out on him, even if it was not his fault. There was a time when she returned every phone call, particularly one from the media. Her calls were carefully screened now. She had others return lots of calls for her. No one called the media back.

Winn knew that whatever she did, it would be appropriate and would be in his best interest. She had passed that test long ago. He recognized the mood. If they talked more, they would fight. It would do neither of them any good. She had suffered enough because of him; he had never given her anything but problems.

"I just thought I'd call."

"Whatever," she said using the word that he knew meant she was on a hair trigger.

"I love you," he said, not knowing why he let the words out. These words would only make things worse.

After a deafening silence, she said: "I know." They hung up the phones and each thought about the other.

JACK SAVAGE BRUSHED HIS HAIR BACK over his head with both hands as he walked into the small ballroom that the Manchester Holiday Inn used for local wedding receptions and school dances. He stepped up on the make-shift platform to the lonely podium littered with microphones. Print photographers were clicking shots as they had each of the last four days during his 3 p.m. media briefing. He wondered what they did with all these pictures. Savage had joked that the national debt could be paid off with all the money spent by the print media on film and developing for thousands, millions, billions of pictures that were thrown in the trash or some equally useless file bin.

He did not dress for such events; he was in jeans, with the sleeves rolled up on a red denim shirt. He pushed his hair back again, as one side fell into his eyes. Most of what he said would be quoted by reporters as background, not played on film with him talking. If they did run footage of the conference, he simply came across as the eccentric campaign hack, and no one would hold Winn responsible for his shortcomings in appearance.

"Jack, what do you have to say about Daily withdrawing?" The cameras were stationed in the rear of the crowd on a platform slightly higher than the one from which Savage was speaking. The television reporters and their print counterparts filled the space in between, all sitting on metal folding chairs, but straining, waving their arms, shouting their questions to get Savage's attention.

Savage knew the art of whom to recognize. He could always find the question he wanted. The Daily question had to be addressed; he intended to take it first and dispose of it as if it was a ridiculous question—his way of dealing with many questions by the media. He also knew the art of getting away with mistreatment of the media. He was hot, so was his candidate. For now, the media needed him as much as he needed them. The media liked a terse give and take—it added some spice to their monotonous job.

"What the hell am I supposed to say?" asked Savage, looking annoyed. "You know a hell of a lot more about this than I do."

"Come on, Jack," the same reporter pleaded, "give us something."

"Fuck you," said Savage. "I am here to talk about our campaign."

The chorus of reporters moaned, begging for more. After letting them work up a lather, Savage gave the response he had intended all along.

"OK, OK, settle down." He looked back at the reporter who had initially asked the question. "The Senator received a phone call from Congressman Daily this morning. The Congressman said he had reassessed the situation with the entrance of the Senator into the race and concluded that the party wanted the Senator to be the nominee. The Congressman expressed that his foremost concern has always been the best interest of the party, and he believed that was served by his withdrawal from the race and the pledge of his support to Senator Winn."

The reporters were scribbling frantically, while they asked follow-up questions.

"Jack, word is Daily has some skeleton," commented one of the reporters.

"Word is you found it," followed another in the silence brought on by the first comment.

"Cut the bullshit, Gary," said Savage frowning at the NBC reporter who made the follow-up comment. "With us in the race, Daily can't raise money. Without money, he can't win. It's that simple. If you want to make up something more titillating, that's your business, but leave me out of it."

"Come on, Jack, level with us. Wilbur Daily never did anything unless it was in Wilbur Daily's best interest."

"I told you what he said to the Senator. I'll leave mind-reading to you First Amendment experts."

"Jack, Daily has done and said about anything to further his political career. Did he meet his match here?"

Savage wanted to smile, but did not. "Wilbur Daily did what any self-respecting politician would do. He quit before he got his ass kicked, so he could go find a more evenly matched fight."

The follow-ups continued, but Savage honed in on another subject and would not return to the Daily topic.

"Rumor is that Lorenzen says he will pull out if he doesn't have a respectable finish in New Hampshire. What do you think is respectable?"

"This race will be over at the Convention in Dallas in August. Benjamin Winn will then get the nomination to be the Republican candidate for President. Make book on it, people." Savage had heard the Lorenzen rumor yesterday, before they knew Daily was out of the race. It amazed Savage how political campaigns would shoot themselves in the foot even if left alone by their opponents. As soon as the Lorenzen rumor hit the street, his money would dry up immediately. No one wanted to spend good money on a guy who would not have any chance of winning because he might not finish the race.

No matter how big the lead, the only sure chance of winning was by eliminating all of the competition. That had been done from the current set of contenders before the first week of the campaign was over. If they kept the wind in their sails, no other contenders would emerge from the Republican ranks.

"So what percentage does Lorenzen need?" The reported pressed.

"Hell, I don't know. If I was in his camp and he couldn't get 40 percent of a two-man race, I'd advise him to quit." He knew Lorenzen would not get half that.

The reporters laughed with their cynicism. They knew Savage would not quit any campaign he had started. But he had given them a number by which they could measure Lorenzen's performance.

"What about the Senator's personal indiscretions?" He saw Nina Steinberg in the front row of the crowd when he entered. He could not ignore the question, but he noticed the generalities with which it was framed. She had reported nothing yet and was obviously timid at being accused of bringing race prejudice into the campaign. It did not fit the NPR image. By now, all the reporters in the Winn entourage had heard the rumor.

"The Senator knows some white women too, Nina. Does NPR only have an interest in making something out of the fact that Winn treats black people the same as he does white people?" He had decided to hit the question direct when it came up. He thought he could scare or shame them into staying away from this topic until after the New Hampshire Primary; by then they would have the nomination in their pocket.

Steinberg was speechless, a rare thing. Savage stared at her, and the crowd was unusually silent. She finally spoke.

"I simply was pursuing some rumors about possible indiscretions of a married man putting himself out for public approval. You will surely admit that his marital infidelities are relevant."

"I won't admit shit. What the Senator or any other public figure in this country does is none of your business unless it affects his job performance." Savage paused, then continued. "But the Senator is willing, against my advice, to live by a higher standard." He had given no such advice, but it had dramatic effect to indicate Winn would tell all even though his consultants had instructed otherwise.

Savage continued. "The Senator is a good-looking, young man who was single for his first 12 years in Washington, D.C. Each of those years, he was touted by the *Washingtonian* magazine, among others, as 'one of Washington's most eligible bachelors.' He had dates and maintained a normal personal life, doing dinner and the theater, and whatever, like any other heterosexual male in America. He became engaged to Mrs. Winn four years ago. I can assure you that since that time, the Senator has not shunned any of his friends, male or female, black or white, but I can also assure you that he has committed no marital indiscretions." Savage paused. He pounded the podium with the palm of his hand to silence the flurry of questions that erupted. The sound echoed throughout the room, causing a screeching in the public address system.

"Note my strong statement, people. The Senator has no reason to make such a strong statement if it were not true. Plenty of people get elected who are known to be fucking around. The Senator does not put his private life in anyone's face, but if you are going to talk about it, get it right. He lives by no outdated conservative notions of family and fidelity; he loves his wife, and has made a commitment to her. Don't fuck that up because you want to stir up some racial animosity that will be interesting to report on. There are plenty of interesting topics to cover in this campaign." There would be no more questions at the conference about Winn's private life. The media would continue to circulate the story among themselves, but nothing would be reported as of the day of the New Hampshire Primary.

Five

H e would get two days off before needing to go to Missouri, the first leg of the Super Tuesday campaign trail. He intended to spend these two days exercising, reading the bottomless file of clippings and briefing papers that was regularly replenished at Savage's direction, and making the fund-raising phone calls from a list that Bill Stevens had provided.

The campaign was moving like a freight train. He had received an unprecedented 80% of the vote in New Hampshire. No candidate who was not an incumbent President seeking re-election had ever come close to these numbers. Although he withdrew, Daily's name was on the ballot and he received 3%

of the vote from people asleep at the wheel or who found themselves at the polls because they had a relative running in the
state primary for dog catcher or something. Lorenzen finished
with a dismal 9% of the vote. He was almost beaten by the 8%
that did not make a selection in the presidential primary.

Winn had spent the evening in New Hampshire giving an
acceptance speech at the Holiday Inn, followed by key media
interviews set up by Bill Stevens. Stevens had two rooms arranged for the interviews and ushered Winn into one room to
the designated reporters while the players were changed in the
other room for another round. Winn had done ABC's *Nightline*
live from the same rooms. The next morning he did all four of
the morning network news shows live from Manchester. The
sun was setting by the time the private jet, a corporate plane
provided by one of his supporters, returned to National Airport.

Julia, who had been Winn's housekeeper for years, now
served as the cook as well and had dinner waiting for Winn
and his wife when he arrived. George, his driver, had picked
him up at the airport and was followed by a car of Secret Service agents to the Winn residence in Georgetown. Until he was
nominated, they would let him go, once he was "put to bed,"
and as Winn walked into the house, the Secret Service men
were heading up M Street, grateful for a couple of days off in
their home city.

They had been cordial at dinner. Andria asked appropriate
questions about the campaign; she almost seemed interested at
times, but was distracted at others. Winn had grown used to
their distance. He helped her clear the table and put the dishes
in the sink for Julia to clean up tomorrow, then followed her
upstairs to the bedroom.

Without saying anything, Andria started taking off her clothes
and turning back the flowered bed cover on the king-size canopy
bed. Winn had not thought about sex, and while they performed sex enough to probably be in the "normal" range, he
was surprised at her actions, mechanical as they were. Perhaps
it was his reward for winning the New Hampshire Primary.

Winn felt responsible for the unspoken problems in their marriage. Andria, he thought, would make anyone a great wife. She was attractive, polished, and intelligent—not to mention daddy's money. He had been attracted to her because of loneliness as much as anything; she had been a good companion; someone to travel with, sleep with, share experiences with—a reason to ignore his loneliness. He may have even loved her, although he was never "in love" with her, a distinction that was clear in his mind.

He instinctively turned on the big screen Mitsubishi television in the corner of the huge master bedroom, but turned the sound down. The 11 o'clock news was just going off. He noticed that Georgetown had lost a basketball game—he was shocked at their 15 and 11 record. He had not been paying attention lately, but did not think they were doing that badly.

"Come on, dear, let's get in bed," she said. Andria did not know if she was feeling guilty or just performing her wifely duties as long as she was in the relationship. She was proud of Winn's victory in New Hampshire. When she was with Tony, everything was clear; she knew what she wanted. When she was home, however, she was confused. Was it her fault that Winn did not respond to her? No, it was that black "bitch's" fault. Or was it her fault that she could not be more like Dorothy Wallace? It was all too confusing, and if she let him have her body, somehow it would allow her to avoid the issues for now.

Winn hung up his suit in the large walk-in closet that was at his end of the room; her closet was by the bathroom. At this end of the room was the fireplace and a large straight-backed chair with a reading lamp that only Winn used. The closet had one section for ties and one for suspenders. Winn had a system for putting the most recently worn items at one end so as to get more use and more diversity out of his wardrobe. He did not put the suit in the row of neatly pressed suits that hung down the long expanse of the closet, but rather hung in the section where Julia would know to have it cleaned and pressed before putting it back in its appropriate place. George had tossed his suitcase and hanging bag into the closet before leaving. He would let Julia unpack in the morning.

When he walked back into the bedroom in his boxer shorts and dark blue robe, Andria was already under the covers. He bent down in front of the fireplace, turned on the gas and struck a match to light the flame. Wood was already arranged in the fireplace, and soon the blaze would take the chill out of the air.

He tossed his robe on the foot of the bed and pulled off his boxer shorts as he slid into the bed. She barely moved, but put her hands on his back and rubbed them just enough to qualify for participation. Foreplay was a long-ago abandoned item. She did not enjoy this, and he really did not want to be a burden. As he penetrated her, she thought of Tony and let out a brief and uncharacteristic moan. He ignored the sound, lost in his own fantasies of Dorothy's beautiful black body. Soon, he was finished and rolled over.

Andria got out of bed and put on his robe; she looked so innocent in his big robe with her short boyish haircut. She went into the bathroom for a few minutes and then walked out of the bedroom, asking him perfunctorily if he needed anything from the kitchen. It was her way of escaping until he went to sleep. The less time spent together, the better the chance of no confrontation. He said no, shaking off the whole experience without evaluating it.

Winn quickly showered off, then pulled on a tee-shirt and pair of sweat pants and sat down in the chair by the fire that was beginning to burn nicely. He opened up the file and began to read news clippings.

WINN STARED AT THE BLOOD as it ran onto the white marble kitchen floor, illuminated only by the small light under the range hood. He gagged as he stepped back to avoid the moving pool of blood as it spread across the floor and into the cracks of the squares of marble. Her body was lifeless, sprawled face down on the floor with her arms and legs spread awkwardly like those of a rag doll. He could barely see the wound, but detected the darker spot on the navy blue robe below her left shoulder, which ran down her side and into the blood that seemed to be running onto the floor like wine. The smell was sickening, and he gagged again.

He noticed that his body was trembling as he first became aware of himself and tried to shift his focus away from the wretched sight of Andria lying dead on their kitchen floor. Then it registered with him, like a jolt of electricity bringing him to consciousness.

He stared at the gun in his hand, raising it up to examine it more closely for the first time. It was a Colt .45; he had lived this nightmare before. The gun had plain black plastic grips, and was blued, not stainless steel. He slid back the chamber of the automatic weapon and then released it after finding that a round was in the chamber. Instinctively he cocked the weapon and held it to a ready position. He thought about the large .45 caliber slug that had surely gone through Andria's heart and was lodged somewhere in the wall or maybe the floor. He pictured her body hurled through the air like he knew a .45 at close range would do.

He surveyed the room, then noticed the time. It was 12:15 a.m. He stood staring at Andria's lifeless body, then what he thought was only moments later noticed that the clock on the microwave displayed 12:40 a.m.

"Fuck," he said aloud, "now what?" He considered calling an ambulance, but Andria was dead. He could tell that. He thought about calling the police, then thought about the gun again. Using two hands, he lightly depressed the trigger while letting the hammer back down on the chambered round. He grabbed the dish towel off the island in the middle of the huge kitchen. The room was beyond eerie, with the dead body still bleeding on to the floor, but slower, as the blood began to co-agulate, in the soft amber glow of the single light over the stove. With the towel he wiped the gun thoroughly. He laid the gun on the island and wiped where his fingers were holding it. He picked up the gun with the towel, thought about hiding the gun until he could throw it away, then laid it on the floor beside Andria.

He walked to the kitchen table and sat down by the wall phone. He picked it up, still thinking about whom to call. Almost by default, he dialed the Alexandria extension.

"Savage," he answered, obviously still awake.

"Jack, I've got a big problem."

"Ben." He could hear a strain that he had not heard before in the unmistakable voice. Savage instantly knew this was serious. "What is it?"

"Andria's been shot." He paused briefly, then said, "She's dead."

"Where are you, Ben? At home?"

"Yeah. In the kitchen."

"Who did it?" Savage braced himself. He thought he knew Winn well enough to rule the possibility out that he did it.

"I don't know."

"Not you?" Savage asked, but it was almost a statement. He had to confirm what he already knew.

"No."

"Did you call the police?"

"I haven't done anything. Some time has passed."

"How much?" asked Savage, taking charge like a field general who had been given orders.

"I don't know."

"What do you mean, Ben?" Savage was not good at being gentle. Winn was obviously in shock. He was trying to work with him.

"I don't know when she was killed."

"Where were you, Ben?"

"In the bedroom, I guess. We had sex, she came into the kitchen." Winn was trying to recreate the events. "I suppose I wondered what was keeping her, came in here and found her dead on the floor."

"What time was that, Ben?"

"I don't know, Jack," said Winn collecting himself a little with the passage of time. "I first noticed the time at about 12:15."

"Jesus Christ, that was 30 minutes ago." Savage imagined Winn in shock while he walked around looking at his dead wife. "Ben, don't touch anything. I'll be there in 15 minutes. Call the police as soon as we hang up. You called the cops, then you called me, got it?"

"Yeah," said Winn.

"I'm on my way," said Savage, followed by a click on the phone. Winn reached down to press the button for a dial tone on the phone, then dialed 911. He was avoiding looking at the body. He wondered what he should do about the gun.

"911," answered the female voice after five rings.

"My wife has been shot."

"Is she breathing?" asked the voice in a monotone.

"She's dead," said Winn.

"What is your name, sir?"

"Ben Winn."

"Oh," he thought she responded with recognition. "And what is your address, Mr. Winn." He told her. "You are at that address and so is your wife?"

"Yes," responded Winn.

"Please stay there, Mr. Winn. I have an ambulance and the police on their way."

WINN HUNG UP THE PHONE, still considering whether he should hide the gun. Before he moved, however, he heard the distant sounds of sirens. As the noise increased, he saw the flashing blue and red lights of a police cruiser coming down the street. The car pulled in front of the prominent Georgetown house. Quickly, a second car arrived. Then four cops got out and started walking toward the front door.

Winn turned on additional lights for the first time as he walked through the Victorian dining room and into the foyer of the two-story home. By the time he opened the door, a third unmarked car had arrived, and the older of the two plain clothes detectives was barking orders to the uniformed officers to shut the flashing lights off on their vehicles. He knew what he had here; otherwise he would not have jumped out of bed, scaring his wife half to death, and rushed to the waiting unmarked car that picked him up and drove him the 20 blocks to get here. He knew this was Senator Benjamin Winn, maybe soon to be President Winn, and some sense of decorum was needed until this mess could be sorted out. He recognized Winn instantly.

"Senator, I'm Chief of Detectives Oliver Thorn," said the black man dressed in a suit, but without a tie. He was about 55 years old and out of shape at 230 pounds from sitting behind a desk all day and eating junk food. "Where is your wife, Senator?"

"She's in the kitchen," said Winn as he turned to let the group follow.

As Thorn followed him into the kitchen, he held up his hand and gruffly told the uniformed cops to stay out and not touch anything unless the younger plain clothes detective instructed otherwise.

Thorn stood over the body, while the younger man squatted down. Byron Lane was only 29 years old, but had been a homicide detective for five years. He was viewed as a star in the department, largely because of his conviction of the mayor for murdering a man in what was supposed to be a friendly card game. Lane pursued the Mayor when it was not politically popular to do so. Finally, he coerced one of the other players to confess and disclose the cover-up scheme that the Mayor convinced them to use. No one ever corroborated the story, but it was enough to get a conviction.

Lane was stocky, over six feet and over 200 pounds. When older, he would look fat, but now he was an intimidating presence of bulk. His face was expressionless, almost the "b & d" look. He wore a dark shark-skin, double-breasted suit, and the short ponytail from his slicked back hair hung over his collar. He could tell the victim was dead, but as a matter of routine confirmed that there was no pulse.

"Been dead an hour or so," said Lane to his boss.

"Yeah, well, we'll let the coroner tell us about that," said Thorn. He hated the young know-it-all types. They had not put their time in like his generation. They all wanted to rocket to the top on the back of some sensational case, acting like newspaper reporters and assistant United States Attorneys. Cops did not used to play that game.

"Senator, this is Detective Byron Lane. He will be in charge of this investigation, that is, except for me."

Winn instinctively extended his hand to Lane, who looked at him for an awkward moment before shaking it.

"How do you do, Detective?" asked Winn routinely as they shook hands.

"Not bad, Senator," said the young detective with what Winn took to be a cocky, disturbing smile.

Lane looked around the room again, then squatted down to pick up the automatic pistol with a handkerchief he produced from the outside breast pocket of his suit coat. He produced a large plastic bag, like a zip-lock bag, from the one of the side pockets on his jacket and gently dropped the gun inside the bag.

"Is this your gun, Senator?" he asked without looking at Winn, as he stood back up.

"No."

"Do you own a gun, Senator?"

"Yes." There was something too smug about this guy, thought Winn. He looked at Andria and decided the least he could do, however, was put up with the hassle of these people. It would all quickly be over, and then he could focus on how to grieve and how to get his life moving forward.

"Ben," said Savage, as he walked through the mildly protesting uniformed officers. "I got here as quick as I could."

"Jack, thanks for coming," said Winn as he reached out and grabbed his hand, holding it for a moment, but not shaking it. He had not realized how vulnerable he felt alone here until he felt the sense of security from having Jack arrive.

"Jack, this is Chief of Detectives Thorn and Detective Lane.

Gentlemen, this is Jack Savage, a friend of mine." Savage shook Thorn's hand as they nodded greetings to each other. Lane was kneeling near the body again and did not respond to the introduction.

Savage looked at Andria Winn lying dead on the floor, then said, "I'm so sorry, Ben."

"So how did you know she was dead, Mr. Savage?" Lane stood up again as he shot the question.

"Ben called me," said Savage, trying to assess the situation. "Right after he called you," he added.

"Right after, huh?" repeated Lane.

"When he called, he said he had just called the police," shot back Savage, not willing to put up with much from some young punk who obviously thrived on the power being a police detective gave him. "He said someone had shot Andria. I said I would come right over."

"Because you're his friend," said Lane with some sarcasm that did not seem to have any place here.

"That's what the Senator just told you."

"And, you're his campaign manager," said Lane, as if he had revealed some secret that Savage and Winn were trying to conceal.

"So?" responded Savage stepping in Lane's direction. The cocky cop watched more on TV than "America's Most Wanted," thought Savage. There was a silence in the room. Lane was acting like there were several secrets here, and he would quickly uncover them all.

Thorn cleared his throat, then moved to get some order. His boy was irritating people who would soon be calling the shots from Pennsylvania Avenue, which definitely was the most important address in his jurisdiction.

"Gentlemen," Thorn said, looking to Savage and Winn. "We will do this as quickly as possible. Detective Lane here needs to ask some routine questions. We need to have the lab people go over this place. We'll get out of here as quick as we can. It's fine for you to be here, Mr. Savage, if that is what the Senator wants."

Winn nodded that it was. He sat down at the oval oak kitchen table. Savage continued to stand. Without asking, Lane pulled a pocket tape recorder from his inside coat pocket and put it on the island in the kitchen as he pressed the record and play buttons.

"Do you know who killed your wife, Senator?"

"No."

"Did you see her get shot?"

"No."

"Why don't you just let him tell you what happened," said Savage, irritated as he intervened.

Lane looked at Savage without any particular expression, then continued as if Savage had not uttered a word.

"You said you own a gun, right, Senator?"

"Yes."

"What kind of gun?"

"A Colt .45"

"Like the one on the floor?"

"Not exactly," said Winn. "Mine is a stainless steel Officers Model."

"So you got a close look at the gun on the floor?" asked Lane.

"Look," interrupted Savage, "what is going on here. I will insist that the Senator not respond to this non-consentual, recorded interrogation without a lawyer unless you begin to make some sense out of what you're doing?"

"Are you a lawyer?" asked Lane.

"No, but I can get several here pretty fucking quick," shouted Savage.

"OK, let's settle down," said Thorn frustrated. This was not going well. He did not need this. "No one is interrogating the Senator. Lane, shut that fuck'n tape recorder off. Take notes if you want to record something." Like we did in the old days, he thought, but did not say. "Senator, tell us what happened." Thorn gave Lane a strong look of disapproval, but got no outward response from the young detective.

"I don't really know what happened. Andria and I went upstairs to the bedroom after dinner, probably about 11. I was working when she left the room. I thought she was going to the kitchen to get a drink or something. She asked me if I wanted anything. Time passed. I suppose I became concerned about what was taking her so long and came down to the kitchen. She was lying there dead." Winn dropped his head in anguish.

"So you didn't see anything or hear anything?" asked Thorn.

"That's right, Detective," answered Winn.

"What time did you find her?" asked Lane.

Winn paused, silently stumbling. Savage tensed up, knowing that the delay in phoning the police would not look good.

"I don't know exactly," said Winn deciding to be vague rather than expose the time delay.

Lane nodded his head as if doubting the response.

"Did you check her pulse?"

"No," said Winn. He had not considering touching her. She was obviously dead.

"How did you know she was dead?" asked Lane.

"She looks dead," said Savage loudly. "What kind of a question is that?"

"She may look dead now," said Lane knowingly, "because she has been lying here over an hour; bleeding has coagulated, and her body is beginning to stiffen. She didn't look like this an hour ago. Then she was a warm body, bleeding. How did you know she wasn't alive?" asked Lane as he stepped towards the kitchen table confronting Winn.

"I just knew," Winn answered, trembling. "There was too much blood. I just knew." Winn hung his head again, re-experiencing the ordeal.

"That's enough," said Savage, who was politely cut off by Thorn raising his hand.

"You're right, Mr. Savage. We have enough. Senator, is it safe to say that you don't have any hot prospects on who would want to kill your wife?" asked Thorn.

Winn shook his head no.

"Give that some thought, please. We will need to have some of your time tomorrow, when the shock is worn off some, to talk. We'll figure out how the killer got in and see if we can find some clues about who it was," said Thorn. The last thing he needed was the Mayor or Chief of Police on his ass about mistreating Winn. They, and everybody else, would be all over this case, wanting a quick and tidy arrest of some burglar or other social derelict for the murder.

"I would suggest that you sleep somewhere else this evening," continued Thorn. "We will be here awhile doing the lab stuff. Tomorrow, please look around to see if anything is missing, to substantiate the burglary angle. It looks to me like Mrs. Winn surprised somebody. You are probably gone a lot. Whoever came in probably did not expect anyone to be home. The house was pretty dark when we drove up. I take it you can't see the bedroom lights from the street."

Winn shook his head affirmatively. Lane was staring at him.

"Well, then, Ben can pack up a few things and we'll get out of here," said Savage, looking for approval from the Chief of Detectives.

"Sure. Senator, I'm sorry about your wife. I know this must be difficult," said Thorn, looking sympathetic, but mainly wanting to cover for the antics of his subordinate.

"Chief Thorn," said Savage, "how will your people handle the media?"

"We will put out a statement with a few facts. We have a policy against any off-the-record comments by department personnel," said Thorn, knowing all the while that the department leaked like a sieve. What the Department did not leak, the U.S. Attorney's office would.

"So, what will you say about the killer?" pressed Savage.

"Let us look around and find something to support a break-in or robbery or something. Then we can do a routine statement that Mrs. Winn probably surprised someone in the house. The Senator was in another part of the house, and the killer was gone before the Senator found her. Something along those lines."

"I am surprised that the media is not here already," said Savage. "Whoever is listening to the police scanner is probably fucking off or something. Can we see the statement before you put it out?"

Thorn had that constipated look that government bureaucrats get when someone asks them to deviate from their standard practice, "procedure" as it was called.

"The statement will come out of the Public Relations Office. I will see to it they get your request," said Thorn. "From there it's out of my hands." He shrugged to underscore that it was not his responsibility.

"Who is in charge of the Public Relations Office?" asked Savage.

"Chuck Carroll," said Thorn.

Savage would contact the office directly. There was still a presidential campaign going on, and going well. This would be touchy if there were any screw-ups at all. Winn and Savage started toward the foyer to take the stairs to the master bedroom.

"What about Andria's body?" asked Winn as he stopped in the doorway.

"We will take care of that, Senator," said Thorn. "We will need to do an autopsy. You will be contacted before any procedures are performed. I assure you we will take care of her." Thorn tried to sound as sincere as he could. It was sometimes difficult for a homicide cop of 25 years to remember that murder was not routine to most people. His comments made Winn feel sick again.

"Where is your Colt .45?" asked Lane, staring as Winn and Savage turned back at the sound of his voice.

"It's at our condo in San Antonio," said Winn. "Of course, it's against the law to possess a firearm in the District of Columbia," added Winn, thinking that this guy would arrest him for a weapons violation.

Six

THEY SAT IN WAR ROOM on King Street. It was 3:00 in the morning, but Winn had seemed to regain his senses in the car on the way back to Alexandria. It was Winn who insisted they consider the political implications of Andria's death. Savage agreed that the media would be calling the campaign office soon, if they had not already.

No phone messages were waiting when they got there. A few college kids were working on a mailing to Republicans in South Carolina in the big outer office that was filled with borrowed desks and tables. There would be plenty of all-niters between now and November. The volunteers were shocked to see Winn in the office at this time of night. He greeted them calmly. They were still high from the New Hampshire victory and did not notice anything unusual about Winn's demeanor.

Savage picked up the phone on the cluttered credenza behind his desk and dialed a number.

"Bill, it's Jack. Yeah, I know what time it is. Now, send her home and get to the War Room as quick as you can. Ben is here with me. This is urgent. Get here." Stevens had taken an apartment in Old Town Alexandria, and his red Alfa Romero pulled up to the vacant parking meters in front of the Bank of Virginia building on King Street within ten minutes.

Savage had made coffee in the meantime and poured them each a cup. He gave Stevens the facts as he knew them.

"You have to get a hold of this Chuck Carroll guy first thing and work with him on their release," said Savage. "We will have our own by then; try getting the police to just use what we put out. We want our statement out before the East Coast 7 a.m. news so we spin the story first."

Savage paused, then addressed the issue that had yet to be raised.

"We need to treat it this way, Ben, no matter what you decide to do. It keeps our options open," said Savage.

"I know what I'm going to do, Jack. I'm going to finish the campaign we started." Winn paused as he saw the relief on their faces. "Look, guys, I will grieve for Andria in my own way. But the marriage had a lot to be desired. She was not a part of my decision to do this, and she was not a part of the campaign. She didn't want anything to do with politics. Life goes on, and the best thing I can do for everyone, including myself, is just keep going."

"Great!" said Stevens, then was embarrassed for showing such excitement only hours after Winn's wife had been murdered.

"We may have a problem, however," said Winn. Savage knew what he was thinking; it had been his primary focus since Winn called, exasperated after hearing the questions asked by that punk cop.

"I think this Lane guy wants me to be the killer," said Winn.

"Arrogant son-of-a-bitch," added Savage. "It's a big case for him. It's the kind of case he gets his head handed over to him if he can't solve it. But, if he can make people think you did it, it becomes a mega case, the kind that will make him Chief of Police, or so the stupid fucker thinks."

"It was definitely a hostile exchange," said Winn, commenting on his interview with Detective Byron Lane.

"Shit," was all that Stevens could think to add.

"This guy is a peon," said Savage confidently. "We can put pressure on the cops to keep him under control, while we control the spin with the media. Hopefully, they will quickly find the killer. Then I will see to it that this Lane guy gets to trade in his shark-skin suit for the blue uniform of a beat walker."

BY 6 A.M. THE STATEMENT WAS FAXED to Stevens' list of television and radio networks, other prominent local radio and television stations, the print services, and the major newspapers. It read:

"EMBARGO, immediate. Around midnight, Andria Hamilton Winn was shot and killed by an intruder she apparently startled in the Winns' Georgetown home. Senator Ben Winn discovered the body after the killer had fled. District of Columbia police have assured the Senator that they will not stop until the intruder is apprehended."

To their surprise, no one called until the fax began to make its way into the offices of news directors with their early morning coffee. Since then, Savage and Stevens had been constantly on the phone. "Yes, the Senator was doing well, though deeply saddened by the tragic death of his wife." "No, the Senator had not talked about politics; it was expected that the campaign would continue, but the Senator would focus on nothing but his wife for the next few days." "No, the Senator was in no way a suspect in the killing; it was a burglar whom Mrs. Winn discovered. The Senator was lucky that he too was not shot and killed." "No, the Senator would not be available to the media." "No, the Senator would not be campaigning for the next few days, although he was expected to return in plenty of time for Super Tuesday." "Yes, the Winns were happily married." "No, Mrs. Winn was not pregnant."

It was the lead story for all of the electronic media. They took the spin put out by the Winn campaign. Broadcasters used their fake, soft tone of sympathy like they did for earthquakes and assassinations, reporting that the Winn home had been burglarized in the middle of the night. Confronted by Mrs. Winn, the intruder had shot and killed her. Most of the reports implied that Winn had barely missed being killed by the burglar as well. Listeners had the impression that he too had been part of the surprise to the intruders. It was reported that the Senator was in mourning and that he refused to discuss politics, although it was expected that he would continue his race for the nomination.

Savage and Stevens smiled at each other as they paused to take in the 7 a.m. news shows. They then returned to the phones, taking media calls, but now began to call key supporters and contributors identified by Savage to assure them that Winn was fine and was still a candidate for President. Other campaign staff had been called in and were allowed to call many of the important, but lesser, people on Savage's list. Mary Ellen Barker, Arnie Walker, and Sarah Riley were all working the phones. "Yes, the Senator was fine, although grieving over his wife of four years." "Yes, the Senator was emotionally strong and would be back in stride quickly. Remember, this is the guy that stopped Red Surprise." "Yes, the Senator is definitely still in the race." "Unequivocally, still a candidate." "Count on Winn being the nominee." "If anything, he is more committed than ever to the race."

Stevens had managed to get Chuck Carroll on the phone by 7:30 a.m. He had been called at home by the Public Relations Office, which was being deluged with media inquiries since the early news broadcasts. Savage had made a call to someone, that resulted in Carroll getting a call from the Chief of Police before he talked to Stevens. Carroll agreed with Stevens that the department would cooperate; they had no desire to cause the Senator any further harm—he had suffered enough with the loss of his wife. They would put out a statement similar to the one used by the campaign. Stevens could see it before it went out. Carroll would stress to the media that the Senator was definitely not a suspect and the Senator was helping them try to locate the killer.

"YOU'LL LIKE THIS," said the young black girl dressed in a white blouse and short, tight black skirt as she tossed two pages stapled together on Byron Lane's desk.

He looked up at her, but said nothing as she stood there for a moment, then walked away in a huff at his lack of appreciation. His desk sat in the middle of a small room, surrounded by the desks of other detectives. He was the only homicide guy at this precinct in Georgetown except for his boss Thorn, who was also in charge of all homicide detectives throughout the District. Most of the plain clothes guys worked burglary and robbery, which was Georgetown's number one serious crime. A couple were vice guys who worked drugs and prostitution. Most of the bar room assault and batteries that occurred throughout the upper middle class area of the District were handled by the uniformed guys, and seldom prosecuted.

He picked up the report and slowly read it.

"Fuck-in-A," he shouted and grinned broadly, gaining the attention of the other detectives who made it in before noon.

"Something make you cum, Lane?" joked one of his colleagues. None of them liked the pompous, holier-than-thou bully. He was a loner, which was fine with his peers. There were conflicting rumors. Some made him out to be a hero, fighting city hall, laying his career on the line to go after a popular mayor of the city for murder; that image was completely at odds with the Byron Lane they knew. Others said he climbed the ladder by beating a false confession out of a guy and then threatening him with either jail or using the false story to help Lane put the mayor of the District in jail. Now sitting in prison, the mayor still claimed he was innocent and had a small but earnest vigil that waited for his vindication.

"Fuck you," Lane said as he rose from his squeaking chair. He smiled condescendingly on these poor bums; he would not have to put up with them for much longer. He would soon soar above this place.

Lane walked into the empty office of his boss, Oliver Thorn, for some privacy. If this became his office, he would start by wheeling in the trash barrels and hauling the stacks of paper and memorabilia out. Why were cops such pigs? Lane knew he had obsessive/compulsive behavior patterns, but boasted that it made him a clever detective; he kept things organized and sorted out, throwing away what was not needed, keeping only the important pieces of the puzzle. He was not as quick as he liked to think, and his method of sorting things down to a few facts was his only hope of keeping a grip on the picture. Important pieces were lost along the way. Sometimes the picture looked like it was supposed to when he was done. Sometimes it did not, and people were in prison because of the distorted portraits he had pieced together. Lane did not consider this possibility, but it did not really matter to him. He got what he wanted either way: a conviction. And convictions were the rungs that his ladder of success was made of. He believed that everybody was guilty of something anyway. If not what he nailed them for, then something else. Justice was done either way.

"Sybil Stephenson," Lane said smoothly into the phone. Sybil Stephenson had only one personality. The 38-year-old prosecutor hated men and hated law firms. Both had denied her the recognition due and rewards earned. A graduate from the middle of her class at George Washington University, Stephenson was a local Maryland girl who managed after law school to get a job with one of the mid-sized law firms in D.C., but after two years was told she was not on the partnership track. All but one of the 23 partners at the firm were men, and she knew they would keep it that way. Men had tried to control her, keep her in her place, beginning with her father. Stephenson had joined an incest survivor group, deciding during law school that even though she could not remember it, sexual abuse by her father was the only explanation for certain dysfunctional parts of her personality. Her family had disowned her on hearing the story, and it ultimately led to the early retirement of her father and the moving of her parents to Florida to get away from their crazy daughter.

Men were always abusing women, and now she was in a job where she could make them pay. The United States Attorney's Office in Washington, D.C., was different from other U.S. Attorney's Offices. Like the others, it handled all of the federal crimes in the District. In the District, however, it prosecuted what would be state crimes in the other jurisdictions—real crimes like rape and murder. Crimes committed by men, usually against women. The U.S. Attorney's Office was a hot spot for law school graduates. Young lawyers were able to get into court and get litigation experience that would take years to get in a law firm. After getting three or four years' experience, they were then hot lateral prospects for the law firms. They could move in and be the lead chair on minor civil cases. Other than the U.S. Attorney, who was a political appointee by the President, in every District there were a few senior lawyers in the office. At 38, Stephenson was the senior female in the District, and junior to only three of the civil servant lawyers. She could bully her way into most any case she wanted to prosecute. She picked cases that were high profile, with men as defendants, and usually women as victims. She prosecuted like a bulldog, keeping her case simple, and hammering at it until the jury could take no more. Her record was impressive only to herself. Slick private lawyers, usually men, were able to make a case complex sometimes and confuse the jury. It was not her fault. Her biggest headline, however, was for convicting the mayor of murder. She did not have much evidence, but she had an eyewitness. In the end, and in a flurry of media activity that lynched the mayor, the jury came in with a conviction. Several of the jurors cried, saying later they had been intimidated by their fellow jurors and by the Marshals letting in news clippings showing that the world had already decided what their verdict should be. The conviction would stand, however, in spite of the defendant's efforts to appeal.

"This is Ms. Stephenson," she announced in her whiny, motherly voice.

"Sybil, it's Lane. I need to talk to you about the Winn case."

Her face lit up; like everyone in the Office that morning, except the U.S. Attorney himself, she was exhilarated about the case. It would be high profile. She wanted it. A conviction in a case of this level would launch any prosecutor's career.

"Have you got a suspect?" she asked.

"I got the killer," said Lane, smiling as he boasted and stopping for dramatic effect.

"Well?" she asked impatiently.

"Senator Ben Winn," he said extremely proud of himself.

"My God!" she said, briefly losing her composure. This was too good to be true. She could take out a major political figure for killing his wife. It would make the mayor's case look insignificant. No telling what kind of dirt the investigation would kick up. "Are you shitting me? None of the reports back that up; even the statement your office issued said there was an intruder." She was beginning to doubt the whole thing, even though Lane was not the practical joking type. Their relationship was not that kind; she did not have that kind of relationship with anyone.

"Fuck the news stories, and fuck the department," said Lane, sounding convincing.

"Who knows? Does Thorn know?" she asked the second question before he could answer the first.

"Nobody knows but me, and now you. Thorn can't keep anything. There will be pressure to bury this deep unless we expose it. Nobody wants to rock the boat." Of course, there were plenty of young detectives and young prosecutors that

would sell their souls to get this case. But, Lane always operated with the crusader mentality.

"Jesus Christ. We'll be famous throughout the whole
Goddamned country for putting him in jail," said Stephenson
with glee.

"Fuck-in-A," said Lane. "I don't want to talk about it on the
phone." He operated in a state of paranoia; there were only
bad guys and him. "Let's meet in your office."

He hung up the phone and headed towards the men's room.
He felt like he needed to urinate; it was really just pressure
from the sexual stimulation he was getting from the process he
was setting in motion.

Seven

S avage sat behind his desk. As usual, the two doors to the brain center of the campaign headquarters were open. He liked operating with an audience. People walked in and out, relaying messages or handing him materials while he talked on the telephone.

The day had gone well. The police finally seemed to be cooperating. The media had bought his spin with little resistance. His candidate was getting free media around the country, as the murder was the lead story. Jerry Swords had already given him preliminary numbers, and the sympathy factor was causing Winn's already good numbers to soar even higher. In a head to head with Hardy, the likely Democrat nominee, Winn was now getting 10 points over yesterday's numbers, which were already pumped by the hype off the New Hampshire victory. He would run the campaign through the motions of the primaries, but he was now running against the Democrats, probably Hardy. The Republican nomination was a done deal.

"Harry Helm is on line four," shouted Mary Ellen Barker, sticking her head into the open door. Savage had told her to place the call.

"Harry, I want a national buy, television only, but you can't do it through the networks. I want it to look regionalized, like it's a buy for states holding primaries." Savage held in his hand the photocopy of a map of the United States that he had marked up with his red pen. "In the next 60 days there are 19 primaries. I am faxing you a map that divides up the states into 19 regions. Buy in each region, telling the sales directors that you are buying for which ever primary I have put in that region. If it's a state without a primary, tell them we believe their station spills over into the primary that I have marked for that state."

"What are you talking about, Jack. It will take forever to contact all of these stations directly," protested the marketing consultant that Savage was using for the campaign.

"Shut up and listen, Harry. You get paid to work hard. I want as much available evening news time and prime time in 30-second spots as you can get on Thursday and Friday; go for as many rating points as you can buy. Make the same buy for Tuesday and Wednesday of next week. Then buy morning shows and local news times for the stations in the 19 states having primaries on every other day between now and a week from Sunday."

"This will cost a fortune, Jack," said Helm, not protesting, but complaining.

"Money is my problem, Harry. Buying time is yours." Savage was on a roll with this, feeling the exhilaration of a moving campaign. Helm knew he had no alternative but to get the job done.

"So, is the Senator all right, Jack?" asked Helm, wanting some inside information about the murder.

"He's fine, Harry. He's going to be President," Savage added, not making clear whether the two comments were related. "Now get busy," Savage added as he hung up the phone.

"Mary Ellen," Savage shouted, and she instantaneously appeared. "Fax this to Harry Helm," he said, handing her the map. "Get me Margaret Hartley on the phone."

Winn scribbled some notes on his legal pad while he waited the brief time for the call to be placed.

"Margaret Hartley on line six," Mary Ellen shouted, enjoying the thrill of the pace.

"Margaret, I want to shelve everything we have for now and put together a new spot. I want it in Harry Helm's hands by noon tomorrow, with copies for a national distribution."

"That's impossible, Jack," she responded with her New England accent of precision.

"Nothing's impossible, Margaret. I'd like to hear the ad people just once say 'Great, I'll get it done.' " They always complained that it could not be done that way, or it could not be done that quickly, or it could not something.

"This is. Even if we had the spot, we couldn't make the copies ...."

"Margaret, if you don't want to do it, say so. I'll get someone who will."

There was a pause on the line. Winn would be their biggest client this year, even surpassing their silk-stocking traditional business clients.

"What do you want?" she asked.

"It's not that tough," said Savage, unable to resist the final dig to which he knew she would not now respond. "I want you to find footage in the archives of a man that could pass for the Senator standing alone at a grave." It was amazing what these people could come up with, and Savage knew it. You could find footage of anything if you looked at enough film. "I want ten seconds of this, preferably with a cold, gray-looking setting;

really somber."

"This is really tacky, Jack," she said, not daring to guess where he was going with this.

"This is brilliant," Savage said, as much to himself as her. "I want the footage to run with no sound, then I want a black screen for 20 seconds with white lettering that says 'In Memory of Andria Winn.' At the end, the last ten seconds or so, I want a narrator saying, 'Senator Ben Winn had intended to be here asking for your support in the upcoming primary. He needs to be elsewhere and appreciates the thousands of calls and letters of support you have given in this time of bereavement.' Flash on the bottom of the screen the 'paid for' stuff, leaving it there only as long as you have to, to keep the FEC off our ass. For the voice, use that guy you used on the South Carolina Meet the People spot that you canned. If he is not available, use someone solemn and patriotic. I want to see it before you copy it."

She was astonished, then rationalized that Winn had not caused the murder. He had to do something to keep the campaign going. Maybe Savage was right. This was fair game. Everything is fair in politics and war.

"I'll see what I can do, Jack."

"Get the fucking thing done, Margaret. Timing is everything here."

Savage took the stack of pink slips from Mary Ellen Barker who had eased in to hear the conversation. He looked through the messages as he considered his strategy. It would keep the media focus on Winn as the bereaved widower, while feeding the sympathy current that Swords' numbers had shown. Winn could stay under cover and avoid having to deal with anyone publicly on this thing until the police came up with something. He lit a cigar, an event he usually saved for much later in the evening, in honor of his plan.

IT WAS DECIDED that Winn should not do this alone. Definitely he did not want a lawyer; that would send all of the wrong signals to the media if they got wind of it. Savage was too confrontational. Bill Stevens was elected for the job.

Stevens had worked it out with the cooperative Chuck Carroll to have Winn driven into the underground parking garage of the Federal Building at Judicial Square that housed the U.S. Attorney's Office. Winn was at first uneasy with the idea of an Assistant U.S. Attorney being in the meeting. He was assured that it was routine, however, and convinced that the Federal Building would be the most discreet place for his meeting with the police. Winn agreed to ride in the Secret Service car because it could not be traced by some reporter to him. Undoubtedly, the media would have the Federal Building staked out to watch any activity that might have something to do with Andria's murder.

The basement was used for parking by the judges that also held court in this building and a few members of the U.S. Attorney's office. The car pulled up to within a few feet of a waiting elevator, being held open by Chuck Carroll. Stevens jumped out of the car, looked around the area, and seeing it clear asked the Senator to follow him into the elevator.

Winn shook Carroll's hand and thanked him for his courtesies in his time of personal crisis. Stevens then filled the time talking to Carroll about the media inquiries that the Police Department was getting.

The elevator opened on the fourth floor, and Carroll ushered them into a conference room that overlooked the Metro Station entrance. The room was vintage upper-crust government, ornate in its 1940s' work-project detail. It contained a long mahogany table, where four people were seated, rising when Winn entered the room.

"Senator, I'm Jake Butler," said the Democratic appointed U.S. Attorney. Butler liked big cases, but not ones where the down side was this big. He wanted this one to go away quick and orderly. "I don't want to stay around and clutter this thing up, but I wanted to express my sincere apologies to you and let you know we are working with the police department to wrap this up as quickly as we can."

No one noticed the knowing glances that Lane and Stephenson exchanged.

"Thanks, Jake, I appreciate it," said Winn humbly.

"I believe you know Chief of Detectives Thorn and Detective Lane," said Butler turning to the group still standing at the table. "This is one of my most experienced prosecutors, Sybil Stephenson. She will be heading this up for our office." Stephenson had blind-sided him with this earlier. He did not know why she was so hot to have the case; they did not even have a suspect. She had worked well with Lane before, however, and some of his people had problems with this guy. So he agreed.

Stephenson nodded with a brief smile, but did not move to shake hands with Winn.

"With that, I'll leave you to wrap this up," said Butler, again shaking Winn's hand, giving him the presidential respect that he was due.

Winn and Stevens sat at the opposite end of the table, unconsciously taking hostile positions to the law enforcement people at the other end.

"Thanks for coming, Senator," said Thorn. "I'm sorry we had to meet under the circumstances we had last night. Again, let me extend my sympathies, and we will try to get this over as quickly and painlessly as we can."

"What did you find at the house?" asked Winn.

The law enforcement people looked at each other, and then Lane took over.

"This works best, Senator, if you just let us ask the questions. When we are done, you can cover anything you think we have left out," Lane said.

"Do you mind if we record this interview?" asked Lane, as he turned on the portable recorder that Stephenson had brought from her office. He smiled, knowing that he was being only slightly more diplomatic than he had last night when Savage jumped him. Winn nodded that he did not mind, even though he did.

"OK, let me state some things for the record then," said Lane as he repeated the introductions at his end of the table, along with the date, time and location. "And your name is?" he asked looking at Winn.

"Andrew Benjamin Winn."

"And you have brought counsel to this interview?" asked Lane.

"No," said Winn. "This is Bill Stevens. He is my friend and works on the campaign."

Lane smiled arrogantly, again recalling his exchange with Savage.

"As you know, we are investigating the murder of you wife, Andria Winn, which occurred at your home last night in Georgetown," said Lane apparently intending to complete the interrogation himself. Winn had tried to size up the Assistant U.S. Attorney. She was short and slightly overweight. She was not attractive and did nothing to make the most of what she had. She wore little make-up and could be credited only with her stylish, short blond haircut. She wore a dark blue suit, which was appropriate, but rumpled. Motherly and mousy seemed to be the only descriptive words that came to Winn's mind.

"Were you there when your wife was shot, Senator?" asked Lane, forcing Winn to again remember the events of the evening before.

"I was in the house. I was not in the kitchen when she was killed," said Winn calmly.

"Did you hear the shot?" asked Lane.

"No."

"How do you explain that, Senator?" Lane asked quickly adopting his interrogation style.

"I can't explain it, Detective. I was hoping you could shed some light on that."

"You saw the murder weapon?"

"Yes."

"How do you know the gun you saw was the murder

weapon?" asked Lane.

"Wasn't it?" asked Winn, unbalanced by Lane's question. "I guess I assumed it was the gun."

"What gun are you talking about, Senator?" asked Lane.

"The Colt .45 that was laying on the floor," said Winn, the annoyance beginning to show in his voice.

"Have you ever heard the sound when a Colt .45 is fired, Senator?"

"Yes," said Winn. He had shot his own Colt .45 on a regular basis at a local shooting range with Dorothy Wallace. Before that, he had shot his sidearm many times at the Air Force Academy.

"Pretty loud, isn't it?" said Lane, beginning to taunt a little.

"Yes, Detective, it is pretty loud."

"So how do you explain that you didn't hear the shot?" asked Lane.

"I said I did not have an explanation. I hoped you would." Winn wondered what this guy was doing. He was treating Winn like a suspect, not asking any of the expected questions about who might have killed Andria.

"Was that your gun, Senator?"

"No."

"That's right, your Colt .45 is in San Antonio, isn't it?" stated Lane.

"That's correct."

"And, you never saw this gun, except when it was laying on the floor by your wife?"

"That's correct."

"Did you touch the gun, Senator?"

This was not what Stevens had expected. He wondered if he should do something. Winn was right; this guy considered Winn a suspect.

"What is your point, Detective?" asked Winn with irritation.

"I'm not trying to make points, Senator. Did I ask a difficult question?"

What a prick, Winn thought. That "Goddamn" gun; he knew

he should have thrown it out.

"Detective, I did not shoot my wife," said Winn.

Lane smiled at Stephenson. She could not help smiling back. Winn and Stevens were appalled at what they were seeing and hearing.

Stephenson spoke for the first time, her voice fitting the image Winn had settled on.

"Are you having an affair, Senator?" Stephenson asked.

"No."

"Did you sleep around on your wife?" she asked.

"No."

"Was your wife having an affair?"

"No."

"Did you and your wife fight, Senator?"

"No, Ms. Stephenson, not in the way you are implying. We had what I would consider to be normal marital disagreements."

Lane and Stephenson again exchanged glances. Winn was considering shutting this meeting down, when Lane stood up.

"I believe that is all we have for now, Senator," said Lane. "We may want to talk with you later."

Stephenson rose as well. Thorn looked about as shocked as the people at the other end of the table.

"Detective, I don't understand what's going on here. Are you trying to find out who killed my wife?"

"You bet we are, Senator," said Lane with an arrogant smirk.

"Do you have any real leads?" asked Winn.

"We have better than that, Senator," said Lane.

"Can you tell me what you have, Detective?" asked Winn, irritated, and maybe scared.

"I believe we have said all we can for now, Senator," said Lane. "Rest assured that we will be in touch." Lane walked to the door, opened it, and stood back for Winn and Stevens to exit.

Eight

Stevens and Winn did not talk in the car because of the Secret Service agents. Winn considered the interview, better described as an interrogation. They were not looking for a killer; Lane was trying to pin it right on him.

Stevens called Savage from the cellular phone installed in the agents' car. He was sitting in front of Winns' Georgetown home in his black BMW by the time they made their way through the rush hour traffic up Pennsylvania Avenue.

Winn used his key to open the door, hung up his gray wool top coat in the foyer closet that was packed with Andria's coats, and walked into the elegantly finished living room. He was usually a good host, even to those who worked for him. This time, however, he offered Savage and Stevens nothing as he silently built a fire in the large bricked fireplace and sat down in one of the wing-back chairs that faced each other in front of the fire, slightly opened to the sitting areas in the rest of the room. Savage had taken a seat on a love seat that was close to Winn and was chewing on a cigar. Stevens was pacing the floor, looking out the front window into shadows created by the street lights in the early evening.

"I take it things didn't go well," said Savage, breaking the ice.

"I'd say that pretty well sums it up," responded Winn. Winn took the poker from the rack of fireplace tools and moved the wood around to allow some space between the logs for the gas flame to emerge.

"I can't believe they think you killed her," said Stevens, shaking his head and still looking out the front window.

"Believe it," said Winn.

"OK, let's hear about it," said Savage, wanting the facts before he participated in forming a plan. There was silence as Winn still played absent-mindedly with the fire.

Stevens considered recounting the events. Before he could decide where to start, however, Winn began speaking.

"Thorn was there, but Lane did all the talking. John Butler put in an appearance, but left before the show. The prosecutor was Sybil Stephenson; she was older for the U.S. Attorney's office, maybe 40, probably a supervisor or something. She was matronly and unimposing, but had this scowl like she lived to put people in jail who thought they were better than she was."

"Great, the post-divorce working woman syndrome," chimed in Savage as he played with the end of his cigar to keep the hand-wrapped leaves in place in spite of the damage his chewing was causing.

"Something like that," said Winn.

"She never took her eyes off you," said Stevens, now turning to Winn and looking to decide where to sit, "except for those 'looks' she and Lane were exchanging. They acted like they have a thing for each other or something."

"My guess is it's the 'or something,' " said Winn. "In a nut-shell, I'd say they are two of a kind—crusaders, who think they alone can protect the world. Narrow minded, not too intelligent, and once their mind is focused on something, they are like bulldogs." Winn paused, hanging the poker back on the rack as he looked at the fire that was burning nicely.

"Lane focused on me last night," Winn continued. "I don't know why. Maybe most women are killed by their husbands. Maybe he just took the first convenient alternative. Maybe he sees me as his big stepping stone. Maybe he hates all politicians and thinks we are corrupt. I don't know. But he has me in his sights and is not looking anywhere else."

In spite of his normal style, Savage was a good listener until he had enough information to make a decision. He rarely found himself in a situation where it took him long to accumulate all the information he needed. He now sat patiently on the love seat, letting Winn tell the story at his own pace. This was perhaps the single most important moment in the campaign.

"From the beginning he asked me implicating questions. Did I hear the shot? How could I explain not hearing a Colt .45 fired in the same house? Where was my gun? How come I got such a good look at the gun?"

Winn got up and tossed another of the small walnut logs on the fire. He sat back down and continued.

"Then Stephenson asked me if I was having an affair? Was Andria having an affair? Did we fight?"

Winn stopped for what seemed like an endless silence. Stevens concluded that he was done.

"Then they cut it off," said Stevens, staring at Savage in disbelief. "They would not tell us what they found in the house or anything, but Lane arrogantly announced that they had identified the killer and they would be in touch. We then got led to the door."

After another pause, Winn added: "Pretty grim, huh, Jack?"

"They're pea-brains," said Savage, acting less affected by the story than he was. "We have got to put on pressure and shut these guys down."

"I don't think they work that way, Jack. These are the Woodwards and Bersteins of the District of Columbia Law Enforcement Community. The more pressure they get, the more they will be convinced they are pushing the right buttons."

"Then we have to talk them out of it," said Savage seeing the sense in Winn's assessment. He knew the type; young know-it-alls that had to be co-oped to be beaten. Lane was definitely that type; he had to decide it was his own idea to back off.

"They won't even talk to us," said Winn.

"They will talk to your lawyer," said Savage.

Winn looked at Savage, his eyes flickering as if he was shifting gears and moving to a level closer to reality.

"Once I hire a lawyer, the media will eat us alive," said Winn, thinking about the political implications of this ordeal.

"The media is running pretty hard with the story as we put it out," said Savage. He knew Stevens had briefed him on their morning efforts and how the media was playing the story. "We won't tell them you have hired a lawyer, and by the time they find out, this thing will be in the can. Or if it's not, we will have bigger problems than the fact that you've hired a lawyer."

"Yeah, like I'm being indicted for the murder of my wife." No one had wanted to recognize this possibility, even though Winn and Savage had both considered it since the encounter with Byron Lane last night.

"And because that is a possibility, you need a lawyer anyway, Ben," said Savage with sincerity. He had not wanted to raise the issue, until Winn seemed willing to accept the possibility.

"Jesus Christ," complained Winn, "how many murders do I have to be accused of in this lifetime? This is Tina Adams all over," he said referring to the young assistant who had been murdered and raped by KGB agents who tried to frame Winn for the crimes four years ago.

"Hopefully no more than two," said Savage with a smile. "If there is a third one, I will have a tough time getting you elected President." Winn returned the smile.

"Look, Jack. If they push this thing very far, the campaign will go up in smoke," said Winn.

"Don't be so sure," Savage said confidently. "Right now you're benefiting from this whole thing; I don't mean to be callous about Andria's death, but politically it is working to your advantage. If the public decides that the government is picking on you in your time of grief, that will play well, too." Savage actually believed what he was saying. "You let me worry about the campaign; I can not only keep it a float, but I can keep the steam flowing for quite a while. Unless you confess." Savage had only meant to inject some humor with the confession comment, but Winn looked at him, wondering if Savage thought he killed her.

"Your focus needs to be getting a lawyer who can sit down with these guys and their superiors and talk them out of this witch hunt," said Savage.

"Butler was real sympathetic," added Stevens, trying to find a ray of sunshine in the dismal ordeal. "He told us they would not stop until they found the killer. Nothing he said showed any signs of what Lane and Stephenson followed up with." Stevens paused, thinking, then added hurriedly to get it in before anyone else could talk. "And Thorn was sympathetic. These are the guys in charge, and they may not buy this bullshit story."

"Lane and Stephenson are lone wolves," said Winn. "They won't shut down easily because their superiors tell them to."

"But someone can talk them out of it," said Savage still being upbeat. "I know their type. Aggressive, but not real quick. It's like working the media; someone has to massage them a bit and let them conclude that this is a dead end that will damage their careers."

Winn and Savage knew that this was the next step. Savage began to consider potential lawyers. They needed someone polished who could be pushy, but not overbearing. Someone bright, but not condescending. Someone discreet, and preferably well-connected.

"How about Roger Atchinson at Henderson and Hall," said Savage. "He represented the key Clinton people charged by the special prosecutor with the health care insider trading stuff—got them all off, when they were guilty as hell.

"Most of his work has been white collar stuff, I think, but that makes him better suited if the media does ever find out. Plus, he's a Democrat and has a kind of professorial manner that might work with these guys."

Winn did not respond. Savage knew he was considering other alternatives, and waited patiently.

"I know some people at Hogan and Hartson that do criminal stuff, too." said Stevens. "They hire a lot of people out of the U.S. Attorney's office, and are probably wired with the civil service lawyers over there."

Winn knew he needed a lawyer. Somebody who could talk these people down, if that was a possibility; somebody that he could entrust his life with, if it was not. After a long silence, he spoke.

"I want Dorothy to do it."

"Fuck, Ben. This is complex enough," said Savage. He had not even considered the possibility. He knew the story well; it had been summarized repeatedly by the media, where it was almost a folk story. It had been printed in great detail today, as the media retold the Ben Winn story as part of their expanded coverage of Andria Winn's death. Four years ago, Winn's college room mate at the Air Force Academy was killed while working at the CIA. Before he was killed, he told Winn about a secret project the Russians had to make a first military strike against the United States and use an elaborate Star Wars system they had effectively developed, the "Red Surprise," to repeal the American response. The Russians had allowed the apparent disintegration of the Soviet Union into fragmented "independent" states, to throw the United States off its Star Wars quest, in fear of the Americans developing the same technology. The story was buried at the CIA by its Director, who later killed himself because of the embarrassment. The KGB had tried to silence Winn by framing him for the murder of a young female assistant who worked for then Congressman Ben Winn.

Winn had gone to Dorothy Wallace, the young, attractive, former Supreme Court clerk, for help. The facts about his relationship with Wallace at the time were sketchy, but the media implied they were lovers and had been since Wallace worked on the Hill for Winn. In a thriller that was better than fiction, Wallace and Winn were chased around the country by the FBI and KGB, until they uncovered enough facts to convince Texas eccentric billionaire Ralph Monroe that the United States was in imminent danger of nuclear disaster. Wallace and Winn had accompanied Monroe and his private army on a midnight military attack on the Kremlin, where they kidnapped the commander of the Russian military and stole intelligence information that would enable the United States to defend against the attack. With the Russian General and a Russian scientist to prove their story, Wallace and Winn had convinced President Carson to act. The Russians made their first strike, but it was destroyed by the system put in place at Wallace and Winn's direction. NATO forces had occupied the former Soviet territory since, and continued the process of setting up real democratic rule in the various satellite countries. Russia was still kept under NATO military rule.

At the time, the media romanticized the relationship between the national hero Winn and the young, attractive black heroine Wallace. Something had happened, however. It was speculated that the relationship ended for fear that its interracial implications would hurt Winn's career. Some speculated that his marriage to Andria Hamilton was always a front, a political convenience, and Winn and Wallace continued their affair beyond the view of public consumption. Winn had told Savage that he was not having an affair. Savage had operated from this position in deflecting the "personal indiscretion" questions in New Hampshire. Even if Winn was lying, Savage would have handled the questions the same way.

"She's not a criminal lawyer," said Savage, hoping to stomp out the idea with an objective fact.

"Jack, this is non-negotiable," said Winn. "My life is on the line here. I was willing to put my political life in your hands. I am not willing to put my 'other life' in anyone's hands but Dorothy's."

Savage knew it was a done deal, and even understood it. He and Winn were alike in many ways. They felt they were more capable than almost everyone. It was not arrogance in their opinion, just factual. They judged people by their own high standard, and you did not pass unless they were willing to give you a problem with confidence that you could solve it as well as they could. Almost nobody passed the test. Winn joked that he had met less than a dozen people in his life that he considered as capable as he, that he would turn over his own problems too. He and Savage joked about the group as being "The Club." Savage was in "The Club." He did not know Dorothy Wallace well, but he knew that Winn put her in "The Club" as well. From what he knew about the Russian crisis, Savage saw no reason to doubt Winn's assessment. Besides, Winn was in "The Club" as far as Savage was concerned, so by definition, he had to accept Winn's characterization of Dorothy Wallace.

"This is red hot, Ben," said Savage. "If the media ever turns on us over this, they will look to dig up dirt on you, and Dorothy is the first place to go. They will have you killing Andria to be with the sexy black girl that sits at the lawyer's table with you in court."

"I know," said Winn calmly. "With Dorothy on our side, we have some chance that it won't get to that point." He paused, then added. "If it does, the media is the least of my concerns, and with Dorothy at that table, I have a chance of avoiding the electric chair." Only recently had the death penalty been enacted for the first time in the District of Columbia. Its passage by the Congress of the United States evidenced a definite change in the wind, the same wind that Winn had intended to ride into the White House.

Stevens was seldom shaken, but he now sat stunned, wondering what he was witnessing and where it would end.

Nine

"**W**as she afraid of him?" asked Byron Lane, sitting across from him with a small tape recorder held in his right hand. Lane's voice was direct, yet almost without expression as usual. He reminded Tony Baroni of Sergeant Friday on the Dragnet reruns.

Baroni thought about his response. He sat back in his chrome-plated desk chair, with his thumbs cupped under his suspenders. Andria Winn was dead, but she could still turn him into a celebrity. Maybe more now than ever.

"Of course she was afraid of the guy." Baroni paused for effect, trying to look as sincere as possible. He cleaned up

106

well, and Lane did not doubt that he was a ladies man. Winn was stylish, but this guy had playboy written all over him. The office was contemporary and expensive, just like Baroni's clothes. Lane was impressed with the Nicole Miller tie that Baroni wore; he would like to have one, but could only afford the cheap imitations.

"He was not home much, but when he was, he was constantly abusive," said Baroni.

"Physically abusive?" asked Lane, still matter-of-fact, but now holding the tape recorder forward a bit, as if to ensure that he picked up every word that Baroni was uttering.

"Can I have a copy of that tape when we're finished?" asked Baroni, slipping out of his emotional over-wroughtness for a moment.

Lane looked at him with annoyance, but decided he should placate a key witness.

"Department policy does not allow for me to give you the tape," Lane said mechanically. "When you testify before the grand jury, however, the U.S. Attorney's office will give you a summary of the relevant information you've given me." Baroni had never been involved in a criminal case; in fact, he was not a lawyer except for the bar certificate on the wall. He was a lobbyist, a politician. He was unfamiliar with the process Lane alluded to where the prosecutor would coach a witness before the grand jury, give them written answers to study and to refer to when challenged by the defense lawyers at the trial. Without a script, witnesses constantly contradicted themselves and looked bad in front of juries.

"OK," said Baroni, not really sure if what Lane said was adequate. Baroni knew he had to be careful. He was making this up as he went along and needed to remember the story for when it had to be retold.

"So, anyway," continued Baroni, again looking like the bereaved boyfriend of one of the victims, "he was physically abusive. I would see her with bruises a lot, usually in places where they would not be seen when she was dressed and in public.

He was very concerned that she not look battered, and he would never hit her in the face or anything." Baroni was proud of himself with that line; it was good, he thought.

"You saw the bruises when you had sex with Mrs. Winn?" asked Lane. He knew this guy was scum, but this scum would be useful in cleaning up other scum.

"Andria and I were in love," said Baroni, telling at least a half-truth. "We spent as much time together as we could. Yes, we had sex, and I saw her naked in normal relationship kinds of ways, like in the shower and getting dressed and such." He thought he might write a novel; this stuff was coming quick and natural.

"Did he ever threaten to kill her?" asked Lane, showing a slight increase in the octave of his voice, to indicate the importance of the question.

"She said she was afraid he might kill her," said Baroni, stumbling in his thought process a bit. "She never came out and said that he threatened to kill her, but she was afraid he might." Baroni squirmed in his chair, and picked up a ball point pen, clicking it, to release some of the anxiety.

"Why was she afraid he might kill her?" asked Lane, unable to resist his confrontational style.

Baroni paused, thinking, although he had already decided on the gist of his story. He thought he detected some suspicion in Lane's voice.

"Because he was crazy; he would bitch at her all the time. It's like he had to be perfect in public so he took out all of his frustrations on her." Baroni, inappropriately smiled, pleased with himself. Then he added the key to his story. "She loved him at first, before we fell in love. But he never loved her. He continued to have an affair with this black chick that he was seeing when he met Andria. She figured out that he married her for her money and because it wouldn't fit his political image to be seen in public with the black chick."

"But Andria was only window dressing," continued Baroni. "She knew that if he ever got out of politics, he would leave her for the other woman."

"What black woman are you talking about?" asked Lane, although he already knew.

"You know, the one that the papers talk about, Dorothy Wallace. The one that he was with during that Russian stuff."

"When did you last see Mrs. Winn?" asked Lane.

"The day he killed her."

"Where did you see her?" asked Lane.

"She came to my place; we never met at her place."

"Did you have sex?" asked Lane. It was not relevant, but his prurient interests prompted the follow up.

"We made love," said Baroni, sounding offended at Lane's casual use of the phrase "have sex" to describe the special relationship he was portraying.

"Did Mrs. Winn say anything unusual to indicate she felt in more danger than usual?"

"She said he was acting more crazy before he went to New Hampshire and that he had not called her at all, even after winning the primary. She did not know what to expect when he got home."

"Why did she stay with Winn?" asked Lane, knowing that it was because of the power, but wanting to see what Baroni would say.

"She intended to leave him," he lied. "We were going to get married. He did not give us a chance," he said pathetically. What an actor, he thought.

"Why did you call the police?" asked Lane.

"When I heard about it on the news, I cried. I am not too proud to admit that it was difficult to pull myself back together. But I knew from the first minute I heard it that he had killed her. I had to get my shit together for Andria; I had to ensure that her death was avenged." He would need a publicists, he thought. He was certain that every daytime talk show would be bidding for his story.

SAVAGE DROVE OVER the Fourteen Street Bridge and, as he often did, thought about the February airplane crash of Flight

401 that occurred during a snow storm that killed most of the passengers and decapitated several of the commuters stuck on the bridge in rush-hour, snow-packed traffic. He had been a young intern on Capital Hill at the time; like many Washingtonians, he had considered the possibilities of his being on the bridge at the time of the crash. But for working late that night to get out a draft of bill, he would have been pushing through the traffic for his Arlington apartment.

There was no snow on this February day, however. It was bitter cold, but the sun was shining, glimmering off the Dome of the Jefferson Memorial. It had been a dry winter, El Nino, Savage recalled from his days of physical science at Tulane.

It was mid-afternoon as he pushed up Fourteen Street and took a left on Pennsylvania Avenue. He looked at the White House as he turned the corner and considered the possibilities of being there. People would probably find it odd that he had never been in the White House, not even for one of the popular Congressional tours that the members of Congress dole out to their constituents.

There were protesters, as always, across the street at Lafayette Square. Signs saying "Free Russia," "Stop Abortion," and "No more taxes" had long-established places of prominence. Savage thought they should pay rent if they were going to be there this long. The small park in the middle of the city was for the public, not for a bunch of radicals that scared off normal people.

Savage turned right on Seventeen Street and then left on Connecticut. He stopped at a stop light, looking for a parking place on the street in the next block. Seeing none, he pulled ahead when the light changed and turned into the parking garage marked "public parking" with an official-looking neon sign. He pressed a button and took a ticket and searched for an empty spot. If the machine gave him a ticket, surely there was one somewhere, Savage thought.

DOROTHY WALLACE SAT WORKING in one of the small conference rooms that she often used to work in. Her office was

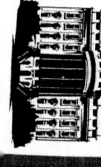

ed with another deal. She was using this space to com-
 e materials needed for the litigation she had upcoming
 he FDIC. The government's lawyers had begun to talk
 settling for a lesser amount, but Wallace insisted her cli-
 uld pay the original contract price and not a penny more.
 s the way business is conducted," she had said indignantly
 d the conversion with one of their lawyers.

orothy, Mr. Savage is here," said Staci, peeking her head
 door, as if she could interrupt without being intrusive.
 had worked for Wallace at Jones & Day, coming with her
 they formed the new firm. She was indispensable.

ll get him," said Wallace, knowing that Savage would be
 waiting room down the hall. No one was allowed to pass
 eceptionist until a lawyer was ready to meet them. There
 a lot of drawbacks to having clients, let alone adversaries,
 around your offices unattended.

allace laid down the purple felt-tip pin that she was fa-
 s for using to obliterate the work of her associates, and
 idered the call that Savage had made. It was brief, but
 enough to get her mind spinning. Savage wanted to talk
 her, but he did not want to talk on the telephone. "You
 r know who's listening," he had said. She did not really
 w Savage, having met him only a time or two on social
 sions when Winn had hired him to run the Senate cam-
 n. He had a reputation for his brilliant mastery of the art of
 tics.

he had been following the story in the newspapers. She
 n picked up the telephone once to dial Winn, to express
 sorrow and let him know that she cared. She had resisted,
 ever, confident that he knew she cared, and feeling it some-
 y inappropriate. But for the brief call from Winn last week
 a brief call the week before when he called to say he was
 ng to run, she had not talked to Winn for months.

She was not sure if she had made the right decision for her-
, but she was confident that she had made the right one for
 nn. Besides, Wallace was not the type of woman to second

guess herself. You make a choice, and you live with it. Regrets serve no purpose.

She and Winn had ignored their love for years, letting it emerge in the form of a close, but very private friendship. That had been Winn's call, although not said in so many words. As a Congressman he was a single, young, good-looking man living alone in Washington, D.C. He knew the voters would ignore his sleeping with some of the women he dated—they would be happy that his bed partners were not men—but, he was not sure they would understand his sleeping with a black woman. Race continued to be a white-hot issue in politics. Besides, if Winn let himself go that way, he was not sure he could stop with just sex. An interracial marriage would be political suicide. Wallace took out her hostility by joking with Winn about what the voters back home would think, and other nonsense to make a serious issue seem less important. It was her way of dealing with stress. Whining was not allowed. Accept the facts, and live with them.

When on the run with Winn, trying to save his life by proving his innocence in the murder of Tina Adams, and then discovering that only they could save the lives of every American, their guard had been down. A sensuality broke through when they thought there might be no tomorrow. They had confessed their love and consummated it.

Then Winn was a hero; her, too, for that matter. His political career was more alive than ever. She knew a part of him would die inside if he had to give it up. She knew he could not have both her and politics, and never considered what might die inside Winn if he had to go on without her. She made a unilateral decision and broke off their relationship. He had tried to contact her, but she avoided him. She had wanted to cry and grieve, but Dorothy Wallace did not act that way. She went on, burying herself in her work more than ever.

After he gave up, she began to occasionally take his calls. Their conversations were brief, but began to assume their pre-affair form, where topical issues were discussed and flirting allowed. He always called if he was going to be doing something that the media would find noteworthy; he wanted her to hear it from him first. When he called to say he was getting married, she was stunned, but did not show it and wished him well. She would never forget the one sentence, "But you know I will never love anyone but you." He gave no explanation. Briefly, she wanted him to protest her decision, declare that he would end his political career if necessary to have her.

In spite of the huge problem hanging over his head, which had dominated all of his thoughts since Winn had called the night Andria Winn was killed, he forgot about all else when she walked into the reception room. Savage, a single man, too busy to have a serious relationship, was of above average intelligence, with considerable money and even more power. Hanging around campaigns, there was never any shortage of "talent" if he had the time and interest. Even to a man of such assortment, Dorothy Wallace was a show-stopper.

He remembered that she was attractive, but apparently did not remember it as clearly as he should have. She was graceful and at ease as she walked from the catacombs of her own offices—the law firm where she was Queen. Still young at 31, she was for the first time in her career—the first time since college—no longer anyone's "girl wonder" to parade and show off. She was in charge of her own shop, bringing in business to keep 30 lawyers busy, and making well in excess of half a million dollars a year.

The power and the ability added to the attraction for a man of Savage's sensibilities or, Savage thought, to a man like Winn. She was, however, gorgeous enough to turn the head of anyone. At five feet, three inches, and weighing no more than 110 pounds, she was petite, but possessing the sexy curves and long legs that would compete with any model, a business at which she could also have succeeded.

Dressed in a black suit with a peplum coat to accentuate her tiny waist, she looked like a picture out of *Vogue*. Her thin but shapely legs, which revealed the workouts and running that she did daily, were covered with black stockings; black heels completed the picture that Savage found himself taking in an embarrassing silence after she had said hello. Her make-up was stylish, putting only a sheen on her dark black face, with her eyes done only with black liner and her lips covered with a dark maroon gloss. Her long black hair extensions were pulled back and loosely tied with a black hair do.

"Earth to Jack Savage," she said, trying to start the introductions over again. She was used to men looking her up and down; it was mildly annoying, but something she took in stride unless the gawkers were obnoxious. Then she could make any man feel two inches tall.

"Dorothy, thanks for taking the time to see me," said Savage, as he stood up from the purple cushioned chair in the reception room.

"I assume it's got something to do with Ben," she said. Savage wondered if that meant she would not see him if it were about his own business, and considered being mildly annoyed. It was no never-mind, however. He was here on Winn's business; besides, Dorothy Wallace could get away with treating people like Savage in ways that nobody else could treat them.

'Yeah, it's about Ben," he said.

"Come on back," she said, as she turned and led him through the closed double doors that protected the lawyers offices.

"Nice space," said Savage as he looked at the plush accommodations. "The War Room on King Street does not compare well." She had read about the reference to the Winn headquarters in Old Town as the War Room.

"We are already outgrowing it," said Dorothy Wallace. "We've been here about two years. Not very good planning, I guess," she said modestly, knowing that the space problem was a clear sign of their success.

They walked down the long corridor that had lawyers' offices with windows to their right. To their left was an open area that housed secretarial people, and small windowless offices on the inside wall where the paralegals worked. Every desk had at least one computer terminal. Savage noticed that even most of the lawyers had computer terminals inside their offices. The firm increased its turnaround time considerably by letting lawyers get into the documents on their word processors to make drafting changes, then letting the clerical help pull the documents up from the central processing system to polish off and print the documents.

The offices were all done in tasteful art deco colors—greens, purples, blues. It was trendy, but stylish and expensive. "Just like Dorothy," thought Savage.

The lawyers' offices went completely around the floor of the building. The paralegal offices built in the interior prevented Savage from seeing the bull pen for secretaries and the lawyers' offices on the other side.

Wallace led him past the small conference room where she had been working and into her spacious corner office. It provided a panoramic view of the downtown Washington. The Capitol Dome and the Washington Monument were also visible.

Although larger, the office was similar to that she had decorated at Jones & Day. Not because she wanted them to be similar, but because it was what she liked. The walls were covered with gray-textured cloth wall coverings. The two walls that were not covered with windows prominently displayed large colorful abstract original paintings. Both were done by local artists and had been purchased for the aesthetic impact they had on Wallace, not for their name, nor their impact in impressing others. One of the artists was, however, now being touted by Georgetown art deals as an up-and-coming guy whose work was a wise investment. The walls no longer displayed any of Wallace's credentials, including the boxes and boxes of American Jurisprudence and West Publishing Company law school awards that she had in the basement of her condominium building. Everyone who came in this office knew who Wallace was; she no longer needed to sell herself to any one.

Savage sat down in one of two cushioned purple swivel chairs that, together with a dark blue love seat, surrounded a glass and chrome coffee table on one side of the room. The glass and chrome desk, flanked by a tall and slender black leather executive chair, was covered with stacks of paper and pink phone messages.

"How is he doing?" she asked, ending the small talk they had made on their way into the office.

"We have a big problem, Dorothy," he said, watching to assess her reaction. She gave none.

"And what is that, Jack?" she asked, wanting him to come to the point.

"The cops think Ben killed Andria." He paused, then continued. "There is this young egomaniac, save-the-world type homicide detective who made his mind up the night he came to Ben's house. Now he has some woman prosecutor who seems to be his kindred spirit." Savage rolled his eyes to emphasis the exasperation that these two were causing.

"What's her name?" asked Wallace, wondering if she knew the person Savage referred to as the "woman prosecutor." It was a common type characterization that mildly annoyed Wallace, but she let it pass. She was used to being identified as the "cute black lawyer" or similar epitaphs.

"Sybil Stephenson."

Dorothy Wallace shook her head no; the name did not ring a bell.

"So, how is he doing?" she asked again.

He realized that her first concern was how Winn was doing emotionally. He indicated that, as expected, Winn was playing the hand he had been dealt. Winn was doing fine, but if he did not get these law enforcement people straightened out soon, the political damage could be astronomical.

"So why are you here?" she asked getting to the point, which was her style.

"He needs a lawyer," said Savage seriously, but with the air of amusement that people have when faced with a dilemma they still cannot believe is real.

"So you want me to make a referral?" she asked. Dorothy

uncrossed her long sexy legs, then crossed them the other way. She was reluctant to hear the answer to the question.

"He wants you to be his lawyer," said Savage as he found himself focused on her legs, then looking back into her dark brown eyes.

"Fuck," said Wallace, using her infamous foul mouth that was so incongruous with the dainty feminine presentation she made. "Ben knows that I don't do any criminal work. He isn't stupid enough to let a virgin do the case if he really needs a lawyer. He cannot be serious."

"Oh, he's serious," said Savage. "You know how he is; nobody is going to talk him out of this once a decision has been made."

"I can talk him out of it if I don't take the case," she responded instinctively, defending against a statement that indicated she had no say in the matter.

Savage paused, considering where to go next. He then turned the conversation to another subject, a tactic he often used in negotiation. He would later return to his purpose.

"Aren't you going to ask me if he killed her?" Savage regretted the question. He thought that she had undoubtedly talked to Winn; indeed, he believed that surely she and Winn were having an affair. She was gorgeous. Besides, Savage thought, he was not sure whether he knew the answer to the question.

"I know he didn't kill her," she said calmly.

"So you've talked?" asked Savage, wondering if he was at a disadvantage in this conversation.

"We haven't talked," she answered. "But I know Ben," she said. "Besides, if I had any doubts, I'd ask him, not you," she said with a glare that reminded Savage he was not dealing with your average campaign bimbo who asked "how high" when he said jump.

"Look, let me back up," said Savage, now wishing for sure that he had never started this line of discussion. "What we need here is not a criminal lawyer. We need someone to meet with these people and convince them that they should get off this kick before they ruin their careers and Ben's. They need to be looking for the real killer," he said, hoping that they had not really picked the right guy already.

"I'll talk to Ben about it," she said. Her tone indicated that he would get no further. It was a humbling experience, like none Savage was used to any more. He felt like an errand boy who was being sent home with a scolding for not bringing an adult with him to do the job.

"We were concerned about the media ...." Savage started to explain the concern of the media seeing Winn with a lawyer, particularly this lawyer.

"I think you can pull off a meeting in secrecy," said Dorothy condescendingly. It was settled. While annoyed, Savage could see why she was the right girl for the job. It would be up to Winn, however, to sign her up.

Ten

SALLY MACARTHUR was 42 years old. Compulsively concerned about her appearance, she presented the best body
that money could buy. In spite of over $25,000 of work, which
had bought implants for her now firm and ample breasts, and
provided a facelift and nose job, she stood in front of the mirror
each evening after dinner and convinced herself that her frame
of five feet, six inches, covered with 100 pounds, was fat. She
then locked the bathroom off the bedroom that she shared with
no one, and went through the ritual of sticking her finger down
her throat and vomiting. She was certain that one day she would
look in the mirror and the obese woman that was always there

would not be staring back. When she had asked the plastic surgeon about liposuction, he had rather awkwardly suggested that she see a psychologist instead. Eventually, she would find another doctor.

Sally MacArthur was twice divorced, collecting periodic payments resulting from property settlements from both. She married well, and divorced even better. Her "idiosyncrasies," as she referred to them, could be well disguised during the whirlwinds of a romance. Marriage was, however, another matter. Her insistence on a separate bedroom had come early in both marriages; the marriages ended in substance, if not form, shortly thereafter.

Without children, she now lived alone in the Georgetown townhouse that her last husband had owned when she met him. Harry MacArthur had been a partner and member of the managing committee of the Washington, D.C. office of Ernst & Young when he met Sally. At age 54, Harry found the young slender brunette to be irresistible, and after a short but whirlwind affair, Harry immediately divorced his wife of 21 years and immediately went to Las Vegas where he and Sally were married.

The honeymoon was wonderful. Sally was young and full of life, always on the go, seldom taking time to eat or sleep. They had spent their honeymoon at the Mirage, frequenting the room for sex once or twice a day, then moving off to the tables or a show. They had stayed in Vegas for seven days—normally an eternity in Las Vegas. When the week was up, however, Harry was not ready to leave. His new wife was spending his long-saved money at a record pace though, and he decided to moderate his new bliss by returning to the office and keeping a claim on his clients.

The first night home was great; sex again, then while Harry slept, Sally was off somewhere in another part of his tastefully furnished townhouse that his wife had left, returning to her family in Milwaukee. When Harry returned home from work the next day, he found that Sally had, as planned, moved all of her things in, but instead of to the master bedroom, she had moved all of her possessions into the guest bedroom on the second floor that had its own private bath. She said it was just for his convenience; she did not want to upset his routine. She would sleep in the master bedroom but use the guest room for her clothes and make-up and stuff. He accepted her explanation in spite of its fallacy; the master bedroom had been stripped by his departing ex-wife. A large walk-in closet in the master bedroom was almost empty. Sally MacArthur sleep in the master bedroom with her new husband for two nights before retreating to the privacy of the guest room she had taken over. For the first few months, she would sleep there only part of the time, although that part grew continuously. Six months into the marriage she was sleeping there all of the time. There was no sex; Sally was too strung-out on diet pills and tranquilizers. She claimed that her husband was suffocating her and used violence to push him away. Several times the Georgetown police were called by Sally, who claimed that her husband was abusing her. Always finding more evidence of violence inflicted on Harry, the police would leave with Harry's assurance that he would be fine and needed no outside help with his wife. Quietly, she sought some treatment at Harry's insistence. In the end, Harry offered her anything she wanted just to let him go. She took his Georgetown home after he paid off the mortgage, the BMW he had bought her, his membership at the Chevy Chase Country Club, and agreed to $5,000 a month in maintenance. The marriage lasted three years; it was the worst business deal Harry had ever done. In the end, however, he was struggling to keep his reputation, his business, and his sanity. If he could walk away with those, then he could pay the losses. Combined with the payments from her first divorce, Sally managed an income of over $100,000 a year. Together with the closely monitored money she received from a trust fund set up by her father, but tied up in the control of a stuffy financial institution as trustee, she managed to live well while contributing nothing.

She was hardly Andria Winn's best friend. Andria did not

have a best friend in Washington other than Tony. Her roots were in Houston, and she had longed to return there. Sally was always looking for friendship, however, and managed to work her way in to the group of women that Andria Winn lunched and played bridge with at the Club weekly. She called Andria at all hours of the night, confessing the abuse she received at home, and seeking pity. In uncharacteristic form, Andria tolerated the inconvenience. Indeed, Sally became quickly useful as an ally in contriving stories to deceive Ben Winn about his wife's whereabouts. Sally gladly played the role, feeling important to someone, needed by another human being.

Sally knew why he was there. Tony had called. He said that it was a certainty that Winn had killed "their" Andria. Andria had confessed to him the abuse she took, and the fear she had for her life. Sally was empathetic. She had no idea, but she had been through the same thing. "I thought Harry would murder me for sure," she had said. She now believed these lies. Baroni said the police could not go with his story alone, however. He was, after all, her lover, and a jury might frown on that. Sally, however, was Andria's best friend. He lied, but it made her eyes sparkle. Surely Andria had confided her horror in Sally; if only she could corroborate his story, they would put that "son-of-a-bitch" away for taking their Andria. "Of course, Andria, told me all about it. Called me in the middle of the night sometimes, scared to death—for her life," she added, lying. She could not believe that Baroni would be saying this if it were not true; and if it were true, she could not confess that her "best friend" never let it be known to her. Besides, Baroni assured her that the police had hard evidence, and all they were doing was providing motive to help strengthen an already airtight case.

"You knew her well?" asked Lane, sitting in Sally's well furnished living room as he flipped on his portable tape recorded, not asking permission as usual.

"Of course, I knew her well. She was my best friend," said

the frail-looking woman. Lane thought that she looked sick. He would remember to check into it, make sure she was not an alcoholic or something. It would not be devastating, since they had Baroni, but it would be something to prepare for to rehabilitate her as a witness.

"And you knew about her relationship with Mr. Anthony Baroni?" he asked.

She paused, not sure what the right answer should be, then agreed that she knew. Lane explained that they had solid evidence indicating that Winn had killed his wife, and that Mr. Baroni had given corroborating evidence primarily concerned with motive and the state of mind of the victim.

"Baroni said that you were her best friend and would be able to corroborate his story."

Sally said nothing, trembling a bit, waiting for Lane to lead her down the right path.

"Did Mrs. Winn ever say to you that she was in fear of being hurt, even killed, by her husband?" he asked in an even monotone.

Sally stumbled as she spoke. She knew what she was supposed to say, but did not want to make any mistakes.

"Yes, she was afraid. He hurt her badly sometimes." She paused briefly, but was getting a head of steam. "She would call me in the middle of the night and ask to come over. He would be in one of his fits and she was afraid if she did not leave he would hurt her, maybe kill her." In no time at all, Sally would convince herself that all of this was true.

By the time Lane was finished asking questions, he had a tape lasting over an hour that put the icing on his cake. Winn was a dead man, figuratively and maybe literally.

"We may need to have you testify at the grand jury. Will there be a problem with that?" he asked.

"Will there be press coverage?" asked Sally MacArthur.

"Probably not for the grand jury; their proceedings are in private." Sally looked disappointed, but seemed pleased when Lane added that there would be media coverage of the trial, probably a lot of media coverage.

SHE RAMMED ON THE BRAKE of the black Porsche when she saw the District of Columbia patrol car sitting off to the side of the Amoco station as she rolled over the bridge into Georgetown. She raced down Pennsylvania Avenue each day listening to Usher, Will Smith, or something with a good beat on her CD player. She always moved to the music, in the car, in the shops, at the club, or wherever. Chair dancing, she called it. Wallace said that her motto in life was to "never miss a beat."

The cop sat motionless in his unit. He was probably on a donut break, she thought. Instead of cruising down to the Georgetown Mall where her condo was, she moved the Porsche into the right lane and turned up Wisconsin Avenue. A couple of college boys standing on the corner waved their arms wildly, shouting something. She did not look directly, but recognized them with a smile; they were cute. They thought she was hot.

As she parallel parked in a space that looked too small but ended up being plenty big, Wallace looked at the house. She immediately thought about Andria Winn lying dead inside. They never really knew each other. She gave Andria the benefit of the doubt, figuring that Winn would not have married her if she were not special. There were few facts, however, that had come to her attention to support the conclusion that she was in Winn's league. Wallace wondered if Andria had been jealous, but concluded she was not. Andria had nothing to do with why she and Winn were not together. It had been all her doing, or it had been all his and she had merely acted accordingly.

He was in the house alone; it was what he wanted in spite of Stevens and Savage arguing for a private meeting to be arranged somewhere outside the watchful eye of the media and the cops. Winn was putting a lot of non-negotiable items on the table lately.

She stepped up to the door, dressed casually in a short black skirt, with black tights and chunky-heeled loafers. She wore a black turtleneck under her off-white Gap cardigan sweater. She had no clients in the office this afternoon, and hearing the winter storm watch on the radio, had changed clothes accordingly. She had a private bath at her office and a closet that would be the envy of most women as their main wardrobe.

"Hey, Dot," said Winn as he opened the door. Dorothy Wallace was called Dot only by her family in Illinois and Winn— it was her name until she went to Yale. He glanced up and down the street. Wallace assumed he was looking for TV cameras; there were none.

"I wasn't followed," she said a bit sarcastically.

"I was just looking," he responded defensively. "Habit, I guess. Seems like I'm on the run again." He smiled. She did not.

"Are you doing okay?" she asked. Once safely in the door, she lightly embraced him and patted him on the back as a sign of caring.

"Yeah, I'm OK," he said, then added, "for a guy whose wife has been killed and who the cops think did it." He smiled at the irony.

"When you get your life fucked up, Ben, you sure go all the way," she said easing some of the tension, but still not smiling. She followed Winn into the back of the house, through the kitchen where Andria had been killed and into the sun room that overlooked the well-groomed private back yard. They each sat down in the large high-back white cane chairs.

"So aren't you going to ask me if I did it?" he asked.

"Fuck you, Ben."

"So where is your usual light-hearted good nature?" he asked grinning at her as only he could.

"I left it at the office," she said dryly.

"You have always been my salvation, Dot. You're supposed to make me see the bright side or something. Cause me to laugh while my life goes to shit."

"That was then, Ben," she said as she folded her arms to match her crossed legs. It was not an inviting picture in spite of her physical appeal. Body language says it all.

"No mercy?" he asked.

"Come on, Ben. Quit fucking around. We had our chance. We had two, in fact. We got on with our lives the way adults do."

"So you're seeing somebody?" Winn asked. He felt like she had never been away. Her personality was like a magnet to him. When he was around her, he was drawn in like groupies to a rock star. He idolized her; she was his Barbie, his baby; and he loved her, too. Like he had never loved anyone. Why had he let her get away, he wondered. Maybe he could get another chance.

"Snap out of it, Ben," she said, ignoring his question. He was in a zone that had nothing to do with the reason for their meeting. She could tell. "Get back to reality, Ben. The way Jack tells it, you need a lawyer. This time I'm not the right 'guy.' "

He sat there looking at her. He did not need to use words to convey his feelings; he wanted to be rescued and he did not trust anyone but Dorothy Wallace to do the job. It was crazy. She answered his unspoken question.

"I have never worked on a criminal case in my life, Ben. You know the saying that 'a lawyer who represents himself has a fool for a client.' Well, some derivative of that is applicable here. You're a smart man, Ben. You know I can't do this job."

It still seemed like forever before he talked. When he finished, she agreed to take the case. At least, until she could have a meeting with these people; surely she could convince them that they were crazy.

Eleven

H E SAT IN HIS HOTEL ROOM at Hilton Head, South Carolina staring at CNN. The fund-raiser had looked good,
but over half of the 1,000 seats had been discreetly given away
by his staff to make the event look good. There were two
goals at every fund-raiser. First, raise a lot of money; campaigns, even with the matching funds, were quests for money—
asking people to give you something for nothing, except that
brush with potential power. On the first goal, this fund-raiser
had failed liked most of his fund-raising efforts had gone south
in the past few weeks. No one wanted to invest in a losing
cause. Just as important, no one wanted the winner to see

them as a foe. Many people, particularly the political actions committees, play both sides of the fence but, as they say in politics, it costs twice as much to buy in late. Well before Ben Winn formally declared his candidacy, his people were making his intentions known and lining up financing. He was a national hero, and the bandwagon picked up steam quickly. The money had begun to flow Winn's way, like the thawing snow finding its way to the mountain crevices.

The second part of every fund-raising event was the show. There had to be a crowd, no seat left unattended. An old political tactic was to know how many people you would have attend, and then prepare seats for 100 less. Nothing made an impact on a crowd like the last-minute setting up of tables and chairs—a standing room only sell-out. Randy Hardy's people had discreetly given away enough tickets to pull off the crowd size, but the locals knew how hard it had been to raise the money, and nobody believed that the crowd was a paying one.

After Hardy had given his stump speech, he did the obligatory handshaking, then came to his room to be alone. He had been sitting on the bed since, with his back propped up on three of the thin institutional white pillows. He was still wearing his blue pin-stripe suit, including the jacket, although he had loosened his blue and red striped tie and unbuttoned the collar of his white shirt. He stretched out with his legs crossed, staring at the television, partially listening, partially in another world. He looked more like a ward boss than a presidential candidate, something along the lines of a Hubert Humphrey. His round face and balding head portrayed a fatherly type, even though he had never had children. His wife had died from cancer five years before. He was not the type to marry again. For all of his faults, sexual promiscuity was not one of them. He was a driven man, and his drive was to be President of the United States.

He had worked his whole life to get to this point. He had paid his dues. Elected 25 years ago, when he was 30, as the county clerk of Maricopa County, he then ran for Congress and became the first Arizona Congressman who also served as the State Democratic Party chairman. He was a party man through and through, eventually serving on the platform committee for the national party and as the coveted majority whip in a Congress where Republicans remained a minority party. He was the only man in the race who had earned the job. In spite of this, he was being ignored; they were all flocking to the boy-hero. The ladies man, who dressed like he walked out of a GQ photo shoot, not out of the hallowed chambers of the U.S. Congress. He hated Ben Winn. Hardy spent a lifetime to get in this position, the odds-on favorite to receive the Democratic nomination for President. Now at 55 years old and high blood pressure that was discreetly withheld from the media, he was soon to be a has-been. It had been clear for months that if Winn entered the race, Hardy would provide no more than token resistance in a general election. Winn would take the oath of office that should have been given to him.

He came fully back into awareness as he saw the black and white footage of the man in a long dark overcoat standing over the gravesite. The sky was gray and overcast; it was a moving scene. Instinctively, he focused his attention on the television screen. The picture changed to a black screen with large white capital letters burning the words, "IN MEMORY OF ANDRIA WINN." He listened to the deep baritone voice of the narrator.

"Damn," he said as his face reddened. He bit his lip as he watched the commercial. He drew blood. He liked the salty taste of his blood. He had come to the room to watch for updates—developments—in the Winn case. He had not expected this. He picked up the phone and dialed a zero. The operator knew by the room number on her console who was calling and jumped to transfer his call to the room he wanted.

"Are you watching TV?" Hardy asked in exasperation.

"We saw it," responded his campaign manager. Hardy could hear the moans of the crowd in the other room. They had been gathered to go over the staggering numbers that the absentee candidate was posting.

"That Goddamn son of a bitch is using this. Can you believe it?" Hardy groaned the rhetorical question. There was no response. Hardy hung up the phone. He could not believe this. What had gone wrong?

DOROTHY WALLACE REACHED her long slender black arm to the nightstand to hit the snooze button on her Sony radio/alarm. The second time around, she turned off the alarm and switched on the radio. A Spice Girls song was playing. She pulled the white and black checkered sheet and white electric blanket up closer to her neck to ward off the morning chill.

She wondered if she was crazy. She knew little more about criminal law than a third-year law student. She had read the briefs on her share of Fourth and Fifth Amendment cases while clerking at the Supreme Court. She had even written a majority opinion for the Court on a Fourth Amendment case concluding there was no reasonable expectation of privacy on a small yacht in the Gulf of Mexico, and, therefore a search and seizure without a warrant was reasonable. This, she thought, hardly qualified her to be representing a target of a grand jury murder investigation.

As Wallace pulled herself out of bed and on the floor for her morning ab work, she convinced herself that this would all blow over. Winn had enough bad luck with the murder of Tina Adams four years ago. Lightning could not strike twice in the same place.

While lying on the floor, Wallace pulled up her Washington Redskins tee-shirt to look at her abs. She was never satisfied, even though her stomach was hard and her ab muscles gently ribbed. With indifference rather than satisfaction, Wallace pulled her tee-shirt down and then rolled over to do four sets of ten push-ups. Her arms were thin, but the definition of her muscles was clear. The shape of her muscles became more pronounced as she pumped blood into her arms and chest. Wallace had run the night before, doing her short track—three miles through the residential streets of Georgetown that she had measured out with her Porsche.

After a shower, Dorothy looked in her large walk-in closet to decide what would be appropriate for the occasion. At 9:30 a.m. she would be meeting with Jack Butler, Byron Lane, and Sybil Stephenson. The closet was shaped like a "L," displaying four walls for clothes and accessories. One of the walls was filled with suits. Another had dresses and casual outfits. A third wall was filled with single pieces, such as shirts, jeans, and the like. The final wall had built-ins filled with shoes, sweaters, and other accessories. What a prize she was for Saks Fifth Avenue. Wallace alone could support the value of their stock.

Standing there in her white bra and bikini briefs, Wallace glanced back and forth between the clothes and the full-length mirror on the back of the door as if imagining what different outfits would look like on her body. She finally selected a navy silk suit, laying it on the bed with a pair of navy high heels. She pulled a white shell over her head that would be exposed at the top of the suit, then sat down on the side of her king-size bed, gathered up one leg of a pair of navy panty hose, and slipped her toes into it. She pulled the panty hose up to above her knee, repeated the process for the other leg, then pulled them up to her waist. Wallace then sat down at the vanity in her bedroom to finish her make-up and hair before putting on the rest of her clothes.

She turned on the CD player in her Porsche to the first one available—it was Janet Jackson. As she bobbed and weaved in and out of the morning rush-hour traffic, she went over in her head what she would say.

WALLACE WAS USHERED into the same room where Winn had been interrogated three days before. Butler got up to greet her; Stephenson and Lane remained seated and thereby set the tone of the meeting.

"Thanks, Jake, for agreeing to see me," said Wallace. She had worked with Butler when she was at the Supreme Court and he was a young attorney in the U.S. Attorney's office arguing FOIA cases. He was impressed, if not intimidated, by her skill then. This view had only been reinforced as he followed her career in the *Washington Post.*

"This is not an easy one on any of us," said Butler, as if he was ready to pronounce someone dead.

"Frankly, I'm not sure what purpose is served by a meeting at this point," said Stephenson. Awkwardly, Butler pointed to a chair for Wallace to take a seat. Wallace slowly put her brief case on the table, opened it and removed a file and legal pad. The file had nothing to do with Winn. It was, however, obvious that this was going to be a hostile meeting. Wallace knew to use props to slow down the meeting and keep some element of control on her side of the table.

"We were pretty surprised to see that you would be representing Mr. Winn," said Stephenson as she grinned at Lane.

"And why is that?" asked Wallace. She would set the tone early that cheap shots, irrelevant and prejudicial information would not go unchallenged.

Stephenson looked flustered as she fumbled for a reply but could think of nothing to say, intelligent or otherwise.

"Because you may be an issue in the case," said Lane, not to be outdone by some small, attractive black woman.

"And what case is that?" asked Wallace.

"The case against your client," responded Lane smugly.

"Jake, if you have a case in which my client is the defendant, then I insist that under Brady vs. United States and the rules of the District Court you open that file up to me immediately."

Stephenson looked angrily at Lane. He knew little about the law and nothing about the rules binding a prosecution. He should leave this to her and everything would work out. Lane disagreed, knowing that the black lawyer would hide her client behind any procedural barrel she could find. Lane was not about to let that happen.

"Dorothy, there is no case against your client," said Butler, trying to be calm.

"That's not what your lead investigator says. Would you like me to play it back?" asked Dorothy, as she reached inside her briefcase for a portable voice activated tape recorder. She knew about Lane using a recorder at Winn's house and at the meeting he had here.

"You can't record this meeting," said Lane angrily.

"And why not?" asked Wallace.

"Can she?" Lane pleaded for help, finding nothing better to say. Stephenson again gave him a condescending look.

"Dorothy, regardless of what Mr. Lane said, there is no case pending against your client. This is hard on all of us," repeated Butler as if this helped.

"Let's cut out the bullshit," said Wallace, surprising Lane and Stephenson with her language. "What is the status of your investigation with respect to my client?"

Stephenson and Butler exchanged looks. "We are collecting information in the investigation of Andria Winn's death," said Stephenson. "That information will be presented to a grand jury. I have no idea what the grand jury will do."

Wallace smiled sarcastically. All in the room knew that the grand jury process was an archaic procedure that hid the prosecutor's machinations from the light of day. The grand jury would do what any decent prosecutor wanted it to. It was a playground for prosecutors where they made the rules.

"Jake, if you make any move against my client, it will cause irreparable harm. You know that. I have no doubt about the innocence of Ben Winn in the murder of his wife. If I am right and anything to the contrary leaks out of this office to the media, you will be responsible for irreparable damage."

"Our responsibility, Ms. Wallace, is to Andria Winn," said Stephenson condescendingly.

"Your responsibility is to the people of the District of Columbia," said Wallace sharply.

"And that responsibility is to bring the killer of Andria Winn to justice," said Stephenson.

Wallace sat back in her chair and took a deep breath. This was going no better than the last meeting Winn had reported. It would be a nightmare fighting with Stephenson and Lane.

They were jealous, stubborn people who wanted to see others fall. They could care less about Andria Winn; in fact, they would be glad she was dead if it meant they could bring down her husband.

"OK, Ms. Stephenson, let's try looking at it your way," said Wallace. "Can you assure me that any information presented to the grand jury will be kept from the media?"

"All grand jury proceedings are closed."

"Yet I read in the paper about them every day. I am asking what precautions you will take here because of the media's unique interest in this case?"

"Ms. Wallace, we will do our job correctly."

There seemed to be no way to talk business with this woman without her taking it personally.

"Are the police looking at other possible motives and killers?" asked Wallace, looking at Lane.

"We are doing a thorough investigation," said Lane, smugly thinking that he had the guilty party and he would nail him.

"What evidence do you have that leads you to believe my client is involved?"

"We have no obligation to tell you that at this point in time," said Stephenson smugly.

"If my client is the target of a grand jury investigation, you have an obligation to send us a target letter immediately and open the investigative file for our inspection."

Stephenson and Butler looked at each other, then Butler asked Wallace to give them a few moments to talk. On her return, Stephenson led the conversation.

"Ms. Wallace, once the grand jury decides that your client is a target, he will be notified. Until that time, we see no reason in this office carrying on a dialogue with you or your client."

"Jake, you fuck up on this and I will have your ass," said Wallace as she got up from her chair, closed her brief case and left.

Twelve

LANE RECOGNIZED Henry Rothstein when he walked into J. Paul's in Georgetown. Lane had asked for the meeting; Rothstein named the place. J. Paul's was an upper middle class bar on M Street that served fresh shellfish from the Chesapeake Bay and served as a watering hole for the up-and-coming behind the scenes people in Washington. It was a hot place to find an interesting date. It was an even better place to find young government employees whom, after a couple of beers and a crab cake, wanted to show their importance by dropping inside information. In his earlier days, Rothstein hung out here regularly to find tantalizing leads for new stories concerning trash on the Hill or in Administration.

Rothstein did not know what Lane looked like, but he had read his name in the paper. He knew he was the homicide detective on the Andria Winn case and that his only other claim to fame was his role in prosecuting the popular former mayor of Washington, D.C. Rothstein did not like cops; they were too much of the conservative autocratic system that he despised. If Lane could lead him to a story, however, his personal views on cops were irrelevant. So far, Rothstein was not covering the Andria Winn investigation. While it was a high profile item, it had no direct political consequences. He had done some stories on how the death of his wife had pulled Winn off the campaign trail; remarkably, it did not seem to be affecting his numbers. In fact, Winn was getting stronger in the polls every day. Rothstein could sense that he was following a winner.

"Mr. Rothstein, I'm Byron Lane with the D.C. Police Department."

"My pleasure," or at least he hoped it was. "Can I buy you a drink?" asked Rothstein, as he raised up his Long Island Iced Tea. He had a large CNN expense account that he freely used in the pursuit of a story.

"Maybe a beer."

"Is it true you guys really don't drink on duty?"

"I don't think there are any written rules on it," smiled Lane. "Can we sit back there and talk?" asked Lane, pointing to a table in the rear of the bar.

"Sure," said Rothstein, while he sized up the cop. Big and dumb, pretty typical.

"So you're in charge of the Winn investigation?" asked Rothstein as they sat down.

"Yeah, it's my case. But I've never seen anything like it. The pressure to tie up the department is coming from every direction."

"What do you mean?" asked Rothstein with more than casual curiosity.

"Let's get some ground rules straight, OK. Everything I say

has to be off the record."

"An unidentified source in the department," smiled Rothstein.

"No. It has to be attributed to someone else." Lane spoke confidently. He felt himself a breed apart and assumed those he dealt with could sense that he was "special." He had real power and he knew how to use it to get what he wanted.

"You mean I have to confirm anything you say with someone else?" Rothstein was used to these punks; they wanted to be important, but did not want to get caught at it.

"I don't care whether you confirm it or not. I wouldn't tell you something if it weren't true. You just can't say you got it from a cop. Say it came from the Winn people or something." Lane knew that any leaks identified as coming from the department could be too easily traced to him.

Rothstein got the idea. This guy had an agenda; he did not care what rules he played by to get the agenda completed. He wanted a story on the air; he did not care if Rothstein attributed it to any source. That was Rothstein's problem.

"OK," said Rothstein.

"Second, if we meet again, it can't be in public. We have to come up with somewhere private to talk."

Rothstein sipped on his drink to avoid drooling. This guy had something hot and he intended to be a steady supply, a real "Deep Throat."

"OK, Lane, or can I call you Byron? You call me Henry. Now, I'll agree to all that. What is it you want me to know?" Rothstein would decide later whether to keep his word with Lane. He would see what the guy had, assess whether he would be useful later, and then figure out how to satisfy his producer.

"I know something that Winn and the political forces are trying to keep smothered. I have never seen something this hot kept under wraps for this long. I keep waiting for you guys to dig it out on your own." Lane looked disapprovingly at Rothstein.

Rothstein said nothing. He simply starred at Lane waiting. He was irritated that this jerk would insinuate that the media was not doing its job. If the guy had something, he should just say it and cut out the games.

"Ben Winn killed his wife."

"No fucking way!" said Rothstein with total surprise. It had been almost a week since the murder. No one had speculated that Winn was involved. This was too good to be true. "But you guys said it was an intruder."

"The Department used the press release that the Winn campaign used. I told you that Winn was clogging up the whole system here. Somehow his people have the department acting like a puppet, saying whatever they want. Who knows who's pulling whose strings. This is Washington, remember."

"You gotta be shittin' me," said Rothstein with a smile, not really believing what he was hearing. He pulled his dog-eared notepad out of his pocket and began to take notes.

"Look, I'm only going to tell you that we have hard evidence, you know, like fingerprints on the murder weapon."

"Are you saying that Winn's fingerprints are on the gun?"

"I did not say that; I said we have hard evidence like that."

"Cut out the crap, Lane. Do you have fingerprints on the gun or not?"

Lane smiled. Rothstein knew that was a confirmation. Lane had a plan here. He would build public pressure to bring Winn to justice. He would become famous in the process. Rothstein would be right in the middle of the action. It could be a Pulitzer. No one so famous had ever been charged with murder. Would the government have the guts to do it?

IT WAS THE LEAD STORY on the CNN World News Tonight.

"It has been six days since the murder of Andria Winn and seven days since her husband won the New Hampshire Republican presidential primary. Creating a tremor in the nation's capital, it was today reported by sources inside the beltway that Ben Winn is a suspect in the murder of his wife. CNN has learned that Winn's fingerprints are on the gun used to kill Andria Winn. Only a few minutes ago, the U.S. Attorney's office refused to comment on the case, but said that it was presenting evidence to a grand jury and expected an indictment to be forthcoming. This is Henry Rothstein in Washington, D.C."

Rothstein had thought about saying less the first time he aired the story. He decided, however, that if the investigators were talking to him they would talk to others. He did not want to be scooped. His producer did not raise any objection to the story. Since it aired, the news industry around the country was in chaos.

A STRANGE UNION between the Secret Service and a private security company that Savage arranged for right after Rothstein's report was trying to hold back the hoards of media people lined up in the neighborhood around Winn's Georgetown home. Over 20 television vans with satellite dishes on top were double-parked up and down the street. One crew tried to come in over the fence in back and had been arrested by the Secret Service and then turned over to the D.C. police where they were taken to the police station, then released.

Instantaneously, media coverage had consumed the airways like no other story in history. All normal programming on the networks was suspended as the network anchor men were hurried to the studio to begin their marathon coverage of the event. Each network arranged to have an assortment of experts to be hooked up by satellite to help the anchor analyze the story. They all waited for more news. Meanwhile, the experts each speculated on whether an indictment would be issued and, if so, when. They instructed the viewers on the criminal process that led to the charging of a defendant. They speculated concerning whether Winn was too popular to get convicted, and if he was convicted, whether a jury would put him in the gas chamber.

Before any official word had come down, the nation was following and discussing the Ben Winn murder case. The networks and print media were scurrying for other leads and leaks. Rumors ran wild. One station reported that Winn had confessed; another reported that the police had an eyewitness. One reporter said he learned that Winn had, in fact, hired someone to kill his wife, but had not done it himself. It was a circus and Ben Winn was the main attraction. He was fair game for anything, and just about everything was thrown into the pot that cooked nothing but rumor and innuendo.

The master bedroom upstairs in the rear of the house was considered the safest from the telescopic lenses of the media, and was being used by Winn, Savage, and Wallace. Both had come to Winn's house as soon as the CNN story broke.

"So, how's the campaign going, Jack?" asked Winn with a smile. Somehow he managed to rise up under pressure. When there were fewer alternatives, he was able to be more focused.

"Pretty funny, Ben. We have to say something. Every news agency in the country is on 24-hour alert for breaking stories. Rumors are flying all over the place. If we don't say something soon, the momentum of this will wash us completely away."

"You can't make a statement," said Wallace.

"So my lawyer says don't talk; my political guru says talk. She's a lot cuter than you, Jack."

"I didn't say the campaign can't make a statement," said Wallace.

"Where did CNN get the tip?" asked Savage out of intellectual curiosity.

"The government," said Wallace pointedly. "Pick one, it really doesn't matter."

"So what's with the gun, Ben?" asked Wallace.

Winn paused. He looked at Wallace, then at Savage. He lowered his head, and Savage wondered if he was about to confess. Many in the Winn camp were accepting the story and figured Winn to be the killer; Savage was not sure where he stood.

"That damn gun." Winn shook his head back and forth. "I suppose I should have said something to both of you, but I wasn't thinking clearly at the time and then I guess I forgot about it—wanted to forget about it."

"Forget about what, Ben?" pushed Wallace.

"The gun. I picked it up. I don't know what I was thinking. I don't even remember picking it up. I remember checking to see if a round was in the chamber. I guess instinctively I thought the killer could still be in the house. Later, I wiped the gun off and laid it down by Andria." Winn hung his head shaking it back and forth, wishing he could do it over again.

"And you didn't think the cops would find it suspect that the gun had been wiped clean?" asked Wallace.

"Pretty stupid, huh?" responded Winn.

"They are going to eat you up over this," said Wallace, overwhelmed momentarily by the news.

"Who are they? The cops or the voters?" asked Savage.

"If we lose with the first, the second doesn't really matter, does it?" added Wallace.

"Hey, I could be the first President to pardon himself."

"Nixon considered that; you see where it got him," said Savage.

"OK, guys," said Winn straightening up and taking some control. "First, I didn't kill Andria and I don't have any idea who did. We have to convince the cops or the prosecutors or a jury of that. Second, assuming that truth prevails, I'd like to keep the campaign afloat so that we can finish what we started." Winn paused as his braintrust considered his words. "Now, I'll go to some warm island beach while my lawyer accomplishes the first and my campaign manager the second."

"Look, Ben, if you want to keep the campaign going, I'm not going to try to interfere, but you can't do anything in the campaign that in any way endangers you with the prosecutors. Agreed?" asked Dorothy as she sipped on the Diet Pepsi Winn got her from the refrigerator.

Winn looked at Savage, then said "Agreed. If we have to jump off the campaign ship to keep my life afloat, it's a fair trade."

"How in the hell can you keep the campaign alive in his hell?" asked Wallace, looking to Savage for answers.

"Beats the hell outta me," said Savage.

"But he'll figure out something," added Winn.

"You need a real lawyer on this case," said Wallace, changing the subject.

"I've got a real lawyer. You can read her name in any newspaper in the country."

"The ones I read referred to her as your black babe," said Wallace, cringing at the accounts of her relationship with Winn and the possible implications of her relationship in any motive Winn had to kill his wife.

"I'll not agree to your resigning, Dot. You'll have to quit."

"OK," she said already prepared for his answer. "But you'll have to agree to the hiring of co-counsel."

"Anyone you want, as long as you're lead counsel and don't let go of the control switches."

"Jack, I'd agree to your releasing a statement that says the Senator is grieving over the death of his wife, is shocked at rumors that he might have been involved." Wallace paused, then continued. "Categorically deny that the Senator killed his wife, or that he had anything to do with her death. Say that the prosecution is causing irreparable injury to the Senator and the country by leaking information about their investigation and that they should charge the Senator or find the real killer. If political pressures result in them charging the Senator, then we will categorically prove his innocence in a courtroom."

"You should have been in politics, Dorothy," said Savage smiling. "I'll show you the statement before it is released."

"Fax it to my office any time of day. We will have someone on 24-hour watch for a while."

"I'll get to work on it, if I can part the media sea outside," said Savage as he got up and left.

Wallace slipped out of the winged-back chair she was in onto her knees in front of Winn who was sitting in the matching chair. She took his hands inside both of hers. She looked at the contrast in colors as she always did.

"When you get in a mess, you really do it right, Ben." She squeezed his hands tightly, feeling his pain, wishing she could take it away.

"The only way we can prove I didn't kill Andria is to find out who did."

"I know. I'm meeting with a private investigator tonight. He comes highly recommended."

"So you never intended to get off the case."

"Not if you felt you needed me."

Winn put his arms around her and held her tight. They did not move and said nothing until Wallace needed to go.

Thirteen

THE GRAND JURY PROCESS defies most of the traditional notions of justice. In a grand jury proceeding, the blindfold is not on the guardian who holds the scales of justice; the eyes of the public are covered so the prosecutorial process can work in secret.

The District of Columbia, like most states, has two methods by which it can charge a defendant with a crime. The most commonly used method is to hold a preliminary hearing before a trial judge, where a prosecutor must produce enough evidence to show that it is more probable than not that the defendant is guilty of the crime to be charged. This "probable cause" test is an easy one to pass, but must be done in a forum bound by the normal rules of evidence and one where the defendant and his lawyer can challenge the admissibility or credibility of the evidence. Lawyers can be artists, who take the materials available and paint the picture as they want it to be seen. The adversary proceeding of a preliminary hearing ensures that an impartial judge sees the pictures as presented by opposing parties. It is much like the ensuing trial, except no jury is present and the standard to be passed by the prosecution is much less because the defendant's liberty is not yet at stake.

The second avenue by which the defendant can be charged is with a grand jury indictment. If the grand jury issues an indictment, then no preliminary hearing is required. There is no impartial judge present at a grand jury hearing. Neither the defendant nor his lawyer is allowed to participate; in fact, the process may be almost over before the defendant is aware that the proceeding is taking place. There are no rules of evidence. There is no one to ensure that both sides of a story are presented. The grand jury is little more than a group of 25 ordinary people who are told what the rules are and what their duties are by a prosecutor. They are presented with whatever evidence the prosecutor deems appropriate, which need not include anything that could exonerate a proposed defendant, even if the prosecutor knows that such exculpatory evidence exists.

The grand jury members, the substitute for the impartial judge, are entitled to ask questions, but a skilled prosecutor can easily cut off a questioner from going down a direction that does not support the desired result. The prosecutor has decided what that result should be before the grand jury is convened. The prosecutor does not use the power and secrecy of a grand jury to pursue the truth. A prosecutor has determined what he wants the truth to be long before the grand jury is convened. The grand jury process is the prosecutor's tool to bring about a desired result, to take a man or woman to trial on a criminal charge, without considering the impartial opinion of a judge or the adversary opinion of the defendant. When the prosecutor first approaches a case, he is trying to determine how the pieces fit. Once the prosecutor paints that one picture, however, he ignores everything that distorts it and encourages only that which is compatible with it. From that point forward, the job of the prosecutor is not to find the truth; it is to win, and winning is defined by the number of convictions—the number of men and women put behind bars.

Almost as a prize inside the crackerjacks, the prosecutor does not have to share any of the evidence presented to the grand jury with the defense. The longer the defense is kept in the dark, the more difficulty they will have painting their own picture. Much of the prosecution's evidence will not be turned over to the defense until the eleventh hour. Although there is an obligation to share all information with the defense after an indictment is brought, the prosecution has a legion of ways to avoid this mandate and still be within the letter of the law. The prosecution will share as little as possible as late as possible. The less time the defense has to do its own research, the more likely the prosecutor will win. To the defendant, his reputation, his liberty, and perhaps his life are at stake. To the young ambitious prosecutor, it is only another rung in his career ladder. As he climbs it, he will not consider the men and women who have suffered because of the power he wields.

Sybil Stephenson looked over the group of 25 residents of the District of Columbia. They were about as ordinary as you can get. Grand juries, like juries, end up being filled with lower class and lower middle class people who cannot get out of service by having someone call the prosecutor's office to get them excused. They are typically the powerless. This often works against the prosecutor because these are people who have been kicked around by the system their whole lives. They are suspicious. They are, however, easily intimidated, often overwhelmed by the power and grandeur of the judicial system. As Stephenson looks over this group, she knows they will do what she wants. She wishes they could skip to the end and avoid the waste of time that she perceives the proceeding to be. She has already determined that he should be charged with murder. That should be enough.

They were meeting in Grand Jury Room No. 4 in the Federal Courts Building on Constitution Avenue. The room was little more than three rows of chairs faced by a table at which Stephenson sat. It looked more like a classroom than a courtroom. It was a disappointment to what many of the grand jury members had expected. Television has shaped the views of many on several things, not the least of which is the judicial system. To these people, this may be the most exciting event they have ever participated in. It will provide a story to tell in their mundane lives for years to come. It will only make a story, however, if what they do leads to a trial. They can only validate their importance in this process by issuing an indictment. Otherwise, their very existence will never be reported.

As usual, Stephenson had worked to get as many females on the grand jury as possible; she managed to end up with 18 women of the 25 grand jury members. Stephenson did not trust men; she did not realize that this opinion, which most men readily became aware of, might have something to do with why she seemed to do better with women than men on juries. Sixteen of the grand jurors were black, more than Stephenson wanted, but considering the racial make-up of the District of Columbia, she was lucky the number was not higher. She was convinced that white people would be offended with Winn's relationship with a black woman, as she was. Black people, she feared, might somehow give Winn some credit for this. Over one-fourth of the grand jurors worked for the federal government in one capacity or another. Half of the grand jurors did not work for anyone, with eight housewives and four people who were unemployed until they received the prospect of getting a check for jury duty. Five were college educated. Nine had less than a high school education.

At the table with Stephenson sat Tanya Ball, a young black female lawyer in the U.S. Attorney's Office that Stephenson had selected to assist her in the Winn case. Ball was chosen by Stephenson to counter some of the effect of the stylish Dorothy Wallace on the other side. Men in the office thought Ball was attractive. Stephenson assumed that meant she slept around. Ball wore short skirts and stylish outfits that Stephenson abhorred. Ball wore her long black hair extensions in stylish corn-rolls that Stephenson thought to be too ethnic. The only thing she disliked almost as much as men were cute woman. And Stephenson thought that it went without saying that black people simply do not operate from the same values and pursue the same goals as white people.

Ball was smart, but not a very hard worker and would be content to be a government lawyer for the rest of her career. Ball knew she was a token on the case, but she was excited about the high profile it would give her. She had done all right at the University of Maryland School of Law in its "minority enrichment" program. She could have done much better if the school had required. She was at the time, however, more interested in the All-American wide receiver for the Terrapins and learned no more than necessary to get by. The All-American had gone on to the Dallas Cowboys and to one of the Dallas Cowgirl Cheerleaders. Maybe this case would give her a chance to make a mark in her legal career. For that, she could work with the "bitch," as she and her colleagues referred to Stephenson.

Stephenson went over the piles of paper she had organized on the table with Ball so that Ball could help her retrieve them as they were needed. She ignored Ball's comment that Stephenson needed a paralegal, not co-counsel. The members of the grand jury were getting to know each other with idle small talk about the Wizards and the weather until Stephenson rose to call the proceeding to order. It was the first time she had talked to the grand jury since their selection. There was a podium at one end of the table with a microphone used to record the grand jury proceeding. A court reporter, an elderly woman who said nothing and was devoid of expression, was also present. Like any good court reporter, she was simply a fixture in the room, like a witness box or gavel. She was expected to be there when you arrive, and she would be there working on her little machine when you left. Maybe they had no lives of their own. Maybe they never leave the courthouse they are assigned to.

While a record was kept in the grand jury proceeding, it would be sealed unless opened by a judge. There was a vault full of grand jury transcripts that had been diligently prepared by the court reporters and then never looked at again.

The room was warm and stuffy, even though it was a cold March day in the Nation's capital. The room had no windows, secreted away in the middle of the Federal Courts Building. To the rest of the world, this gathering did not exist.

"Ladies and Gentlemen, let me thank you again for giving up your valuable time so that you can sit on this grand jury. I know that you all have children and jobs and spouses and are dearly needed elsewhere. I will see to it that you are detained here no longer than absolutely necessary." Stephenson knew the importance of being the nice guy up front. If they liked her, then they would trust her. If they trusted her, then it was much easier to lead them. She worked best in this type of environment, unfettered by a judge and not harassed by defense counsel. In fact, she was good at doing this, taking the facts she wanted to piece together the picture she wanted to be seen.

"I would like to say first, that the grand jury proceeding is a very informal one. If at any time you have any questions or comments, please don't hesitate to let me know. We will take frequent breaks in the proceeding so that you can rest and collect your thoughts. I will be available during all of those breaks for your questions." She preferred that they tell her what was on their minds in private during these breaks so she could head off any unwanted comments in the open proceeding. It was also a common practice to talk to one of the grand jury members during the break to get them to raise an issue during the proceeding. It sometimes looked better if one of them appeared to reach certain conclusions on their own. "While this proceeding will be recorded by the court reporter you see, this is a secret proceeding and what you do and say will not be looked at by anyone outside of this room except in some very rare circumstances where a judge might read the transcript. So just relax the best you can, get up and move around, get some coffee or soda as you need it." All she needed them to do was put in the time; then she would present them with the already typed indictment that they supposedly composed.

"This is what is referred to as a special grand jury, meaning that we are here to look at only one case. I will help you walk through the evidence in that case and then you will decide whether the defendant should be indicted. Now, to indict a defendant you do not need to determine that he is guilty. That is the job of the trial court and the jury that hears the evidence at trial. Your only job is to determine if you think there is enough evidence against the defendant that a trial court should look further into the case. I think you will make that determination easily in this case and that we will not be here very long." That comment brought a sigh of relief from the grand jury members; none of them wanted to be here a moment longer than necessary. If she would just tell them what to do, they would do it and then they could go home.

"My job is to assist you in looking at the evidence, to help you organize and evaluate it. I will be assisted by another lawyer for the government, Ms. Tanya Ball. No lawyers for the defendant will be here. Their job begins at the trial."

Stephenson grimaced as she saw some of the male jurors smile with glee as she introduced Ball; all men were alike. Ball smiled at the mention of her name. She hoped to get to do something other than sit at the table and push paper.

"The case you will be looking at involves the murder of Andria Winn," continued Stephenson after a slight disapproving glance at Ball. "We will be presenting evidence which indicates that Mrs. Winn was murdered by her husband, Andrew Benjamin

Winn. If there are no questions at this time, we will call as your first witness the lead investigator for the District of Columbia police department, Mr. Byron Lane."

They all knew what the case was; questions at voir dire made it clear this was the Winn case. They had all been taking in the media about Mrs. Winn's death. How could you miss the constant coverage? They would see the story turn towards the Senator over the next few days during their deliberations. With the airways full of speculation about the Winn indictment, they would all be celebrities in their local neighborhoods. Several members of the grand jury would later be paid to appear on the tabloid news shows.

"MS. WALLACE, this is Mr. Pete Smith," said Staci, as she led the white-haired man of 50 into Wallace's office. Smith was an odd mixture of maturity and youth. Although prematurely gray, he was a muscular, physically fit man with the body of a man 20 years younger. He had put on a suit for this meeting, although he more often wore sweatshirts and jeans, and weather permitting would ride his Harley-Davidson as often as possible. He was the sole proprietor of an investigative firm that had 40 employees, over half of whom were field investigators, many former law enforcement officers. Smith did not like the growing size of his firm and refused to expand into the lucrative security work that most private firms were now dependent upon. He was and always would be a Humphrey Bogart investigator looking for the Maltese falcon.

"Mr. Smith, please have a seat."

"You are prettier in person than on television; I would have found that hard to believe." Wallace was surprised that he was so smooth with his statement; she accepted the compliment with a smile, although she usually rebuked such lines as come-ons.

"You come very highly recommended, Mr. Smith." Smith was known for providing investigative work for major cases throughout the country. They did not do divorce work. They solved real mysteries for well paying clients. Much of their work was focused on industrial espionage. Smith, however, liked criminal work. He wanted to solve cases that meant something more than money to people. He lived and worked for the thrill of the solution, and nothing made the thrill greater than saving a man from the clutches of big brother's criminal justice system.

"Call me Pete, please. And, I've been doing this gum-shoe work for a long time. There's not a rock to hide under that I can't eventually turn over." Smith was never modest, and he had the talent to back up his bold statements. He smiled, showing that he had a sense of humor about himself; however, he was willing to laugh if he got it wrong, but he was not willing to quit until he got it right.

"Call me Dorothy, please. And, that's just the kind of talk I need to hear."

"How do you know Winn didn't do it?"

"I've known Ben Winn for almost ten years, Pete. Nobody knows me better than Ben. And I doubt anybody knows Ben better than I do."

"So you're saying you believe him?"

"Yeah, I'd stake my life on it."

"Professionally speaking, you may have." Smith smiled, then they both laughed.

"Tell me about it," said Dorothy. "You couldn't mix this pot up much more if you made the story up. So how about coming aboard?"

"Sounds just like my kind of thing." Smith liked her already. He could tell she was bright; he liked to work with bright people. Besides, he liked a good mystery. That's what kept him in the business. This one had all the markings of real challenge.

"If you've been watching the constant coverage about this case in the media, you know as much about it as I do." Wallace explained the alleged fingerprints on the gun. If they were there, it was because Winn did not get the gun wiped clean. "The prosecutor, a real piece of work named Sybil Stephenson, is taking the case to a grand jury while we speak. I don't know much about what the case will look like. I'd like you to get me a run down on the players personally, at least Stephenson and the cop, Byron Lane. But your real mission is to find the killer. The only sure way we have of getting Ben off is to put the real killer in his place."

"A real Perry Mason kind of deal, huh?"

"You got it," laughed Wallace. She really liked this guy.

"Any suggestions on where I start?"

"Not one," said Wallace grinning.

"Great, then I get all the glory when I figure it out."

THE MEDIA RELEASE that Savage put out decrying the rumor as a political ploy by the Democrats had sufficed for a few days, but the polls were causing Savage concern. Swords reported on the numbers daily. Savage was amazed that even as the numbers began to reflect some doubt over Winn's innocence, they remained strong in the head-to-head political contests. Most of those supporting Winn believed that Democrats in power were taking advantage of Andria's death to push Winn aside. In the behind-the-scenes spin, Savage and Stevens had been pushing this story hard. They needed a boost, however, so Savage had announced a media conference at the Holiday Inn on King Street in Alexandria. It was almost three weeks after the murder, one week before Super Tuesday, and it was the first time that anyone in the campaign had spoken in person on the issue. The candidate was still in mourning. Savage concluded that the media needed some real meat, a sign that the campaign continued—a living, breathing person to tell them that Winn would be the next president. Winn could not do it, so Savage nominated himself.

Stevens had arranged to have the ballroom available at the Holiday Inn. Savage was besieged by media as he walked down the street with a small group of campaign workers and into the lobby of the hotel. Alexandria was littered with television vans, and the ballroom was literally packed with cameras, lights, microphones, duct tape, and reporters. Savage ignored all of the attempts to get his attention and walked immediately down the hallway to the ballroom and onto the platform that supported a podium littered with microphones. Savage was wearing a suit and had used hair spray to hold his hair in place. He knew he would be the lead story on every television station in the country and he had to look good.

"It's been a few days since we held a formal conference," said Savage, as if it was business as usual. "With Super Tuesday coming up next week, I wanted to give you a progress report on the campaign. First, let me read a letter that the Senator wrote by hand this morning." It was not easy getting the letter approved by Wallace, but after several changes from a purple felt tip pen, it received her blessing. Every reporter in the room had a question and was poised to be the first hand in the air when Savage gave an opening. They were all, however, silently waiting to see what he would say. A few pundits expected Savage to announce Winn's withdrawal. Most knew neither Savage nor Winn would walk away from a good fight.

"The letter is addressed to the American people. It says: 'Thank you for your continued support in this time of bereavement. Andria would be deeply touched by all of the cards and letters that we have received. I regret that I cannot yet return to the campaign, but I am sure you understand that I am first needed at home. Let me assure you that the rumors you have heard concerning my role in Andria's death are completely unfounded, and that she would be just as appalled and offended as you that such grandstanding is taking place. I will do whatever is required to prove such accusations untrue and totally without basis. I loved my wife before her death; I love her now. An emptiness has engulfed my life with her passing and I am pained that some would take this as an opportunity to get a political advantage. With your continued support and trust, this will not happen. We will not only survive; we will go on to reach new goals in Andria's honor.'

"The letter is signed Ben Winn. Are there any questions?"

"How did the Senator's fingerprints get on the gun?" asked

Henry Rothstein from the front row.

"Henry, while I know you broke this story and will be considerably embarrassed to accept the truth, there is no evidence showing the Senator's fingerprints are on the gun."

"Are you saying that his fingerprints are not on the gun?" followed Rothstein, holding his pencil and notepad in hand, ready to write verbatim the response.

"Yes, Henry, that's exactly what I am saying." Assuming that he wiped them all off, thought Savage to himself. He had considered the truth, but it was too complex for now. The prosecutors had not yet produced a gun with fingerprints; maybe Winn wiped it clean and the Rothstein story was planted to smoke Winn out.

"Why did the Senator hire Dorothy Wallace to represent him?" asked a reporter that Savage did not recognize as one of the political guys.

"Because she is the best lawyer he knows."

"Does she have any experience in criminal trials?" asked the CBS man assigned to the Winn campaign.

"We do not expect there to be a trial, Sam," responded Savage.

"Why doesn't the Senator withdraw from the race?"

"Because he answered the call of the American people to run for the presidency. Nothing has happened to change that. Remember, folks, the U.S. Attorney for the District of Columbia is appointed by the President of the United States, who just so happens to be a Democrat openly supporting Randall Hardy for the Presidency. If Randall Hardy is elected, it is safe to assume that Jake Butler will keep his job. If Ben Winn is elected, I can assure you that Jake Butler will be looking for work." The reporters laughed.

"So, Jack, you're saying this whole thing has been contrived by the Democrats?" asked Nina Steinberg of NPR with the look of cynicism that only a reporter can portray.

"I'm saying that the Democrats are taking advantage of these unfortunate circumstances and playing them for all the political points they can make. It is an outrageous move on their part, and it simply shows how desperate they are."

"Do you think Daily will re-enter the race?"

"No, not unless he wants to get his ass kicked again."

"Do you think that Lorenzen will now decide to stay in the race."

"You counted Lorenzen out of the race after the drubbing he got in New Hampshire. He announced his candidacy last November. I will consider him our opponent until he says otherwise or until Senator Winn gets the nomination in Dallas."

"Will the Senator be indicted before Super Tuesday?" asked Rothstein, relentless, not giving up. He had a cop telling him how this was going to go down; he wanted to be the one to break Winn publicly.

"I do not expect the Senator to ever be indicted, Henry, or weren't you listening?"

Savage looked at Stevens, who announced that one more question would be taken. Savage had accomplished his purpose; there was no point in continuing to give these guys pot shots at him. Savage sensed that Rothstein would not let up until he had made some news. Savage took a "softball" question from the crowd and then walked out of the room, ignoring the cries for recognition that came from the hoard of reporters.

Fourteen

WINN WAS IN COMPLETE SECLUSION. Not since William McKinley had any presidential candidate hidden himself from the public and press so well. With McKinley it was a political strategy. He was not a good candidate. Modern forms of communication allowed the new breed of campaign strategist to present their own image of the candidate to the people. With Winn, it had nothing to do with his campaign strategy.

The media was still camped out in front of his house. They had been joined by a group of Winn supporters that maintained their vigil from dawn until dusk with signs saying "Find the

Real Killer," "We love you Ben," and other similar expressions of their support. The neighbors were becoming irritated, but there was little they could do about it.

Winn had developed a routine where he would be driven by George every day to Wallace's office on Connecticut Avenue. They would be led by a car with two private security men and trailed by a secret service car in the rear. A new vehicle was used with tinted windows to prevent the media from snapping their daily pictures of Winn. Instead, they showed the three black cars being driven like a funeral procession. It was an eerie scene that served as a good film leader for broadcasts that would continue to feed on the rumor of an indictment.

The floor that housed Heitzman & Wallace was also protected 24 hours a day by the private security company Savage had retained. Winn had been assigned the conference room next to Wallace's office where he spent eight to ten hours a day trying to keep up with developments in the case. He would make a select few political calls from a list prepared daily by Savage. Wallace cautioned him about making any statements that would work their way into the media; she told him to assume that all statements made would end up there.

Most news came by way of leaks or rumors reported by the media. It was usually difficult, if not impossible, to verify whether the information broadcast was true. The media was reporting everything attributed to law enforcement personnel with little regard for verification.

Wallace had cleared most of her other work by assigning it to associates. She met with them first thing in the morning and in the middle of each afternoon to give directions and answer questions. She did not want interruptions throughout the remainder of the day as she read the rules of criminal evidence and recent federal criminal cases. She had talked to her major clients. They were sympathetic, wishing her well in Winn's defense. She was more than a lawyer to all of her clients; they knew she would be back to attend to their matters. They also knew she had to devote herself exclusively to the Winn case until it was over.

Winn sat in one of the cushioned purple chairs in Wallace's office as he read the letter she had handed him. It was printed on stationery from the U.S. Attorney's Office. In two paragraphs it informed Winn that he was the target of a grand jury investigation into the murder of Andria Winn. He was invited to speak to the grand jury if he so desired.

She sat behind her glass table, which was littered with Supreme Court Reporters and copies of the Federal 2d Reporter. She looked calm and composed as usual, dressed in a stylish chocolate brown pantsuit with a denim shirt and brown patent leather loafers. Her long black hair was pulled up and into a stylish pony tail. She sipped on her Diet Pepsi as she tried to read Winn's reaction.

"So do we talk to them?

"It's not a 'we,' Ben. We've talked about this. You cannot have a lawyer present in the grand jury room if you appear. I can go with you; I can wait outside and be available if you want to take a break and talk to me. But you go before a grand jury on your own."

"So, counsel, what do you advise?"

"You know what I think, Ben. There is nothing for you to gain by going before a grand jury. The prosecutor has already primed the grand jury to believe that you are guilty. An appearance by you simply gives the prosecutor a free shot to cross-examine you. There is also some confusion on whether a defendant waives his Fifth Amendment rights for the trial if he appears before a grand jury."

"If there is any chance that I can talk to the grand jury and convince them I'm innocent, how can I pass it up?"

"There is no chance," said Wallace curtly. "You are too filled with notions of justice. The judicial system is nothing more than a form of competition. Think of it like a baseball game, or maybe a hockey game is a better description. The prosecution only wins if they beat you. They could care less at this point about any facts that exonerate you. They could care less about the truth. Their only concern, at this point, is winning. They only win if you get convicted."

"You're one hell of a pessimist, Dot."

"A realist."

"What about the campaign? If the grand jury issues an indictment, the campaign will disintegrate. Maybe I can convince the grand jury that I have more at stake than they have considered."

"They have been meeting with Sybil Stephenson on and off for almost four weeks. They are now her puppets and she has them convinced that you are a cold-blooded killer. They see you as a man who beats his wife, commits adultery, then kills the wife for her money. Don't expect to move them with concerns for your political future."

"So, are you saying that I'm going to be indicted and there is nothing we can do about it?"

"We can get ready to win in court."

Winn was silent, looking out the window. People were walking up and down the street, going on about their business. Their lives were normal and routine. Winn wondered why his life could not be the same. He looked back at Wallace and asked, "So, I'm going to be indicted?"

"Once a target letter is issued, Ben, it's pretty much a foregone conclusion. We can hope for a miracle, but it is no longer likely that we will get it at this stage."

"But doesn't anyone care that I did not kill her?"

"I do, Ben," said Wallace sympathetically. After a pause, she continued. "And, millions of Americans believe in you and care. Should I remind you that you're still rolling up delegates to take to the convention to get the Republican nomination for President."

"So what do we do next?"

"The best defense is a good offense. Pete Smith is coming in this afternoon to talk with you some more. We need a killer, or at a minimum someone who is as likely a killer as you."

"I haven't come up with anything useful," said Winn in frustration. "I don't even know who this Baroni guy is. Who knows what else I don't know about Andria." The media had reported the leak concerning Andria's affair. Lane had tipped off Rothstein at CNN with the story first. It was a shock to the system at first; they had built Andria Winn into the innocent victim killed by her adulterous husband. To soften the blemish on the record they had already created, most of the articles made it appear that her affair was in retaliation for the affair that all of the liberal media now assumed Winn had been having with Wallace. Rothstein reported that an informed source said Baroni was a witness to several beatings that Andria had received at the hands of her husband. Baroni was now talking publicly, becoming a national celebrity. He had a difficult time playing the bereaved boyfriend, naturally glowing from all of the attention.

"Pete is all over this guy. He is our most likely candidate for an alternate killer," said Wallace, who was talking with Smith daily.

"So you don't care who did it; you just want someone who looks to a jury like they are just as likely a candidate as me?"

"Don't get self-righteous on me, Ben. It's their game; we are playing by their rules." She spoke angrily, but knew Winn did not mean for her to take his remarks personally. He was venting anger at the system. She happened to be in the room.

"So, will I be arrested as soon as an indictment is issued?"

"Butler will probably allow for me to arrange for your surrender. I'll find out who the Motions Judge will be and talk to the judge about bail before a surrender. With some luck, we will surrender early in the day and immediately go to an arraignment and ask for bail."

"Will I get bail, or will I spent the next few months in a holding tank?"

"It's 50/50. You are eligible for bail in the District even for a capital offense, but the judge will try to assess the likelihood of flight. We can make a good argument that you are too well known to flee, but expect the prosecution to throw back the run you made during the Tina Adams investigation. We will also argue that you are running for president and therefore have every reason to stay and resolve this issue at trial as soon as possible.

"I am working on a Motion to have the indictment quashed because of prejudicial publicity caused by the prosecution that has tainted the grand jury. That should have some impact on the judge's decision. I am trying to make a case for the prosecutor to turn over the grand jury transcripts for us to assess any such prejudice. Once we have the transcripts, who knows what we will find? Stephenson certainly does not expect us to be able to look over her shoulder. If she has become careless, opening up an argument that the grand jury was unduly influenced by her actions, then we may have some other good arguments to quash the indictment."

"That's rare, right?"

"It's been done," said Wallace confidently. "More likely though, we'll lose on the merits, but if we can make some good arguments we will get points with the judge. Maybe we can cash in with our Motion for Bail."

"Keep me out of jail, Dot. I have cold sweats at night thinking about being locked up in a small room where someone else has the key. It's turning into a nightmare."

"So why don't you get away for a few days?"

"What happened to 'you're the best person to prepare your defense; don't blindly put your fate in some lawyer's hands, including mine?' "

"What's a few days? It will be madness when the indictment comes down. It might be easier for me to arrange for a surrender if you're out of town and the cops can't readily lay their hands on you."

"What makes you think I can go anywhere without the media finding me?"

"Well, even if they do, you'll be out of the jurisdiction. You can take the laptop that you are working on in case you come up with some new brainstorms."

"Are you trying to get rid of me, Dot?   Is there another man?" asked Winn jokingly.

"You won't think those kind of comments are funny when you begin to hear about our 'affair' in a courtroom."

Fifteen

IT WAS A WARM SUNNY Wednesday morning in March when Pete Smith visited the Winn campaign headquarters on King Street for the first time. Winn had won a solid majority of the Republican vote, as well as the overwhelming percentage of delegates at stake in the 19 southern and border states that went to the polls on Super Tuesday. In spite of the media frenzy concerning his involvement in a murder, he was barreling ahead to capture the Republican nomination for President.

It was a surprising result to the media, which continued to lead every newscast and every front page with more speculation about the Andria Winn murder and what seemed to be their foregone conclusion that the prosecution was building an air-tight case against her husband. This generally cynical bunch seemed to assume that the government would not bring such a high profile case unless they had the goods on Winn.

Savage had devoted all of the paid media to a theme alleging that the Democrats in power were trying to deny the Republicans of their only candidate who could beat Randall Hardy. "This is not about justice for Andria Winn; this is just sleazy politics. When the truth comes out, these politicians will be held accountable." It was working for now. Politics is like any emotional subject. Once you make your mind up you consider as credible only that which backs up your decision, all other information is bogus. By the second week in March, most Republicans had made their minds up about Winn. They were vociferously defending him throughout the coffee shops and bars of America; friendships were being called into question, marriages were being strained. It was reminiscent of Nixon, where Republicans refused to admit his malfeasance until the very end. Even then, many did not break down, still referring to Nixon as "The President." On the morning of his death, Nixon was treated with all the respect and regalia of a national hero, rather than a man who was forced from office by impeachment and avoided criminal prosecution only by cutting a deal for a pardon with his predecessor.

Smith was riding his black Harley Davidson fat boy and rolled it backwards, like any proficient Harley rider who parked for a quick getaway, into a parking place off the market square in Old Town. Unstrapping the aged leather saddlebags trimmed in chrome studs, he removed a laptop computer that he used to take notes. He hardly looked like Sherlock Holmes in his blue jeans and Georgetown sweatshirt. He looked like a throwback from the sixties, an image he cultivated and was proud of. Smith lived life for the enjoyment and thrill of it. He did what he wanted, when he wanted. He did not live on the edge, but he could see it from where he operated. He was a man of boundless energy and tireless curiosity. Smith thrived on the excitement of uncovering secrets, solving crimes that lesser men thought had been perfectly committed.

Smith was mistaken for some type of delivery person when he walked into the campaign offices carrying his motorcycle helmet, which he hated to wear but Virginia law required. He handed his card to one of the workers, who delivered it to Savage without offering Smith a place to sit down. Savage quickly came out of his inner sanctum when he found out that the private investigator was in the office.

"Pete, I'm Jack Savage. Dorothy told me you would be coming by." Savage shook hands with Smith and noticed the strong grip from the older man who clearly spent a lot of time in the weight room. Savage had done some research on Smith Investigations, Inc. It was a well-respected firm that hired only experienced and accomplished investigators, most from government agencies, particularly the FBI. Its president was known to be a little eccentric, but was still viewed as the cream of the investigative crop.

"Dorothy told me I would like your wardrobe," said Savage, smiling at the similarity between their outfits. Savage was in jeans, loafers and a blue denim shirt.

"It's what's on the inside, not the outside, I always say," responded Smith. "So where is this stuff you've got?"

Savage led Smith into his office, which was more like the size of a large conference room. At one end was a table that was piled with letters and cassette tapes. "We started getting this stuff the day after the murder. Some of it comes to the Senator's office in the Russell Office Building, but we collect it all here," said Savage, referring to the pile. "Everything that comes into the switchboard is taped, and we have spliced together all of those calls as well. I reviewed it all for a while, but it's a bunch of fruitcakes. We have several people confessing that they killed her. The Russians are a common suspect. Some think that Randall Hardy or Wilbur Daily did it. Others say they saw the Senator pull the trigger."

Some days as many as a hundred calls and letters were received from people professing to have information about the murder of Andria Winn. Undoubtedly, the pile included letters from all of the known "confessors" around the country who took responsibility for this crime like they did thousands of others. It was an unglamorous part of investigative work to rifle through this material; television movies omit this laborious part of solving a crime. Buried deep inside similar piles of lunacy, however, the keys to many locked secrets had been found.

"We tried at first to trace who some of these people were, which ones were known kooks, etc. If we found something out, notes were made. But we gave up early for lack of manpower and the countless dead ends. We kept saving it, however. I was glad we did when Dorothy said you wanted to know if we were getting this kind of junk."

"Have you got a place where I can look over this stuff?" asked Smith eagerly, like a kid who wanted to get into a new box of cereal and see if the prize was any good.

"Hey, just pull up a chair if you can concentrate in here. This place is usually a mad house. You won't bother us."

"Have you got a coffee pot I can get to?"

"Mary Ellen, get Mr. Smith some coffee and show him around," Savage said, as Mary Ellen came through the door before he barely had her name out. "He is VIP, and to be given whatever he wants." Mary Ellen knew what the pile was that Smith was standing over. She wondered if he was a cop.

With a cup of coffee in his hand, Smith sat down at the long table to assess the stacks of letters and tapes. There was no organization to the mess, with more recent items being put on the top of the pile. Smith started by randomly picking up and reading letters to get a feel for what he had. The first letter he picked up was a one-page handwritten letter addressed to Winn from one "John Williams," who said he was a pharmacist in Kansas City. Williams said he knew who killed Andria and knew why. He was afraid to talk to anyone other than Winn and afraid to put what he knew on paper. He gave a post office box where Winn could reach him. Smith's people later determined that John Williams was an inmate in the Missouri maximum-security facility in Jefferson City. He was then put at the bottom of the list.

The second letter looked more respectable. It was typed on letterhead from a business called CalDan Enterprises in Fairfax, Virginia. The letter was from a William Howard Jennings, who said he was the president of his company. He claimed to have seen Mrs. Winn on several occasions at a bar in Fairfax with a man whose picture was recently published as Anthony Baroni. He said that Baroni was abusive to Mrs. Winn, and he believed it likely that Baroni was involved in her death. Smith would later send one of his investigators to talk to Mr. Jennings. If he was legit, at a minimum he would have information that could be useful to Wallace in cross-examining Baroni.

THE SUN WAS DOWN, a new shift of campaign volunteers had come in, and Smith had been reading for several hours when he finally came to something that peaked his interest. It was a handwritten letter from a Gloria Speavy with a Georgetown address. The letter was dated a week ago, about three weeks after the murder. She said that she had contacted the police repeatedly, but that they were not interested in what she had to say. She said a detective named Byron Lane had come to her house at her insistence, but after a brief interview had left, taking no notes, and was unavailable when she tried to contact him later.

Ms. Speavy said that she lived two streets directly north of Winn and routinely walked her dog in the late evening hours. She noted in the letter that it was probably not her safest habit, but one she had been doing for a couple of years. On the night of the murder, Speavy walked in front of the Winn home at around midnight. She heard a loud noise come from the direction of the Winn house. She walked to one of the large elm trees on the street for cover but waited and watched to see if anything seemed amiss. She saw a man running from the Winn house to the street and into a waiting car. She was within 30 or 40 feet of the man, but she did not think she could identify him. She was too panicked to take in any details and did not know what the car looked like. She saw no movement at the Winn house, and assumed everything was all right. She thought maybe it was a burglary attempt, but since they left without carrying anything, she was not overly concerned. At the time, she did not know that the Winns lived in the house. She read the reports in the *Post* the next day and was convinced she had seen the intruder that was reported. She did not think she had any useful information so did not call the police. When the story begin to turn, however, and it was being alleged that Winn was the target of the investigation, she panicked and started trying to get in touch with the police. While she considered herself of no help in identifying the killer, she felt she had solid evidence that confirmed Winn's story.

Smith called Ms. Speavy from the campaign offices, and arranged to meet with her the next morning.

WALLACE FOUND SLEEPING more and more difficult. She sat on her bed re-reading all of the cases she had found concerning abuse of the grand jury process. Several decisions had been written by federal trial court judges and were reported in the *Fed. Supp. Reporter.* State trial court decisions were seldom written and, even if they were, were not published in any regular reporter. As a result, their rulings with respect to grand jury challenges were difficult, if not impossible, to find.

There were very few cases that raised grand jury issues on appeal. By the time a case was appealed, the defendant had usually been convicted and the grand jury issues were, as a practical matter, moot. By then a real jury had viewed the evidence in open court and found the defendant to be guilty. Any remedy for abuse of the grand jury process would be too harsh and not likely to be imposed.

There was a common theme in all of the reported decisions. Prosecutors have wide latitude in the grand jury process, and their actions will not be scrutinized by the courts absent special circumstances that indicate that a defendant's constitutional right to due process has been seriously threatened. Wallace was particularly interested in cases where pre-trial publicity was found to prejudice a grand jury proceeding. There were only two reported cases where the facts were on point. One was from the Southern District of Louisiana where it was determined that the prosecutors had repeatedly leaked information to the media before and during a grand jury proceeding that was not presented at the grand jury. There were no special efforts made to keep the grand jury members from being tainted by such reports. The court ruled that the defendant's right to due process had been violated. Follow-up research indicated that the prosecutor had gone back to the grand jury and re-indicted the defendant, who was subsequently convicted. A second case came from the Southern District of California, a bastion of liberal thought that was vigilant in protecting the constitutional rights of the accused. In a more flagrant abuse, it was ruled that the prosecutors had, in fact, let the grand jury members learn that the public considered the defendant to be guilty and that pressure was applied to convince the grand jury that they would be scorned by their peers if an indictment was not returned. Subsequently, that defendant, a black man charged with the rape of a white woman, was brought to trial pursuant to a petition and preliminary hearing and was acquitted by the jury.

Wallace reached for the remote control to her Sony mini component stereo and changed the CD from the Toni Braxton music playing to Puff Daddy; she needed something more upbeat to keep her spirits up. She was tired but could not sleep; she criticized herself for doing less exercise than she had in years. She was definitely off her routine, but could not resist putting every spare moment into her research and study for the case. She reminded herself that she would be better off—Winn would be better off—if she kept up her exercise to keep her mind sharp and her body less affected by the stress of her work. She promised herself to get up early and run in the morning.

As Wallace laid down the California case that she had now read over a dozen times, she wondered what Winn was doing.

He had taken her advice and gone by way of private jet to Kona, Hawaii, where he was staying at the estate of a supporter and friend. It was determined that he could get more privacy out of the country, but Wallace feared it might be used by the prosecution at a bail hearing as evidence concerning how easily Winn could slip out of the country. The media had determined that Winn was gone when they did not see the caravan move daily back and forth between his Georgetown home and Wallace's office. There was speculation by the media that, fearing an indictment, Winn was in the process of fleeing. Wallace had not been contacted by the prosecutors concerning this speculation, although she was sure they were concerned. The government would be greatly embarrassed if someone with this high of a profile under suspicion was allowed to sneak away. None of this would set a favorable background for her efforts to keep Winn out of jail during the trial. Perhaps it was a mistake to encourage him to go, but he needed a break.

Wallace went into the kitchen and poured herself a glass of Jordan Cabernet Sauvignon. She was drinking one or two glasses a night to help her relax and sleep. She chastised herself for drinking too much, particularly since she was not exercising. Wallace went back into the bedroom and picked up the phone. Pete Smith had his technical gurus check her office and apartment every other day for electronic eavesdropping devices. One had been found on her office phone, connected at the phone company. They did not know if it was the police or the media. If it was the police, it was illegal—a major violation since it involved infringement on Winn's sixth amendment right to counsel—but the cops routinely did illegal wiretaps to find out new information. They would never try to use this information officially, but would use it to find evidence that appeared to be legitimately obtained.

Wallace calculated the time change in her head to note that it was early evening on the Big Island. She dialed the phone number of the private residence where Winn was staying. A house servant answered and politely asked her to hold when she used the pre-selected code of asking for Mr. Longworth.

"Hey, Dot," said Winn, sounding upbeat when he came on the phone.

"Getting a sun tan?"

"It would only be paradise if you were here," he quipped.

Wallace paused, then said, "Maybe soon." Winn was surprised by the seriousness of her response to his joke. He did not pursue it, but would remember.

"So, how are we doing, counselor?"

"We are hearing nothing officially. The media continues to report that an indictment is coming down any day, but they had been saying that for weeks. Who knows?"

"Should I come back?"

"No, it's still better if you're not here if an indictment is issued," she said, trying to sound more sure than she really was.

"I'm sorry that you're left holding the bag."

"I've got plenty of help," said Wallace. "The media reports a second witness with relevant information, a Sally MacArthur. Do you know her?"

"She was Andria's friend. Andria would sometimes stay with her when I was out of town. Best I could tell, she was kind of a kook; I never figured out what Andria saw in her. She used to call Andria in the middle of the night with one crisis or another; she claimed her husband was beating her all the time. Andria said it wasn't true. She was married to some guy in one of the big accounting firms. I think they are divorced now."

"Smith is digging into her background. We are coming up with some pretty good stuff to attack the credibility of her and Baroni. But so far all we have is defense. I am trying to come up with as many procedural issues as I can to slow this thing down once it starts so Pete has more time to find something we can use offensively. I've got a feeling about him; I think he will come up with something."

"Let's hope." Winn suspected that Wallace thought their only real hope was to find the real killer. The police were not helping; it was up to them to solve the crime.

"What are you doing to keep busy?"

"We went deep sea fishing today for blue marlin. No bites; none of the other boats reported any action either. It sounds like paradise, but I'm bored as hell. I have read two novels already, including Grisham's new book. Just what I need, a legal thriller! They do a good job of hiding the newspapers from me." Winn paused, then added from nowhere, "I wish you were here."

When Wallace did not respond, he continued. "I love you, Dot. I want to be with you."

Wallace felt a pleasant chill run up her spine at the sound of his words. "Don't talk like that now, Ben. Even though Pete's checking, you never know who's listening. Remember I'm your motive; by the time Stephenson gets done presenting her case, you're going to wish you had never met me." She loved him, too.

Sixteen

Fittingly, it was tax day, April 15, the day the government gets us all. You wonder how a nation founded on the protest of the Boston Tea Party could end up taking almost half of everyone's income without any serious protest. The U.S. Attorney's Office had announced it was holding a news conference at 3 p.m., plenty of time to get on the evening news around the country. Wallace had waited by her phone all day, expecting a call. It was unheard of that the government would announce to the media an indictment before informing the defendant, but that is what was rumored to be in the works. Wallace got progressively angry as the day continued since

Winn's life was at stake, but to date he was not even a part of the process. For two months now, a bunch of government bureaucrats had run around unwatched and untested, manipulating the media with innuendo and accusations, trying to convince the public that a man was guilty who had yet to be given any voice in the process. What happened to concepts of "innocent until proven guilty" and "justice," she wondered? What was Andria Winn's killer thinking about all of this? He was probably getting a big laugh. She decided that Stephenson would end up calling her at a few minutes before three; even that did not happen.

Three o'clock arrived, and Wallace was joined in the law office by Smith and Savage to watch four televisions that had been wheeled into one of the small conference rooms. The sound was up on CNN, but all of the network broadcasts were being taped. There was plenty of audio visual equipment in the firm; it was common to video tape witnesses or negotiations to ensure that no one tried to recant.

"It would be pretty funny if this doesn't have anything to do with us," said Savage, trying to bring some levity to the situation. Smith smiled. Wallace looked at him with an expression saying, "Shut up and get prepared for this."

The cameras were all focused on an empty platform in the lobby of the Federal Courts Building. This was to be a media extravaganza too large for the media briefing room at the U.S. Attorney's Office to accommodate. The last time they held a news conference in the spacious lobby was when the Special Prosecutor for the Clinton investigation released its findings. The lobby was packed with reporters, cameras, and lights. At ten minutes after three, four people walked into the picture and took the stage: Jake Butler, Sybil Stephenson, Byron Lane, and Oliver Thorn. Butler looked tense. It was not often that a U.S. Attorney was hesitant to get the publicity associated with a high profile case. He felt this one was moving too quick, however, and if they were wrong, he was, politically speaking, a dead duck. Thorn looked like he wanted to be somewhere else.

Stephenson and Lane seemed to have condescending smirks on their face. They were at their zenith. Butler stepped up to the microphone. In spite of his reservations, he knew that if they got a conviction, he would be golden.

"Ladies and Gentlemen, this morning a grand jury reported the following indictment to the United States District Court for the District of Columbia. 'Count I: Andrew Benjamin Winn is charged with willfully and intentionally causing the death of Andria Hamilton Winn on or about February 7 when, it is charged, Andrew Benjamin Winn did with the use of a deadly weapon, that is, a hand gun, shoot with intent to kill Andria Hamilton Winn, all in violation of the District of Columbia Code....' Copies of the complete indictment are being made available at this time."

"Where is the defendant?" asked one of the reporters.

"As of this moment, we have been unable to locate the defendant. An arrest warrant has been issued, and the police department, with the assistance of the FBI, is in the process of finding and arresting the suspect," said Butler.

"Fuck," shouted Wallace. "They're making it look like he's a fugitive when the bastards have not even talked to us."

"Do you believe that Winn is on the run?" asked another reporter.

"I have nothing more to say on that issue, other than we do not know where the suspect is. A warrant has been issued, and we are attempting to execute it."

"Those bastards," said Wallace.

"What is the evidence against Winn?" asked Henry Rothstein.

"We cannot comment on any of the evidence but will be presenting it all in court," responded Butler, still nervous, wanting this to be over.

"Will you now confirm that Winn's fingerprints are on the gun?" followed Rothstein, looking directly at Lane.

Butler exchanged looks with his cohorts on the platform, and by some unspoken tacit agreement Stephenson stepped up to the microphone as Butler stepped aside. "I am Sybil

Stephenson and will be prosecuting this case for the United States. We cannot at this point talk about the evidence against Mr. Winn, but I will tell you that an indictment would not have been returned in a case with this much notoriety unless the evidence against Mr. Winn were not compelling." She smiled with obvious glee that she had compiled a case to put Winn away.

"So you're saying that you have him cold?" asked Rothstein.

Stephenson paused, then could not resist a slight smile as she said, "We are confident that we have the evidence needed to convict Mr. Winn of willfully and intentionally killing his wife by shooting her with a Colt .45 on the evening of February 7."

That seemed to be the statement the media was looking for, as chaos broke out, with reporters attempting to get on the air or file reports with their print services. They were like a pack of wild dogs who had ripped off a piece of flesh for themselves and were running back to privacy to devour it.

THE NEXT FEW DAYS WERE BEDLAM. The media accepted the bait hook, line, and sinker. Except for the few conservative newspapers that still managed to stay alive, the media community assumed that Winn was guilty and was a fugitive. There were reports of sightings all over the country, but the primary opinion was that he had left the United States and would try to change his identify and live in anonymity.

The television media went live with its anchormen and experts to cover the indictment. The experts explained the process and gave their opinions on whether the government would have sought an indictment if they did not have Winn dead to rights. Former prosecutors continuously opined that the U.S. Attorney's Office would not initiate such a high profile case unless it were bullet proof; that the case would be revealed at trial. Members of the defense bar pointed out all the high profile cases that the government had brought and lost in the past. This could be another, and these defense lawyers stressed that Winn should be presumed innocent until proven guilty. The exchange on NBC was typical:

"We are pleased to have with us Mr. Howard Crupp, the former United States Attorney for the District of Columbia," said Tom Brown, the NBC anchorman operating out of New York City. "Mr. Crupp, you have brought some pretty high profile cases in your time, such as the indictment of the former mayor of Washington, D.C. Is this the biggest murder case ever brought in the history of this country?"

The television screen instantly split, as Crupp appeared live via satellite from NBC's Washington affiliate. "Tom, it was widely reported that our indictment of Mayor Barkley was the most notorious case in history. I'd say the indictment of a U.S. Senator on his way to the White House is clearly the biggest prosecution we've ever seen."

"Mr. Crupp, is it possible to get a jury to convict a man as popular as Senator Winn?"

"It will be difficult, Tom. Senator Winn is a very popular man. A jury will not readily forget all the good he has done for this country. Even if the government can prove its case, I'd say there is a chance that the Senator cannot be convicted."

"So you're saying that even if guilty, the Senator may win his day in court."

"That's right, Tom."

"Let's turn to Mr. Richard Stern in Chicago, a well-known member of the defense bar who has received acquittals in several well-known cases. Mr. Stern, do you agree that it may be difficult to get a conviction of Senator Winn regardless of the evidence produced by the government?"

"I strongly disagree, Tom. It is easy for prosecutors to get convictions. Juries expect the government to tell them the truth. They do not expect the government to accuse people of crimes unless they have committed them. As a result, prosecutors around this country get convictions on over 95% of the charges they bring. Senator Winn is running up a steep hill from this point forward."

"Gentlemen, let me ask you this. Mr. Stern, you seem to be

saying that even if Senator Winn is innocent, he could be convicted. And, Mr. Crupp, you seem to be saying that even if the Senator is guilty, he could go free. Doesn't the truth determine the outcome of this ordeal?"

The only thing the experts could agree on was that the truth might have very little to do with the final outcome of the case.

THE GRAND JURY REPORTED its findings to District Court Judge Wilbur Maynard, a reasonable man, who was 67 years old and had sat on the bench for almost 20 years. The District Judge assigned to hear motions on the case was selected by lottery in the clerk's office, a process that was beyond the influence of the U.S. Attorney's Office. They could have done better. Maynard was a no-nonsense judge who did not like grandstanding and did not like the media interfering in the judicial process. He had been appointed to the bench by Ronald Reagan, and while now theoretically apolitical, according to the judicial code of ethics, did not care for President Carson or the present U.S. Attorney. He privately expressed his support for Winn's conversion to conservatism and would like to see his new colleagues over the next four years to be of a similar persuasion. That required the election of a Republican president. Maynard was a fair-minded man, however, who took the judicial process to be something more than a forum for competition. It was a quest for justice, and he would do all he could to neither have a defendant railroaded in his courtroom nor let a guilty man walk out of it.

Discreetly, Wallace filed a Motion the day after the charges were announced with the clerk's office to quash the indictment. She had prepared the Motion in anticipation of the government's move. The Motion was only six pages long and was accompanied by a 30-page Memorandum in Support that argued the law and the facts. Wallace knew from her clerkship what a judge was looking for in a brief — a concise recitation of the law supporting the argument and a good discussion distinguishing any case law to the contrary. Often a good brief would be turned into the first draft of a judge's opinion or order.

The Motion to Quash was made public and available to the media, but was largely ignored, dismissed as a routine procedural matter that any defense lawyer would use. The media was too consumed with speculation concerning Winn's whereabouts and speculation concerning whether he would be given the death penalty if convicted. Maynard set the Motion for an immediate hearing and ruled in advance that the hearing would be in camera, out of the earshot of the media and public.

Wallace worked her way through the hallways packed with media to Courtroom No. 4 where Maynard presided. She was ushered down the corridor inside a mass of reporters and cameramen yelling out questions that she ignored. She noticed that Stephenson was surrounded by another crowd of cameras and reporters as she appeared to be making a statement on her way into the courtroom.

Dressed in a navy blue suit, with nude hose and navy shoes, Wallace set up her materials at the table on the left side of the courtroom. After finishing her talk with the media, Stephenson positioned herself with co-counsel at the other table. Stephenson ignored Wallace. Tanya Ball stared at her with contempt; she viewed Wallace as a "wannabe," a black woman who operates in the white world. Ball figured that Wallace knew nothing about her black heritage and assumed that Wallace cared little about her people. Ball had seen her type before. Ball would not be able to imagine what life had been like for Wallace in the East St. Louis ghetto from which she had escaped. She could only see her for the success she now was. Success breeds jealousy, and Wallace was use to dealing with that.

The courtroom seemed eerie with the empty jury box and empty seats for the media and spectators. It was a large courtroom, built with no windows so that those in attendance would not be distracted. The courtroom was filled with ornate oak trim surrounding the bench, the jury box and the wooden handrail that separated the well of the courtroom from the audience. The spectators would normally be seated in long oak pews fitting for a church. Behind the bench on the right was a flag of the United States; on the left was a flag for the District of Columbia. Above the bench on the wall was a large oak carved seal containing the scales of justice. It was an imposing sight.

The only other person in the courtroom was a U.S. Marshal standing guard at the door to the hallway and a court reporter waiting for the action to begin. Soon another Marshal, an elderly man who was tall and overweight, entered from the door beside the bench.

"All rise. The United States District Court for the District of Columbia is now in session, the Honorable Wilbur Maynard presiding."

Carrying a file that contained the Motion filed by Wallace and the government's response, Maynard walked briskly in his black robe up the steps to the bench and took his seat. He looked old with graying thin hair, but had a sense of energy about him. He put his half-eyes on the end of his nose, as he opened the file. Finally, he looked up to assess the lawyers before him. While he had seen her picture on television and in the papers, he was struck by the beauty of the young black lawyer appearing on behalf of Senator Winn. He had heard the speculation about the two.

"Are you ready to proceed?" he asked, looking to Wallace who had filed the Motion.

"Your honor, if it please the court," interrupted Stephenson.

"Yes, Ms. Stephenson."

"The United States would like to object to the in-camera nature of this hearing. It is our opinion...."

"Overruled," said Maynard gruffly, looking disapprovingly at Stephenson over the top of his half-eyes.

"Your honor, it is the opinion of the United States that this hearing...."

"Overruled, Ms. Stephenson. Did you not hear me?" Wallace did not smile, but was pleased that Stephenson was irritating the Judge right out of the box. It was the first mistake of trial practice. "We are having this hearing to determine whether the prosecutors have tainted this indictment by fueling a media circus around this case. The court is of the opinion that at least this determination will be made outside of the sound bites of the media." Maynard stared at Stephenson in silence, then continued. "I also have a Motion from Ms. Wallace requesting an order to prevent further discussion of this case by those involved with the media. I will give you a few days to reply to that Motion, but will also hold a hearing in-camera to determine that issue. Is that all right with you, Ms. Stephenson?"

She knew that the best course was to agree, but she was not willing to give up any ground. "The United States will have the same objection to that in-camera hearing as well, your honor." Stephenson was tense and red in the face. Her paranoia contributed to her courtroom manner.

"That surprises me, Ms. Stephenson," said the Judge, wondering what it took to get his message through. He then continued. "Now, Ms. Wallace, you have filed the Motion at hand."

Wallace took her cue and started with an oral presentation of her argument. The Judge was known for being an active participant in his proceedings, which was good if he seemed to be on your side. If not, he could direct a case against you with little trouble. At this point, he was not indicating any preconceived notions, but he interrupted Wallace regularly with questions concerning the precedent she relied on. While she had little experience in the courtroom, Wallace adjusted well and carried on a thorough discussion of the issues with the Judge. Stephenson and Ball sat speechless, other than an occasional objection by Stephenson to which the Judge condescendingly informed her that there was no jury present, and the court could determine on its own what it should and shouldn't consider.

Wallace was not pushing for an immediate quashing of the indictment. Her argument focused on the media blitz surrounding the case, the fact that much of the information in the blitz seemed to have originated from the government which made them responsible for any damage it had caused, and that the proceedings of the grand jury should be reviewed to see if prejudice was evident. She indicated that it might also be necessary for the Court to examine the members of the grand jury in camera to see what effect the media coverage had on them. Her argument was cogent and convincing. There was little downside for the Court, for now she was only asking for the transcripts. If there was some evidence of taint, then the Judge would have a tougher decision to make.

"Ms. Stephenson, does the government wish to respond?"

"We do indeed, your honor." Stephenson fumbled through her papers, whispered to her colleague, and rose in an awkward silence. She picked up a photocopy of a case from the prosecution's table, then looked to the Judge. "Your honor, the Supreme Court has said repeatedly that the grand jury process is not to be invaded by the defense, that the defense will have an opportunity to challenge the findings of the grand jury at a trial. In United States vs. Wilson, Justice Walker, writing for a unanimous Court, said, 'The prosecutor is to be given wide latitude in conducting a grand jury proceeding and that latitude will not be called into question except in extreme circumstances.'"

"I have read your brief, Ms. Stephenson," said the Judge with a tone of annoyance. Judges hated to have written arguments read to them in court; they also hated to have the law read to them. Stephenson was not doing well; luckily she had the law largely on her side. She quickly stereotyped Maynard as a male chauvinist who disliked any woman prosecutor.

"The issue here, Ms. Stephenson, is whether these circumstances are extreme," said the Judge in a professorial tone.

"Ms. Stephenson, did the prosecutors do anything to protect the grand jury from the reports concerning this case in the media?" asked Judge Maynard.

"We followed the procedures of the U.S. Attorney's Handbook on grand jury proceedings to the letter, your honor. We specifically instructed the jury that they were not to read or watch any news accounts concerning the case and they were admonished not to discuss the case with anyone outside of the grand jury proceeding."

"Did the prosecutors do anything exceptional in this case because of the exceptional circumstances that resulted in a 24-hour media blitz about the case?"

"We did everything the handbook required, your honor. The procedures set forth in the handbook are used throughout the United States by federal prosecutors and have been routinely upheld by the Courts." The dialogue continued between the Judge and Stephenson, but she was little help. Maynard would have to decide this on his own, without any clever arguments from the prosecutors to help.

After hearing enough, Maynard abruptly stopped Stephenson, then asked Wallace if she had anything to add on the Motion.

"No, your honor," said Wallace, remembering from her trial practice course at Yale that a good lawyer knows when to shut up.

"Ms. Stephenson, the defense has filed a Motion for a Gag Order. I will give you until Thursday to respond to that Motion. I will hold a hearing on the Motion Friday morning at 10 a.m. I would suggest in light of the issues pending before this Court that you use caution in dealing with the media between now and Friday." Maynard did not want to tell her not to talk to the media until he ruled on the Motion, but he was disgusted with the way the prosecution was trying this case in the public arena. He would be further irritated when he saw on the evening news that Stephenson had talked freely with the media both before and after the hearing.

"The Court will take the Motion to Quash the Indictment under advisement and issue a ruling as soon as possible. Is there anything further?"

"No, your honor," said Wallace.

"Yes, your honor. The United States considers Ms. Wallace's client to be a fugitive from justice; we would like to know if Ms. Wallace knows his whereabouts."

"Ms. Stephenson, you surely do not expect Ms. Wallace to disclose that information to you?" said Judge Maynard in a raised voice which expressed his displeasure for the representation the government was getting in this case.

"Your honor, if I may," said Wallace.

"Go ahead, Ms. Wallace."

"Senator Winn is not in flight. Our only contact with the prosecution prior to today was a meeting the Senator had with Ms. Stephenson in February, then a second meeting which I requested with Ms. Stephenson three days later. We first learned of the indictment when it was reported on television on April 15. Ms. Stephenson has known for over two months that I represent Senator Winn in this matter, and neither she nor any representative of the United States Attorney's Office has made any attempt to contact me to arrange for the surrender of my client. In fact, your honor, it seems to the defense thus far that we are no more than a bystander in this process." Wallace paused to let what she was saying sink in.

"Do you dispute what Ms. Wallace is saying?" asked the Judge, turning to Ms. Stephenson.

Stephenson fumbled with her papers, whispered to her colleague, then said, "We have followed all of our regular procedures, your honor."

"Cut the crap, Ms. Stephenson. If you can't carry on a candid conversation with this Court, then bring your superior next time you come here." Stephenson's face was reddening at the chastising she was taking from Maynard. His patience had run to its end. "Now, Ms. Stephenson, were you aware that Ms. Wallace represented Senator Winn in this matter?"

She paused, considering a different answer, but ultimately said, "Yes, your honor."

"Well, I'm glad you admit to that since it has been reported widely over the last two months. Now, Ms. Stephenson, have you made any effort to contact Ms. Wallace to arrange for the surrender of her client?"

"No."

"Unheard of," said Maynard in disgust.

"Ms. Wallace, is your client willing to surrender to the

authorities?"

"Yes, your honor. At this point, we would like the Court to rule on our Motions. If the indictment is quashed, then, of course, there is nothing for Senator Winn to surrender to. Further, in light of the media frenzy that is obviously being fueled by the prosecution, we would like to have the gag order ruled on before the Senator steps into the government's hands."

"There is an arrest warrant for your client, Ms. Wallace. He should surrender."

"Your honor, no arrest warrant has been served on me."

"Ms. Stephenson, this is outrageous. You are making it look in the media like the Senator is fleeing from justice; yet you have not formally presented his lawyer with a copy of the arrest warrant." Stephenson said nothing. She did not care what this man thought; once she got before a jury she would have the last laugh on all of them.

"Once we see the arrest warrant, your honor, we would like to make the customary arrangements to have Senator Winn arraigned and have this Court consider a Motion for Bail. Considering the publicity surrounding this case, we believe that careful coordination needs to occur between us and the government to ensure that Senator Winn's rights are protected when he does surrender."

"Ms. Stephenson, I would expect you to give Ms. Wallace a copy of the arrest warrant before the hearing Friday morning. I would expect both sides to have discussions concerning the Senator's surrender before that hearing, and I would like to know Friday morning what the plan is. Ms. Wallace, the Court would not be insulted if you walk out of this Courtroom and tell the media what you have just told the Court."

"Thank you, your honor. We have tried to limit our contact with the media so that this case can be tried, if at all, in a Courtroom."

Stephenson jumped from her chair, red in the face, overwrought. She would make one final jab. "Your honor, we want it on the record that Mr. Winn has discussed this case repeatedly in his campaign. If the Court decides to issue a gag order, we will demand that the order extend to the campaign that is using this prosecution to win favor with voters."

"Your honor, if I may," responded Wallace, who received a nod of approval from the Judge. "The Senator's campaign was doing quite well before the prosecutors began to leak information to the media suggesting he was a suspect in Mrs. Winn's death. Because of the prosecution's action, the candidate has been forced into seclusion to work on his defense and avoid the media frenzy that has ensued. Surely the prosecution is not suggesting that the Senator's right to run a campaign for the highest office in this land is to be obliterated before his case is heard in court."

"The Court is sympathetic to the situation your client is in, Ms. Wallace." Wallace knew that she did not need to say any more. Maynard, like most Republican appointees, was known as a law-and-order judge. But he was offended with what was going on here. There was a demeanor with which prosecutors were supposed to act. They had the weight and the resources of the United States government on their side. They did not need to cheat. Cheating was just what they were doing in this case.

Seventeen

EXCEPT FOR GLORIA SPEAVY, Pete Smith had eliminated all the other letters and calls to the campaign and to Winn as dead ends. Gloria Speavy was not much more. She provided some confirmation for Winn's "Richard Kimball" defense, but nothing to give Smith any proof.

Smith continued to look at new stuff from the "fruitcakes," however, and now an item that had been received at the Senate office five days ago had his attention. It was an unsigned typed letter on plain white paper. The envelope was postmarked in Phoenix. The letter was short.

Dear Senator:

I am appalled at what they are doing to you. I
know you had nothing to do with the death of your
wife. You must be grieving dearly. An acquaintance
was bragging that he had arranged for the hiring of a
man to kill you. He was pleased that the same result
had been reached even though the killer bungled the
job and shot your wife instead. I am sure the truth
will come out in the end. You are such a good man.
If it does not, I simply don't know what I will do.

Smith sat in his own office where this junk was now delivered. He had bought a relatively small three-story building in
Falls Church where Smith Investigations, Inc. was housed. His
office was large but unpretentious, littered with bits and pieces
of information about the Winn case, most of which led to dead
ends. He got up and got a beer out of the small refrigerator in
one corner of the office, and then returned to his desk where
he reread the letter. After reading it, he studied the paper and
the envelope for some clue as to its sender. Other than the
postmark, he could find nothing. He would have his guys upstairs test it for fingerprints. No telling who had touched it
from the time it was mailed until it arrived in Smith's office. His
boys were able to access FBI files containing known fingerprints. This was a lead he wanted to pursue.

Smith had never really doubted Winn's innocence, although
he tried to keep his objectivity. His job was to help his client
win the case and he needed to know the truth, even if only to
prepare to cast doubt on it. He relied heavily, however, on his
instincts, and he had a "feeling" from the beginning that Winn
was being railroaded. He had seen this type of thing before.
The government needed a quick solution to a high profile case.
Lane and Stephenson were obviously more ambitious than bright
and saw that the best solution for them was to prove Winn was
guilty. They were piecing together a case based on circumstantial evidence, much of which was from witnesses that were

fraught with weaknesses. The government had used the media to prosecute Winn well in advance of any trial. It was laughable to think that any jury could ever be assembled that had not been affected by the trial by media. But based on the evidence as it had been carefully leaked to the media, Smith thought they could win even without finding the killer. He owed it to his client, however, to find the killer of his wife. It did not matter to Smith that Winn was not grieving too heavily over the death of his wife or that Winn and Wallace seemed to have some obvious attraction to each other. Winn had a right to have his reputation restored and his wife's death avenged; these could only be accomplished if they found the killer.

RANDALL HARDY SAT BY THE POOL at his private home in Scottsdale taking a brief and rare break from the campaign. It was a beautiful warm spring day in Phoenix. By the time the summer heat was burning hot, Hardy would be in Seattle accepting his party's nomination for president. He had long ago locked up the nomination, even though the convention was yet several weeks away in July. He had been running against Ben Winn for months now. He was beginning to turn the corner in the polls. Winn's negatives were slowly edging up as people accepted that he had killed his wife. The most recent national poll showed him beating Winn for the first time. If Winn withdrew or otherwise did not get the Republican nomination, the polls showed that Hardy would have a landslide victory over any of the other alternatives. The Republican Party was in such disarray that Hardy might even be able to preserve a majority for his party in both houses of the Congress.

It was clear from the media that Winn would get convicted. The cops were not even considering any other possibility. He smiled to himself about how it had all worked out. Maybe this was an even better result than Winn getting killed. If Winn had been replaced in the race in February, another Republican might have been able to build some momentum. Besides, the publicity over Winn being indicted was ripping the Republican Party apart, as many accepted what the prosecutors were saying. Yet others remained steadfast in support of their boy wonder.

Hardy called for his Mexican house servant to make him another martini while he stepped into the pool to cool off.

JUDGE MAYNARD OPENED THE FILE and reviewed the documents inside as if he were not sure what case he was sitting on. It was a habit of his to make the lawyers wait a few minutes to impress upon them who was in charge. Judges could be overruled, but for the time you spent in their Courtroom, they were God. Anyone who wanted to dispute that could think it over while spending the night in jail.

As Judge Maynard looked up, he removed his half-eyes and spoke to the lawyers in the otherwise empty Courtroom. "The Court has ruled that the prosecutors must turn over the grand jury transcripts for inspection by the defense. An order will be issued immediately following this hearing, which further instructs that the defense is not to copy the transcript and is neither to discuss it nor disclose it to anyone other than the defendant and his lawyers. Ms. Wallace, if you have not filed a supplemental memorandum to your Motion within ten days of receiving the transcript, then your Motion to Quash will be denied. Any memorandum filed is to be sealed and not released for public dissemination."

Stephenson was beside herself. She was on her feet waiting to speak as soon as the Judge said, "Prosecutors must turn over." She was tapping her fingers on the table impatiently, waiting for the Judge to finish his ruling. She heard nothing else he said. No prosecutor in the office during her tenure had lost on a routine harassing Motion to Produce a grand jury transcript. Either the Judge was picking on her, or he was doing this because of who Winn was. Either way, she would not stand for it.

"Ms. Stephenson, do you have something you want to say?"

"Your honor, the government is extremely upset by this ruling and will appeal immediately ..."

"Ms. Stephenson, you have ten days within which to appeal

any ruling of this Court," said the Judge condescendingly. "If you have done nothing improper, then the prosecution has nothing to be concerned about."

"The precedent, your honor; this..."

"Ms. Stephenson, anticipating an appeal by the government, I am issuing a written opinion with my order, which will be part of the public record. You have charged Senator Winn with a capital crime—I need not remind you that his life could be at stake here. Considering the severity of the punishment he faces and the media interest in this case because of his notoriety and position—not to mention the government's actions that have fueled the media fire—I am sure you will be able to distinguish this case from cases in the future."

Wallace knew that the Judge had likely discussed this issue with his brethren, which included the members of the United States Court of Appeals for the District of Columbia that would review his ruling. Unlike most jurisdictions, because of the size of Washington, D.C., all of the district court judges and all of the appellate judges officed in the same building on Constitution Avenue. They shared a lunchroom on the fifth floor where they were served in elegant style at mahogany tables by their own chef and waiters. Wallace knew from her days at the Supreme Court that many decisions were made and agreed to in that lunchroom. A reversal was unlikely. If Butler had any control left in this case, he would probably not allow an appeal. The government would simply look worse if they appealed and lost. Besides, they would look like they had something to hide. To date, they had virtually all of the media momentum. Butler would not want to lose that. If this case ever turned against him, it had the notoriety now to roll right over several members of the law enforcement community crushing their careers as it passed.

"Now, I have read Ms. Stephenson's response to the Motion for a Gag Order as well as Ms. Wallace's rebuttal. I am not going to impose a gag order at this time. I am, however, not going to deny the Motion yet. The Court intends to monitor the behavior outside of this courtroom by both parties, and if it is determined in the future that either side is misusing the media in a way to prejudice the defendant from getting a fair and impartial trial, a gag order will be imposed." Maynard paused, looking at the lawyers to see if any response was forthcoming. Stephenson was still fuming over the first ruling. Wallace sat composed.

"Have the parties discussed the surrender of the defendant?"

Wallace waited. It was traditional for the prosecutor to speak first as the lawyer for the people. When Stephenson did not emerge from her discussion with Tanya Ball where she was chastising Maynard, Wallace rose to speak.

"If it please the court, I called Ms. Stephenson the afternoon after our last hearing with the Court and asked that we arrange a time to have Senator Winn voluntarily surrender, be fingerprinted and booked, then brought to court for an arraignment and hearing for bail. Ms. Stephenson said she would take my request under advisement." It was obvious to the Judge that the government had not gotten back to Wallace. Considering the desire they expressed in the media to get their hands on Winn, they seemed to be taking no action to bring that about. Perhaps for now they liked the media twist better with it appearing that Winn was a fugitive.

"And have you done your advisement?" asked Maynard in a tone that evidenced the tension that was building between himself and the government's lead prosecutor.

"Your honor, the United States will oppose bail, and we are sure the Court will not allow it."

"That comment can wait for the arraignment, Ms. Stephenson. Do you have an objection to scheduling an arraignment in conjunction with the defendant's surrender?"

Of course, she had a problem with it. Winn deserved no special treatment. He was a murderer. He was a classic example of the domestic abuser to which women throughout the country are subjected.

"No, your honor," she said, knowing that there was little she could do. Such arrangements were routinely made, even for defendants in capital cases.

"Ms. Wallace, when would Senator Winn like to surrender?" asked Maynard.

"Any time next week that the Court would like to hold the arraignment, your honor."

"I will schedule an arraignment for Senator Winn at 1:30 p.m. next Wednesday, May 7. I will rule on any Motion for Bail at that hearing, so if either side wishes to file any written memoranda with respect to that issue, I suggest that they be filed with the Court by Tuesday." Maynard looked to the lawyers to see if there was any objection. There was not.

"If it please the Court, your honor," said Wallace as she stood back up. "How much time will the government need to process Senator Winn prior to the arraignment?"

"Ms. Stephenson?"

"A couple of hours." Stephenson was getting testy and dropped the customary address to the Court.

"Will all of the processing be done in this building?" asked Wallace.

Stephenson did not believe she needed to share this information with the defense, even though she would gladly talk to the media about it. Butler had received word that she had angered Maynard in the first hearing and had admonished her about further antagonizing the Judge. The U.S. Attorney was, after all, housed in the same building, which usually led to a relationship with the judges that put the defense at an unfair disadvantage. This might, however, be a case where familiarity breeds contempt. Stephenson knew she had angered Maynard with her response to his ruling on the grand jury transcripts and made a determination to walk through the rest of this as easily as possible.

"Counsel should know that all of the booking procedures take place here," she said.

"And will the government agree to allow counsel to be present with the Senator from the time he surrenders until the arraignment?"

"This may not work when he is being fingerprinted and ..."

"Ms. Stephenson, I have been here for 20 years, remember," said Judge Maynard. It was a standard practice to let a defendant's lawyer walk through the process with his client upon a voluntary surrender.

"We will make whatever arrangements are necessary to allow Mr. Winn's counsel to be with him," she said, knowing that she would keep Winn in jail once he was here and Wallace would have to leave at some point. This she considered some sort of victory.

"And I assume that the government will agree that Senator Winn need not be handcuffed, locked up or in any other way restrained until after the arraignment?"

"Yes, we agree," said Stephenson begrudgingly, even though she relished the idea of a photo of Winn in all the papers in handcuffs.

"Thank you," Wallace said, facing Stephenson. "Thank you, your honor, we have nothing further."

"Ms. Stephenson?"

"We have nothing further, your honor."

THE MAINSTREAM MEDIA EASED ITS PUSH against Winn for a couple of days as its experts evaluated the significance of the Trial Judge's order to release the grand jury transcripts to the defense. The order made clear the defense's concerns. The experts considered the likelihood that the indictment would be quashed and, if so, what the effect would be on the case.

It was becoming more and more difficult to distinguish between the mainstream news media and the now ever popular tabloid news. They separated themselves for these couple of days, however, where the tabloid television shows continued with their scheduled programs filled with paid "friends" and "co-workers" who were willing to say they knew a darker side of Ben Winn and did not consider spousal abuse, and even murder, to be something surprising in the Ben Winn they knew. Most of these people were ex-employees who had an ax to grind or people who simply did not know the Winns at all but were using some past connection in their lives to gain brief fame and a few bucks.

After a heated debate in which Stephenson threatened to "resign and go public" if the U.S. Attorneys Office decided not to appeal the Judge's order, it produced the five-inch transcript of the grand jury proceedings to the office of Dorothy Wallace. Wallace read every word, marking various places where Stephenson had stepped out of bounds, before turning it over to her associates for review and analysis. Not surprisingly, there was nothing so obviously outrageous to ensure the indictment be quashed. There was, however, plenty of overreaching to give Wallace a reasonable argument that Stephenson had abused the grand jury process by taking away its independence. You could tell from some of the questions asked by members of the grand jury that they were well aware of what the media was reporting on the case. None of these instances were accompanied by admonishments from Stephenson that they were to avoid the media reports. There was the possibility that Wallace could get Maynard to bring the grand jury members in for questioning in his chambers to see the extent of the prejudice created by the outside influences.

Wallace dictated the first draft of a new Motion to have the indictment quashed for prosecutorial misconduct and dictated a Memorandum in support of her original Motion in which she requested that the Court talk to the grand jury members individually. She knew that the direct attack on Stephenson's behavior would create further hostility, but had decided that Stephenson did not react well when angry. The more upset she became, the more impulsively she acted and the less methodical she thought. In sum, she would make more mistakes if she was upset.

At eight o'clock she left her office and drove to the Willard Hotel. She parked in back so as not to risk being recognized by the doormen on Pennsylvania Avenue and slipped into the north end of Peacock Alley where she took the elevators upstairs to the 7th floor. She pressed the doorbell and waited until it was opened by Ben Winn. Wallace stepped into the door, where she went into a long embrace with Winn.

"Would you say that I have lost my objectivity?" said Wallace, smiling after they disengaged.

"I know better than to criticize you," said Winn. He had arrived only an hour earlier by a private plane at National Airport, where he was met by Pete Smith and ushered secretly into the Willard Hotel. Smith had registered for the room earlier under an assumed name and gave Winn the key so he was able to slip into the hotel on his own much the same way that Wallace had entered. To the few guests who noticed him, he looked no different than any number of business travelers staying at the Willard.

Wallace said nothing as she looked at Winn. Still standing by the bed, she kicked off her black high-heeled shoes and started to unbutton her gray fitted suit.

"So you may be in prison for the rest of your life starting tomorrow," she said smiling. "I guess the least I can do is lay you. I may be the last 'woman' you ever have sex with."

"Very funny."

Wallace slipped off her jacket, then reached out her long slender black arms for Winn to come to her. She took his face in both of her hands and kissed him gently. Winn moved his hands to her firm slender thighs.

"I love you, Ben. I'm scared."

"Do you know how long it's been since you said you loved me?" asked Winn, knowing that only he had uttered the statement over the last four years.

"About as long as since I last said I was scared," she said with a spunky grin on her face. Both of their expressions then turned affectionate as they embraced and slowly moved onto the bed. He pulled off the white shell that covered her bare breasts and dark brown nipples, then pulled off her skirt. He looked momentarily at her perfect slender body, then with both hands pulled off her black panty hose. He caressed her gently up and down her body while he kissed her smooth skin. She then rolled him onto his back and undressed her lover, reciprocating with gentle touching and kissing when he was naked. Soon he took her by the shoulders more firmly and pressed her closer to him. As he bit her neck, she slightly raised herself into the air as he penetrated her. Passion consumed them, and while they would make love more gently as the evening went on, the first time the bed shook as she responded to his pounding thrusts with strong movements of her own body.

For now, they thought of nothing but each other's bodies and their love for each other. When they finally checked, they realized they had been making love for four hours. Both were covered with sweat, and the sheets were wet from perspiration and sex. Winn was finally the first to push away as he propped pillows up in the bed and leaned back in a sitting position.

"So tomorrow I get booked for murder."

"Let's don't talk about it. There is nothing we can do tonight."

They talked about the old times. The long dinners in her condo when they sipped wine and talked about their work, their ambitions. They talked about what their children would look like if they had kids. They talked about where they would like to spend the rest of their lives raising those kids.

Eighteen

I t had, of course, leaked to the media that Winn would be arrested on Wednesday morning. The parking lot surrounding the courthouse was packed. Constitution Avenue was littered with TV station vans. Cameras were at every conceivable entrance to the building to catch a glimpse of Winn as he entered. It was unclear what the circumstances were. One rumor was building that Winn had been arrested by the FBI and would be brought in handcuffs. Word had spread that whatever was going to happen, it would start at 11 a.m. On the hour, the networks went live to the front of the Federal Courts Building.

Five minutes later a crowd began to stir as someone reported hearing something over a scanner. Within seconds three rented black Ford Lincolns came from the west on Constitution Avenue and turned left into the parking lot. The windows on the cars were tinted and the media was unable to peer in; they were certain Winn was inside. Pete Smith had arranged with the U.S. Marshals that guard the Courthouse to have the three cars pull immediately into the underground parking garage. From somewhere came a circulating news release prepared by Bill Stevens that said Ben Winn's lawyers had not been served with an arrest warrant until last Friday. Immediately, Winn instructed his lawyers to arrange for his voluntary surrender. Today, accompanied by private security officers, the Senator was completing that surrender. He was not in any way involved in the death of his wife, and he was convinced that the truth would soon prevail.

Savage got out of the front passenger seat of the middle car and opened the rear door where Winn and Wallace emerged. Winn looked like he was going to any other political event, dressed in a dark blue suit, white shirt with a tab collar, and colorful, yet politically acceptable tie. His hair was freshly cut and he looked rested, smiling to the guards and shaking hands with those he had come to know over the past few weeks. His lawyer was carrying a thin black briefcase and was dressed in a tasteful olive green-colored suit, with off-white stockings and black heels. Her hair was swept up in a French twist.

As they were escorted into the private elevator and taken to the second floor of the building, Winn commented that this was the same way they had come in last February the day after Andria was killed. He never thought it would result in this. The police officers who handled Winn were polite, most smiling, some wanting to shake his hand. They were not infected with the same venom that ran through the veins of Lane and Stephenson.

Winn took a seat at the desk of an older black woman dressed in a police uniform. She smiled a knowing type smile of admiration at Dorothy and pleasantly asked Winn a series of routine questions as she filled out the standard forms. Once done, she asked Winn and his lawyer if they would follow her to the room where fingerprints were taken. There another smiling police officer, an elderly black man, asked Winn if he would roll up his shirt sleeves. Smiling and joking with the officer, Winn took off his suit coat and rolled up the sleeves on his shirt. As instructed, he reached out his right hand first. The officer took the hand in his own large hands and pressed it against the ink pad, then rolled each finger one by one over the fingerprint card; then he did a print with all of the fingers except the thumb. The officer completed the same process with Winn's left hand, then showed him how to use the soap dispenser to get the ink off of his hands.

After rolling his sleeves back down, then putting his coat back on, Winn was whisked off to another room where his "mug shots" would be taken. He held up a card as instructed that said "Winn, 420066." Winn made several jokes about the number, but tried to have a politically correct expression, not too happy, not too depressed, on his face when the photos were snapped.

Neither Lane nor Stephenson had been present for the ordeal, which went routinely and pleasantly. Once informed they had nothing else to do until the arraignment, Wallace asked if there was a conference room where she could meet with her client. Treated like special guests, they were escorted to a witness room off Courtroom No. 4 where they were delivered coffee, then left alone.

"So far so good, counselor."

"Do you know Judge Maynard?"

"I've met him; nothing that would cause him to excuse himself from the case."

"He seems to be pretty fair. Stephenson definitely rubs him the wrong way. His only ruling so far was the order requiring the government to produce the grand jury transcripts. So we're one for one."

"You know if you win this case, you can quit your criminal

practice saying that you never lost a case."

"Don't remind me of my experience. I feel inadequate enough as it is."

Wallace responded to a knock on the door and was told by the Marshall outside that it was time for them to go into the courtroom. Judge Maynard would be out shortly. They followed the Marshal across the hall and into a side entrance to Courtroom No. 4. It was packed with reporters and spectators. Winn could see the confusion at the entrance to the courtroom, but could not tell that the large hallway out front was just as packed as the courtroom. Spectators stood in line and would be allowed to enter according to their order as people left the courtroom. There was a single camera in the courtroom, which would provide a pool feed to the networks and local television stations. Print photographers were not allowed to use their cameras in the courtroom, although several intended to clandestinely snap a flashless photo of the accused.

Stephenson and Ball were already at the prosecutor's table. They did not look up or in any other way acknowledge the entrance of Winn and his attorney. Winn acknowledged a few of the reporters he knew with a reserved but pleasant smile. Wallace had instructed him not to wear his politician's face; any photos or film used would be in conjunction with a discussion of Andria's death. He needed to have the requisite amount of grief and reverence in his face. Besides, he was not feeling too friendly to any of the media. Although his relationship with them had always been good, they had all jumped on the "guilty" bandwagon weeks ago, never waiting to hear his side of the story.

"All rise, the United States District Court for the District of Columbia is now in session, the Honorable Wilbur Maynard presiding."

Maynard came out, file in hand, and took a seat at his throne. He put on the half-eyes that he was holding, then opened the file.

"First, let me say to the audience that if there are any violations of the rules of this Court by any of the spectators, the court will be immediately cleared and we will continue this hearing without you." Maynard paused to let the words sink in. The media was reporting him as a "hanging judge" of sorts; "Maximum Maynard" was the nickname used by one reporter. They did not think this boded well for Winn.

"Now we have several things to cover here. Let's begin by putting in your appearances."

"Your honor, the United States appears through myself, Assistant United States Attorney Sybil Stephenson, and Tanya Ball, also an Assistant United States Attorney."

You could hear a pin drop in the courtroom as Wallace stood up and indicated to her client to do the same. It was a stunning picture that would be replayed throughout the next few days. Winn was the All-American boy, before this the undisputed next President of the United States. He stood next to a sharply dressed young black woman who was the most beautiful woman to walk into the Federal Courthouse in some time. She looked more like she belonged on a Hollywood set for "L.A. Law."

"If it please the Court, your honor, Andrew Benjamin Winn appears in person and through his counsel, Dorothy Wallace," she said.

"Thank you, ladies," said Maynard indicating that he was from the old school. "Without objection we will start by having the clerk read the indictment."

Wallace stood up again and indicated that Winn should do the same. They listened while the clerk read the now all too familiar words of the indictment.

"How does the defendant plead?" asked the Judge. Wallace had instructed him that this was the only time he was to speak on his own behalf.

"Not guilty," said Winn with a strong and confident voice. The crowd had expected nothing else. Nevertheless, the words created that eruption of noise that spontaneously occurs when a crowd moves around to look at each other, exchanging knowing glances when something unifies their attention.

"Now before we get any new issues on the table, let's dispose of whatever we can. I have two Motions from Ms. Wallace concerning the grand jury proceeding. The first is to quash the indictment because of prejudicial influence on the grand jury by the pretrial publicity in this case. The second is to quash the indictment because of prosecutorial misconduct at the grand jury proceeding. The Court is issuing an order to deny both Motions."

Stephenson was ecstatic. She smiled broadly to Ball, then turned with an "I told ya so" smile to her boss who was sitting in the front row. Maynard did not appreciate her display for the camera and the reporters.

"The Court would like to warn the prosecution, however, that it did not consider the Motions filed to be without merit. The only available remedy, quashing the indictment, was simply too harsh for the misconduct cited. I want the government to know that this Court will not tolerate any such misconduct in the future. The goal here is to ensure that the defendant, Senator Winn, gets a fair and impartial trial. The price to be paid by the government for its actions to date is that this Court will give the defendant great leeway in pursuing its case, and it will hold the government lawyers personally responsible for any action in the future that is on the edge of infringement of the defendant's right to a fair trial."

Quickly, Maynard had deflated her balloon. He had accused her in front of God and everyone of misconduct. She did not turn to see the "I told you so" smile that Butler wanted to return to her.

Wallace was pleased, although she sat expressionless. The best she could hope for from her Motions was to be cut some slack by the Court in the future. Had he granted her Motion, delay would have been accomplished, but it would have been simple enough for the government to convene a new grand jury and re-indict her client.

"Now is there a Motion for Bail?"

"Yes, your honor," said Wallace again rising and drawing the attention of all in the room in a way that Stephenson would never understand. "Senator Winn would like the Court to set bail in a reasonable amount so that he can be readily available to work with counsel in the preparation of his defense."

Stephenson was up before the Judge could say anything to her. "The United States violently objects to bail. This is a capital case. The defendant has already avoided arrest ..." The crowd was on the edge of its seats; this was the type encounter they were anticipating. Wallace remained calm, standing before the Court. Stephenson was ruffled. It would be preposterous for Winn to get out on bail. She would look bad. The Judge cut her off quickly.

"Since this case seems to be dealt with in the media more than anywhere else, let us make this clear, Ms. Stephenson. Are you suggesting that bail is not available in a capital case in the District of Columbia?" Maynard was trying to keep his patience with her.

After rustling her papers and whispering to Ball in a routine that Wallace and Maynard now recognized as a sign that Stephenson had nothing intelligent to say, she responded. "No, your honor."

"So you agree Ms. Stephenson that the United States Code says that the defendant in a capital case has a right to bail unless there is reason to believe that he will flee?" asked Maynard as he was pushed into advocating the defendant's viewpoint.

"Yes, your honor, the United States is familiar with the statute."

"OK," said Maynard, becoming condescending with the hostile prosecutor. "Now, does the prosecutor want to argue that bail should not be granted in this case?"

"We do, your honor. The United States would like the opportunity to submit a written discussion of the law on this issue to the Court before it rules."

It was obvious to all in the Motionroom that she had said something to anger Maynard. The Judge immediately instructed the lawyers to approach the bench for a discussion that could not be overheard by the courtroom.

Maynard talked in a whispering voice but was angry and stern. "Ms. Stephenson, make no mistake about it, if you toy with this Court I will have you dismissed from the case immediately and throw your ass in jail for contempt."

Stephenson fumed, staring speechlessly at the Judge. She did not understand why he was so angry. He was simply picking on her.

"Do you recall what I said on Friday about written memoranda concerning bail?"

"Yes, your honor, but ..."

"No buts, Ms. Stephenson. I'm the Judge. What I say goes. You are on the edge here, and we are not even close to a trial."

"But it is not likely that you will be the trial judge," said Stephenson, even though it was irrelevant and simply reinforced her lack of appreciation for the Judge's attitude. Stephenson knew that the Chief Judge would assign trials separately from the assignment of Motions duty.

"I beg to differ, Ms. Stephenson. The Chief Judge assigned this case to me for trial this morning." Maynard could not help but smile. Stephenson was shocked and speechless. "So here is the deal, Ms. Stephenson. It is certain that I will be here for this trial. The only uncertainty is whether you will be. Do I make myself clear?"

In her abused voice, Stephenson responded that she understood. The lawyers knew they were dismissed and returned to their seats. In small print, Wallace wrote on the legal pad for Winn's eyes only, "She is digging a deep hole."

"Ms. Stephenson, do you have any evidence the defendant in this case was attempting to flee from justice?"

"We could not find him, your honor, when the arrest warrant was issued."

"Did you notify his attorney that an arrest warrant had been issued and provide her a copy?"

"Yes."

Maynard was getting angry again. "When was that, Ms.

Stephenson?"

"Last week," she responded, hanging her head momentarily as if to disown her admission.

"And what was the defendant's response, Ms. Wallace?"

"I immediately informed Ms. Stephenson that Senator Winn would like to voluntarily surrender and asked her to give me a time when the procedures that are occurring today could take place."

"Is that correct, Ms. Stephenson?"

"Yes, your honor."

"And a time for the surrender and arraignment was set in this courtroom last Friday; is that correct, Ms. Stephenson?"

Stephenson nodded her head affirmatively, then when prodded by Ball, orally said, "Yes."

"I told counsel Friday that I would rule on bail today, and that if either side wanted to make a written argument on the issue it should be filed with the Court by yesterday. I have read the memorandum submitted by Ms. Wallace. None was provided by the government. Ms. Wallace makes a persuasive argument that if the defendant were going to flee he would have already done so, that he is too well known to get very far undetected, even if he did attempt to flee, and that the defendant has ongoing business, or should I say political activities that require that he obey the order of this Court. I am also persuaded by Ms. Wallace's argument that much has already occurred in this case to potentially prejudice the defendant, and that he should have the opportunity of working with his lawyers in their offices in the preparation of his defense. Accordingly, bail will be set in this case at $500,000."

Stephenson whispered something angrily into the ear of her co-counsel. It was not overlooked by Maynard, but he would not react to it now. Butler was taking in this embarrassing event and would attempt unsuccessfully to remove Stephenson from the case. She was a bureaucrat who would be there long after him and she knew it. She threatened him with a sex discrimination suit, as well as implied that if he removed her it might be evidence that he was involved in a political conspiracy to obstruct justice. She was clearly out of control.

"Is there anything else?"

"Yes, your honor," said Wallace, rising from her chair again. "For weeks now we have read about certain physical evidence and statements from witnesses taken in this case. While this should be an open file case under the rules of the Court, the prosecutor has turned nothing over to us. We ask that if the government has any such physical evidence that it be immediately made available to the defense for testing and review by our experts." Wallace knew what evidence the government had; she had read about its presentation to the grand jury. Her approach to the question would, however, cause the media to wonder if something in this "cut and dry case" was amiss.

"Ms. Stephenson?"

"Of course, we have physical evidence," she said defensively. "We do not believe that the defendant should be given possession of such evidence where we have already performed tests. We will turn our test results over to the defense lawyers."

"Your honor, we are happy to comply with the traditional rules of the U.S. Attorney's Office which ensure the preservation and protection of any evidence. We believe, however, that we have the right to conduct our own tests with our own experts."

"The Court agrees, Ms. Wallace. This works routinely in thousands of cases, Ms. Stephenson. Will you see to it that all evidence is made available to the defense so that this Court need not monitor the exchange of every item."

After a long silence, Jake Butler rose from the front row of the courtroom, saying, "We will, your honor."

Maynard smiled. "The Court recognizes the United States Attorney who has not yet made an appearance on behalf of the government. It might not be a bad idea if he did," said Maynard. The audience broke into laughter. Stephenson was steaming. Butler smiled, but was now embarrassed for speaking in a case in which he had not formally made an appearance. He sat back down while Stephenson turned her head and stared bullets into him.

"Is there anything else?"

"Your honor, I would just like to make clear that if the government has any 302s or other notes taken in interviews of potential witnesses, we would like to see that material as soon as possible. And, of course, if there are any exculpatory Brady materials, we would like to have such materials turned over as soon as possible."

"Does the government agree to make any such material available by the end of the week and to continue to update the defense with any such new materials it acquires?"

"Yes, your honor, we agree." Stephenson would make the written materials available for inspection in her office. No photocopies would be allowed. Wallace would have to have her associates copy all such material by hand. It was one of the unfair practices that prosecutors were still allowed to get away with.

"Now, Ms. Wallace, is there anything else?"

"Only that at the end of this proceeding we would request that the Marshal help us get to the clerk's office so that bail can be posted." The crowd laughed, thinking Wallace was referring to the hoard of people. She was simply ensuring that Stephenson did not have Winn handcuffed and hauled off to a cell until she could get to the clerk's office. They had come with enough cashier's checks to post as high as $1,000,000 in bail. She had joked that it was like going to a foreclosure sale, something she understood much better than the practice of criminal law.

"The Marshal is so instructed," said Maynard, looking to the bailiff standing to the side of the bench. "Ms. Stephenson, do you have anything further?"

"No, your honor."

"And how about you, Mr. Butler," said Maynard smiling, subconsciously wanting to rub her boss' intrusion in Stephenson's face. He knew there would be a war in the U.S. Attorney's

Office this afternoon. He was sure he would hear about it in the lunchroom.

"No, your honor," said Butler, jumping to his feet, embarrassed again.

"Then, this court is adjourned. A pre-trial conference will be scheduled to discuss trial dates. The clerk will contact you concerning the conference."

"All rise," said the U.S. Marshal as Judge Maynard left the bench and returned to his private chambers.

Stephenson gathered her things and walked silently out of the courtroom, ignoring reporters. Butler was already gone. For the first time since Andria's death, Winn would get the better of the media war tonight. Stephenson would be roundly criticized, and many would speculate her hostility indicated a lack of confidence in her case. There was much discussion about whether the government had all of the evidence it had earlier indicated. Stephenson would be criticized for not arguing that Winn should not be out on bail because he had run from authorities four years ago when charged with the murder of Tina Adams and had been successful in leaving the country undetected by the government. In the final analysis, however, no one seriously disagreed with Maynard's decision to allow bail. Many speculated that based on what they had seen today, the government should be thankful that its case had not been dismissed. Dorothy Wallace was the darling of the news, reported to be cool, confident, and skilled. Experts marveled that this was her first criminal case. There was little discussion on this evening about the widely reported rumors about a romantic relationship between her and Winn. It was widely reported earlier that she might be the reason Winn had killed his wife. For now, she had claimed her place in the story as a talented lawyer who had come to rescue Winn from his government persecutors.

Nineteen

Smith drove across northeast Washington, looking for the three-story brick apartment building at 1322 S Street. Wallace had received the tip. Smith was mildly surprised that she wanted it checked out. If there was substance to it, it was not good for Winn. Smith agreed, however, that the lead had merit. Wallace had received repeated phone calls from the guy before she took his call. He said his name was Bert; he sounded street-wise. Bert said he had sold Winn a Gold Cup Colt .45 sometime before Christmas. Wallace hung up on Bert the first time. She took his call again, however, and heard him out. Bert claimed that Winn was driving a dark blue or black Chrysler.

He was wearing sweatpants and a Redskins sweatshirt and Reeboks. Bert did not know how Winn got his name. He thought Winn was a cop at first, but then he recognized him. He did not ask what a U.S. Senator wanted with a "hot" handgun. Bert claimed that Winn checked out the firearm with expertise and then paid with three $100 bills. If Wallace did not meet with him, he would go to the cops. In other words, he wanted to blackmail Winn.

The story had the kind of detail that an investigator looks for. Wallace said that Winn wore sweats and Reeboks when he ran in the winter. The car described could be Winn's Senate car, even though George usually had the car. Winn always carried several $100 bills.

"So, what do I do when I find this guy?" Smith had asked her.

"You try to figure out if he's telling the truth."

"And then what?"

"Pete, you tell me."

Pete wondered if she wanted to know the truth, or if she wanted to shut this Bert guy up if he knew something. He doubted whether Wallace knew at the moment what she wanted.

"OK, counselor. Let me look into it. We don't have to worry about it unless it pans out. I have run down more dead ends than you can believe over the past few weeks. A lot of them looked more credible than this." Smith smiled. He was trying to make her feel better. She was a stand-up "guy." She wanted to do the right thing.

Even in the daylight, this part of Washington, D.C. seemed threatening. A few black kids hanging out around the street corner were trying to figure out what do to instead of going to school. Smith pulled his Jeep up in front of the apartment building while the kids looked on. One of them shouted something, but Smith could not make it out.

The building was like all the others that lined the street as far as you could see. It was only a few blocks over to RFK Stadium, but no tourists ventured here except with 70,000 fans eight times a year. Bert had not agreed to meet with anyone but Wallace, but Smith said it was out of the question for her to run this down. She had more important work to do. She was also too high profile with the media trying to trail her everywhere she went. She had been instructed to go to Apartment 4. Smith walked up the stoop and through the unlocked front door that served as a common entrance for several apartments in the building. The door was slightly off one of the hinges, and warm, stale air filled the foyer. The stairwell was littered with trash, where kids had hung out to get out of the weather. The building was quiet except for some music coming from somewhere upstairs.

Smith went to the landing on the second floor and followed the music to Apartment 4. A few moments after he knocked on the door, the music was turned down inside. There was no peephole in the door, so whoever was inside would have to open up to see who he was. Smith felt inside his jacket for the butt of the Smith and Wesson that was hanging from his shoulder holster.

After enough time for someone inside to look out front and identify the Jeep, the door opened a few inches, still chained with the inside lock.

"Yeah, man, what you want?" Smith could not yet see the man speaking.

"I'm looking for Bert."

"Who are you, man? A cop?" He knew that he was not; cops do not drive Jeeps.

"I'm here to see Bert for Ms. Wallace."

"She was supposed to come on her own," he said angrily, but making it clear to Smith that "Bert" was on the other side of the door. Smith shoved his shoulder into the door, ripping the chain lock from the rotten wood frame. He was ready to draw his weapon, but "Bert" did not seem to be armed. Smith shut the door behind him to give them privacy.

"Get outta my crib, man. I'm calling the cops."

Smith looked around the room. It was covered with small

appliances, televisions and microwaves. "I'm sure you want the cops in here," said Smith sarcastically. Bert was in his mid-twenties, about six foot tall, and thin. Too thin. Smith figured him for some kind of substance abuse problem—maybe liquor, probably crack.

"OK, Bert, I'm here. Let's talk."

"I said I'm not talking to anyone but that lawyer babe."

"Well I'm the best you're going to get. So take your chance or fuck off."

"I'll tell the cops what I know," said Bert, threatening.

"Tell them what?"

"That I sold that dude the gun, man. He paid cash. Right here, he bought it. I knew he was up to something. When I saw he shot the bitch, I knew what went down."

"What do you want?"

"It ain't easy living here, man. I got a duty to do something. But, maybe if you guys kind of help me out, I can help out some of the people around here and get my conscience clear."

Smith listened to the guy's bull. It was not a surprise. He wanted paid. Once it started, it would never stop. These types never know when to go away.

"So how much do you want?" asked Smith, toying with the guy.

"Not much, man. This dude is rich. I could put him away for life. Maybe a hundred grand. Then I'll go away, man. You'll never hear about me again."

Smith smiled, then pulled his Smith and Wesson, cocking it as he raised it towards "Bert's head. "Who the fuck are you?" asked Smith.

"Fuck you, man."

Smith spun the man around and slammed him face first against the wall before he knew what hit him. Smith patted him down for a weapon. Finding none, he pulled the wallet out of the guy's rear pocket and let him up. He found a District of Columbia driver's license in the wallet with the guy's picture.

"Andre Hayes, huh?"

"Fuck you, man." He had been rousted by cops before. He instinctively adopted his uncooperative attitude.

"Look, Hayes, I'm not fucking around with you. You can still make some money; I just want to know if you're telling the truth."

"Why would I lie?" Smith did not respond with the obvious answer.

"So show me where you keep the guns," commanded Smith.

"Fuck you, man."

"Do you want to make some money or not?"

Hesitantly, Hayes led Smith into the bedroom. It housed the more valuable stuff. Jewelry, guns, and ammunition that Hayes did not want his customers to be able to walk off with. Hayes opened the closet in the bedroom which contained nothing but shelves filled with guns and ammunition. It was a private arsenal.

"Where did you get the Gold Cup?"

"Same place I get everything, man, my boys in the hood. They gotta make a livin'; I gotta make a livin'. It's capitalism, man. It's what made this country great," he said smiling.

Smith asked repeated questions about the transaction. Hayes described Winn to the tee, but who couldn't. He was the most famous man in America. Both the jogging clothes and the car were things Hayes could have picked up off the television. He was unsure; something was wrong with this. If Winn was going to kill his wife, would he come all the way over here personally to buy a hot gun? Wouldn't there be a better way, one that put Winn in less danger?

"OK, Hayes, I'm just a messenger boy," said Smith. "I'll have to take your request back for a decision. You'll hear from me."

"It better be soon, man. I'm calling the cops and spilling everything I know if I'm not taken care of soon."

"Sit tight, Hayes. I'll be in touch." As Smith left, he found the pack of kids out front trying to get inside his Jeep. They ran quickly when he yelled at them. He would go directly to Heitzman & Wallace to tell her what he found.

THEY USED THE REFLECTING POOL between the Lincoln Memorial and the Washington Monument as their meeting place. Both had been in Washington too long to appreciate the beauty as you looked down the Mall to the Capitol Building. The Statute of Freedom had been recently cleaned and, even from this distance, it glittered atop the Capitol dome in summer sun.

Tourists were plentiful, people looking for shade to sit in, wondering how many miles they had walked trying to take in all the sights that seemed to be in such close proximity on the map they bought before coming to town. A few people walked slowly away from the Vietnam Memorial, having located the name of a loved one etched into the scores of dead soldiers' names listed on the dark marble walls.

No regular Washington types ventured this far down the Mall on a hot summer day. A few people took double-takes of Rothstein, wondering if they recognized him from somewhere, but unable to figure it out without seeing him in the coat and tie he usually wore on CNN. None of these people had any idea who Lane was, although they all knew that Senator Ben Winn had been indicted in the Federal Courts Building on Constitution Avenue. This once nameless government building across from the East Wing of the National Art Gallery was now an attraction on the Tourmobile.

"So what new stuff is the government going to show at trial?" asked Rothstein. He had now met with Lane six times. He was weary of this dull, arrogant savior of the world, but he was keeping Rothstein and CNN ahead of the curve on the story. Rothstein had first reported the fingerprints, the Dorothy Wallace motive, and the Baroni story. Rothstein was also the first reporter tipped off to the Winn surrender. The other reporters were now concluding that Rothstein had a deep inside source. It was a business of timely information. If you knew enough, and you knew it before anyone else, you could be a star.

Lane was pleased with the way he had played Rothstein. He trickled out just enough information to keep the story hot and keep Winn against the wall. He might not be known by these tourists, but Lane believed he was the most well-known detective in the city, maybe the country. He was dressing with more pizzazz, ready for his picture to be taken at any time. He was sure the city would convict Winn before any trial. How could you possibly find 12 jurors who had not been affected by this media barrage? Winn was as good as gone.

"You called this meeting, not me," said Lane arrogantly as he wiped the dust from the walkway off of his stylish loafers.

"Cut the bull, Byron. You wanted to be famous. I've made you famous. Now I want something before the trial so that I'm not just one of a hundred other reporters standing around with my hand in my pants holding my dick."

"Do some more shit on the black babe. You seem to get a lot of mileage out of that." Lane grinned. He was amused at the stories about Winn and Wallace. How could a U.S. Senator think he could fool around with some African squeeze and not end up like this?

"You've got to give me something new on them. She killed you guys at the arraignment and is becoming kind of a celebrity herself."

"Fuck that! Give me a break. He fucks her, kills his wife for her, and then has the balls to have her represent him in court. If you can't get another story out of that, you better change professions."

Rothstein had had his fill of this guy, but showing anger would not get him anything he needed.

"Look, I need something cold on the two of them. This Baroni guy plays like the New York Mets. If you guys base your case on him, you may fucking lose."

"Yeah, right," said Lane, never considering that possibility as anything but laughable. "OK, let's say that I had some recordings of them in Winn's house while you guys act like they're up there planning litigation strategy instead of humping like jungle bunnies. If I had it, how the hell could you use it for a story?"

"How the hell could you use it in court?"

"I didn't say we would."

"How did you get a wiretap approved for anything between lawyer and client even if they fuck every night?"

Lane laughed at Rothstein's naivete. He thought of himself as such an experienced veteran. He knew nothing about the way cops operate.

"I didn't say we had an *authorized* wiretap."

"You mean you put in an illegal wiretap?"

"Grow up, man. I thought you were Mr. Sophistication. Nobody says we can't eavesdrop; we just can't use what we find in court." Lane laughed audibly again. "We can only use the stuff we find after we hear where to look." He laughed.

"You never heard of a 1983 civil rights action for violating someone's constitutional rights?" Rothstein was truly appalled. He could imagine a bunch of white cops back at the station listening to Winn and Wallace making love, with the cops trying to outdo each other with racial slurs and cheap sexual quips.

"We're the Federal Government, clown. Those cases don't stick any more." Lane was tired of this. Rothstein would have to take what he had and make a story. "I gotta go. If we get something new, I'll give you a call."

Rothstein said nothing, but watched as Lane strutted away. What a pig, he thought. For a moment, he felt some sympathy for Winn.

Twenty

I t was the first Tuesday in July. Wallace had arrived at Winn's Georgetown home early enough to make coffee. By the end of the week, Randall Hardy would be the Democratic nominee for president. In just four weeks the Republicans would have their convention in Dallas. Winn was the only candidate with a substantial amount of committed delegates, but not enough to ensure the nomination. By the end of the day, Winn would be on trial for murdering his wife. In all likelihood, he would still be involved in that trial when the Republicans met. The worst case was he would be sitting in jail having been convicted for the murder.

The Republicans were scrambling like politicians trying to line up the vote for a pay raise. Most of the power brokers agreed that it was out of the question to nominate Winn if the trial was ongoing. A few diehards dissented from this view, however, continuing to argue that this was a political ploy from the Democrats and could not be allowed to work. The atmosphere was one that did not lend itself to cooperation in trying to find a compromise candidate. They would be heading into Dallas with a disaster on their hands.

There was a standing vigil at Winn's home. The media had backed off some for a while, and only a handful of reporters staked out the Winn residence, agreeing to share information with their colleagues in exchange for the same on their days off. Reports had intensified over the last few days with the impending trial, but they still relied on file footage rather than any new material from Winn or his lawyer. They had not had a public statement from either since this process began. The media did not expect comment any longer. The secret service detail that routinely traveled with a presidential candidate had been dismissed at Winn's request. A few private security guards remained, mostly to keep the media and tourists away.

Winn was driven to the Federal Courts Building by Wallace in her Porsche, where they had arranged for a parking place in the basement. Winn commented that she was particularly relaxed considering what she had ahead of her. Wallace replied that she was a "money player" and it was game day.

In spite of America's overdose of material on the Winn case, the country stood still waiting for the trial. The courtroom was packed to capacity. Wallace had long ago planned her voir dire questions to be used in selecting a potential jury. Their experts had recommended males for the jury, believing they would be less sensitive to the spousal abuse issues that surrounded the case. They disagreed on whether the jury should be white or black. They would normally have said white, but were not sure how any evidence concerning Winn's relationship with a black woman would play with white males. Some of the experts insisted that blacks generally had more experience with interracial relationships. Wallace thought that somehow that conclusion was a nonsequitor.

"All rise," said the U.S. Marshal as he called the Court to order and Judge Wilbur Maynard made his entrance.

"LET ME SUMMARIZE the rules here, although I am sure you are both familiar with them," he said to Wallace and Stephenson. "We will bring in potential jurors in pools of 20. You will each be allowed to examine them as you choose. The Court may have some questions itself. The pool will then be removed and I will move on motions to strike for cause. Each side will then be allowed to strike any members until your pre-emptory challenges are gone. We will continue the process until we have 14 jurors, two of which will be selected as alternates by lot. Are there any questions?" The lawyers indicated that they did not have any. "Please bring in the first pool then," said the Judge as the Marshal opened a side door to the courtroom that revealed a group of 75 potential jurors that had been called for the case.

The clerk handed identical printouts to the lawyers listing the names of the people in the pool, their ages and occupations. The Judge began by delivering a prepared statement about their duties if chosen and asked if anyone felt they could not or should not serve on the jury. One man wanted to be allowed to leave because he was a "life-long Republican" and could never conclude that someone as important to the party as Winn had committed the crime charged. He was excused. The Judge then asked if any of the other jurors had made their mind up about this case. None raised their hands, although they all had preconceived notions. The Judge asked other routine questions, such as whether anyone in the pool was related to anyone involved in the prosecution or the defense, whether anyone had ever had a member of their family murdered or badly beaten, or whether anyone was employed by any law enforcement agency or whether anyone in their family was so employed. Finally, the panel was turned over to Stephenson.

"Are any of you opposed to the death penalty?" The jurors looked at each other to see if anyone was raising a hand. Several of them had misgivings about the taking of a life under any circumstances, including as punishment for a crime, but no one spoke up.

"So if you determined that the defendant committed the crime charged and determined that the law required punishment by the death penalty, is there anyone here who could not vote to have the death penalty imposed?"

No one moved at first, then finally a young black woman timidly raised her hand.

"Yes, Ms. ... Williams," said Stephenson, consulting the scorecard the clerk had given her. "Would you have a problem in voting for the death penalty if the law required it?"

"I guess not if the law required it, but it seems we let a lot of really bad people off for the crimes they commit. It doesn't really seem fair to impose the death penalty on someone who has lived a productive life except for this one crime."

"Thank you, Ms. Williams," said Stephenson, cutting her off. There would be an argument, but the Judge would remove her for cause. Stephenson completed her voir dire with routine questions, nothing that was tailored for any particular strategy in this case.

"Ms. Wallace," said Maynard, turning the proceeding over to her.

"Thank you, your honor. Thank you for coming, ladies and gentlemen." Wallace knew that first impressions were important. Just as she would make hasty decisions about the jurors, they would make hasty decisions about her and her client. She wanted those decisions to be favorable. She talked calmly, with an unassuming tone; she sounded like an understanding person. All of the members of the pool concluded that she looked nice and unabrasive, with her petite figure and simple navy suit. They all had heard about her on television. She did not seem like the home-wrecker she was portrayed to be.

"A brutal crime has been committed here," said Wallace in a

soft tone that had the potential jurors and the spectators on the edges of their seats. "You will see a lot of evidence about the brutality of this crime and the tragedy of Andria Winn's death. Will any of you have difficulty walking away from this trial without knowing who killed Andria Winn?"

"Isn't that why we are here?" said a middle-aged white male who wanted to be recognized by the attractive lawyer.

"No, Mr. Tennenbaum," said Wallace, who had memorized the names of the members of this pool during Stephenson's voir dire. "You are here to decide whether Senator Winn killed her. If you decide that he did not, the fact remains that she was tragically murdered. Your job is done, but the police must still find the killer." Wallace had read numerous articles on this very point. The prosecution will present as much grizzly detail as they can about a death to outrage a jury into believing that somehow they must convict the defendant or the tragedy has gone unavenged. She would work throughout the trial to separate these two issues for the jury. She could see the light go on in their heads.

"How about you, Mrs. Beard, do you see the distinction I am making?" Wallace wanted to recognize as many of them by name as possible so they would realize they were important to her, not just numbers in the judicial maze.

"Yes, I see what you mean," said the juror, surprised but pleased that she was called upon.

"It's a difficult concept," added Wallace. "But you need to remember that your duty here is to the defendant, not the victim. You are to ensure that the defendant gets a fair trial. It is the responsibility of the police, not you, to find the killer." Wallace was surprised that Stephenson had not yet objected. This was opening argument stuff, and would be repeated again during the opening argument. Butler must have drilled her hard on not getting called down by Maynard. She would push until she got Stephenson agitated again; the jury needed to see that side of the prosecutor. She was sure it would not be difficult to get it out.

"Mr. Walker, do you think that Senator Winn should have a white lawyer?"

The 48-year-old computer technician was surprised when called upon. "I guess he can hire whoever he wants; you seem to be doing a pretty good job." The crowd laughed and Walker was pleased with his humor. He began to relax.

"Thank you, Mr. Walker," said Wallace smiling. "I guess what I'm asking is, if you were in trouble would you want a white lawyer?"

"I would want the best lawyer I could afford, even if he was green," said Walker, smiling as he again elicited laughter from the audience.

"Ms. Smith, if you were in trouble would you want your lawyer to be a man?" Wallace asked the 25-year-old black woman who sat on the front row.

Smith knew what her answer should be. She readily confirmed that she too would want the best lawyer regardless of gender.

"Is there anyone here who thinks that Senator Winn made an inappropriate choice in choosing a black woman to be his attorney?" The group collectively shook their heads no. While they might have answered these questions differently before, they were all quite convinced that Winn had made an excellent choice in lawyers.

"Mr. Walker, have you ever dated a black woman?" asked Wallace, returning to the white computer guy.

His wit escaped him as he responded "no" but sincerely wished he could date Dorothy Wallace.

"Are any of you opposed to interracial relationships?"

No one volunteered, but Wallace detected some uneasiness in the body language of a 60-year-old white woman who sat on the panel.

"Mrs. Margione, would you approve of your children dating people of another race?"

"Well, I would not want my children to do it, but I think other people should be allowed to do what they want."

"How many of you have heard some accounts in the media concerning the Senator and myself?" No one responded, and they all looked uneasy now. "Now be honest; it's all right if you've heard such stories. I suspect you will hear more right here in this courtroom." Now a few hands went up, and sensing it was all right, eventually all but one of the potential jurors raised their hands.

"Mr. Hernandez, would you think badly of the Senator or myself if you found out that we had once been romantically involved?"

"Of course not," responded the heavy-set Hispanic man with a deep and certain voice. "I would think the Senator had very good taste." He smiled and again the audience laughed. Slowly, Wallace was disarming everyone.

"How about you, Ms. Ewing?" she asked the middle aged-black woman who drove a city bus.

"I would have no problem with that."

"Of course, your view might be different if you learned that the Senator and I were involved while he was married," said Wallace, knowing that they were all thinking this anyway. "But regardless of what you have heard outside this courtroom, there will be no facts to support the concept that the Senator and I were involved after he got married, because we were not."

"Objection, your honor," said Stephenson rising from her seat. She could not keep the lid on any longer. "Counsel is making an opening statement."

Wallace wanted to approach the bench, but knew that jurors felt you were trying to hide something from them with such a maneuver. She would discuss this in front of them.

"Your honor, the prosecution intends to introduce testimony on this subject; it is therefore imperative that I be allowed to talk with the potential jurors about their views on interracial relationships."

"Objection overruled. I will let you go for now, Ms. Wallace."

"Thank you, your honor," said Wallace to emphasize with the jury that the Judge was siding with her. "Now I know that you have all read about or heard about this case. Mrs. Harper, do you think the American public has made their mind up on this case?"

"It looks pretty bad for the Senator," she said honestly.

"Mrs. Harper, are you able to block out all that you have heard outside this courtroom and make your decision based on the evidence presented?"

"I can do that."

"It's not an easy task," added Wallace. "The media has been full of wild stories, things that are just simply made up and untrue. How will you be able to keep that stuff out of your mind when you are making a decision?"

"We will simply have to do it," said Harper, as if she were now responsible for keeping the jury on the straight and narrow.

Wallace asked more questions concerning the pretrial publicity in the case to create a basis for a Motion she would make with Maynard. She knew he would deny it, but she wanted it on appeal if the case went that far.

Judge Maynard thanked the pool and asked the Marshal to lead them out.

"I presume that no one had a problem with me dismissing for cause the gentleman who was excused," commented Maynard. "Ms. Wallace, do you want any members of this panel struck for cause?"

"Mrs. Margioni, your honor. She will have a preconceived bias against Senator Winn when the prosecution introduces evidence about the Senator's involvement in an interracial relationship."

"I disagree, your honor. She indicated she would not prejudge others for this reason."

"I will dismiss her," said the Judge ruling. "Any others, Ms. Wallace?"

"Not for cause, your honor."

"Ms. Stephenson, does the government want to challenge any members of the pool for cause?"

"No, your honor."

"Does the government want to exercise any of its peremptory challenges to members of this panel?"

"Yes, your honor," she said, while fumbling through her notes and talking with Tanya Ball. "We would like to strike Nos. 2, 6, 7, and 14." She had challenged all of the males under the age of 50.

"Ms. Wallace, do you want to exercise any peremptory challenges?"

"Yes, your honor." She was following advice given in an *ABA Journal* article written by F. Lee Bailey. Don't let the demographics experts influence your decisions; rely on your gut; strike the ones that you "feel" will screw you if they can. "We would like to strike Nos. 4, 8, and 20." Stephenson could not figure out her system. One of the potential jurors was a young black female, another a white professional man about Winn's age; the third was an older white woman.

When done with the first pool, they had 11 of the 14 jurors needed. The process was moving much more smoothly than anyone anticipated. It was four o'clock, so Judge Maynard decided to adjourn until the next morning. With 11 jurors selected, the clerk was instructed to release all of the potential jurors except for the next pool. They would be able to complete the jury with one more group.

THE PROCEEDING THE NEXT DAY looked almost exactly like the first one, as each of the players asked the same questions of the second group. By noon, the jury that would decide Winn's fate had been selected. It included nine women and five men. Eight of the jurors were black; six were white. The youngest man on the jury was 47. The youngest woman was 24. Wallace did not have a clue whether she had made the right decisions, but it was a done deal now.

Maynard gave routine instructions and admonishments to the newly impaneled jurors; the jury would not be sequestered, but was sternly told not to discuss the case with anyone, including among themselves, and not to follow any of the media reports about the case. The lawyers and the Judge all knew that they would do both. Judge Maynard then adjourned the proceeding for the day. They would start the next morning, Thursday, with opening statements.

Twenty-one

I N A RARE EVENT, Stephenson paid particular attention to
what she wore into the courtroom today. She was tired of
reading the comparisons between herself and the stylish, attractive Dorothy Wallace; she always came out on the short end.
One reporter had referred to her as a candidate for the "worst-
dressed women of the year." Another referred to her as
"everyone's old-maid sister." In spite of her contempt for such
chauvinist attitudes, Stephenson intended to look as good as
she could today for the opening day of the most famous prosecution in America. Millions of people would be watching. It
was her big day. Finding nothing in her closet that would do,

Stephenson had actually gone to Nordstrom's and bought a new navy blue suit. She was not going to let Wallace corner the market on style. Fearing accusations that she was trying to look like Wallace, she regretfully passed up the navy blue stockings, but did buy a new pair of navy shoes with one-inch heels. She bought a white shell to go under the suit and wore a simple gold necklace that had a small fake pearl hanging from the end. Stephenson had tried to comb her short, dirty blond hair in several ways and ended up pulling it back on the sides with small pins to hold it in place. Everyone noticed the difference, and while she still looked dumpy in her size 14, she expressed a feminine touch that shocked those who knew her.

The prosecution would speak first. At precisely 9 a.m. Judge Maynard appeared and had the jury brought in. Like all new juries in a violent case, they were eager and excited. This mood would be quickly worn down with the endless expert testimony that few of the jurors understood or cared about. Stephenson was pleased with the group that had been selected. While empirical data did not back up her conclusion, she had the firm belief that she did better with female jurors and there were enough women here to sway the decision.

"Thank you, your honor," said Stephenson in an uncharacteristic graceful and polite tone. She would open her statement with sincerity, finishing with some indignation as the crime was fully exposed. "Thank you, ladies and gentlemen of the jury, for giving the service you are about to embark upon."

Stephenson stood at the prosecutor's table as she began. Then she silently walked to the jury box, looking each juror in the eyes as she continued.

"Ladies and gentlemen, this may be the most difficult thing you ever do in your lives. A man's future, perhaps a man's life, is in your hands. The defense counsel will keep you focused on that issue." Stephenson paused to emphasize what she was about to say. "But let me remind you that a life has already been savagely taken. Andria Hamilton Winn, a young beautiful woman at age 39, was brutally shot and killed. She had no chance to defend herself. She had no chance to hold her killer accountable. That, ladies and gentlemen, is your job, your duty." Stephenson paced silently in front of the jury box, attempting to underscore her point with a moment of silence. She stopped, looking down the jury box into the eyes of each juror, then continued.

"When this trial is done, we will have proved beyond a reasonable doubt that Andria Winn's killer was her husband, Benjamin Winn, the defendant," she said as she turned pointing accusingly at Winn. "Ladies and gentlemen, you will hear the defense tell you what a fine man the defendant is. He is a U.S. Senator; it was thought by many that he would be the next President of the United States. The defense will tell you how he is a national hero." Stephenson would never mention again Winn's credentials and would never refer to him with his official salutation. "But celebrities are subject to the laws of the United States just like you and I. You have an obligation to ensure that just because the defendant is well known, famous, that he is not allowed to escape punishment for his crime — the most brutal crime that can be committed — murder. Whatever else he is, you will determine from the evidence that he is a murderer, the murderer of his wife Andria Winn.

"But, you will also see that the defendant is not the role model that the defense would have you believe. We will show you that he had a long history of abusing his wife. Andria Winn pleaded to her friends that she was in fear for her life—she knew that the defendant could kill her. You will learn that the defendant was involved with another woman, a woman he always compared his wife to, causing severe mental abuse as she always came up short in his eyes. We will show you that the defendant killed his wife so that he could be free to be with this other woman, living in the luxury that his murdered wife's money would buy for him and his girlfriend."

Wallace cringed as she heard Stephenson talk. Everyone in the courtroom, including the members of the jury, knew that the woman being referred to was her. The critics would renew their debate over whether Wallace should withdraw from the case because of her obvious conflict.

"We will prove beyond a reasonable doubt that the harmonious public life portrayed by the defendant and his wife was a mask for an arena of spousal abuse. Your verdict will make a statement that such spousal abuse will no longer be tolerated. Had it been acted on in this case earlier, Andria Winn might still be alive.

"Andria Winn paid a price for this turbulent relationship well before her death. You will learn that her response to her husband's infidelity was to have an affair herself. We are not arguing that Andria Winn was right in seeking comfort from another, a man who loved her like her husband did not. But you will understand and empathize with Andria Winn for retaliating against her husband's own affair and her desire to find companionship with someone who would not abuse her.

"Ladies and gentlemen, you will learn that on the evening of February 7, the defendant, with malice aforethought, took a Colt .45 revolver, a gun that fires a bullet twice as large as standard police issue, and walked into a dark kitchen while his wife was getting something from the refrigerator and shot her in cold blood in the back. In what must have been a gruesome sight as her body went hurling through the air from the force of a .45 caliber weapon and the blood gushing that you will see from photographs of the crime scene, the defendant calmly tried to wipe all fingerprints from the gun, arranged the crime scene in a way that he thought would support his story, then an hour later finally called the police. Calm and composed, belying any grief for his dead wife, the defendant then told his false story to the police, assuming that because he was an important person they would accept his story and his life could go on, without interference from Andria Winn, running for President with another woman at his side." Stephenson paused, again reinforcing her statements with a visual polling of the jury.

"Well, ladies and gentlemen of the jury, we will show the defendant that important people are subject to the law as well.

The defendant is guilty of willfully and wantonly murdering his wife; we will not let him walk away from that act unpunished."

Stephenson paused, still standing in front of the jury. They looked uneasy, beginning to feel the weight of their responsibility. There was a rumble of noise in the courtroom, as reporters passed notes to runners to get her opening remarks on the wire and their comments to the television commentators operating from the studios. The case was being carried live on every network, including CNN, with anchor people and experts commenting like sportscasters. Stephenson took her seat. Judge Maynard slammed his gavel on the bench to restore quiet to the room. The crowd quickly silenced, for all were waiting to hear the response of Winn's lawyer, the beautiful woman who the prosecution said it would prove was his motive for the killing.

"Ms. Wallace?"

"Thank you, your honor," she said as she rose from the table. She patted Winn on the shoulder for all to see, making clear that hers was the role of a lawyer concerned for her client, not for herself. She also wanted to emphasize to the jury that whatever her relationship was with Winn, it was nothing for which she was ashamed.

Dorothy Wallace approached the jury box before speaking. She then smiled demurely to the jurors, saying: "You probably can't wait to hear what I have to say in response to that." The jurors smiled; the audience laughed. Wallace did not want to appear insincere, but she did want to release some of the tension in the room—eliminate some of the suspense. The jurors loosened up, but still sat on the edge of their seats waiting to hear what the young lawyer would say.

Stephenson had presently colored the way the jury looked at her. She was a perfect size attached to a beautiful face. While she wore a more conservatively cut black suit than was her trademark, the curves could not be hidden. Her attractive slender legs were hidden by the skirt that hung to her ankles, and she topped her outfit off with a pair of short-heeled black shoes with a gold buckle. Her hair was hanging freely with loose curls. Was she beautiful enough to kill for? The jurors agreed she was, except for an older white man and middle-aged white woman who could not fathom a white man desiring a permanent relationship with a black woman. Wallace knew that she had to refocus the jury away from the image that Stephenson had artfully created.

"Let's not mince words," said Wallace, changing her smile to a serious look. "You have all heard plenty about this case in the media. The prosecution has indicated it intends to feed on that media frenzy by focusing much of its case on rumor and innuendo. I don't think you will be fooled."

"I have known Ben Winn for almost a decade. I know of no man who is more decent. I care for Ben like you care for those close to you. But let's get it on the table. I did not sleep with Ben Winn during his marriage; the prosecution can talk about it, but they can't show that it happened because it did not. Do they really expect you to think that someone as well known as Senator Winn could have an affair without anyone knowing. Well, let's see if they have any direct evidence. I assure you they will not. You can hold me to that." The crowd burst into noise in disbelief of the corner Wallace was backing herself into; most assumed that Winn and Wallace had been having an affair during his marriage. Judge Maynard banged the gavel to restore order.

"Now I am hesitant to make such a statement, because the prosecution is trying to shift your focus in this case. I am buying into that to an extent. They want to focus you on their speculation as to why Senator Winn might have a motive so they can avoid the fact that they have no evidence that he committed the crime charged. Well, I'm trying to get it out in the open. There was no affair. I'm asking you to forget about it until the prosecution shows you some proof to the contrary. Focus on the weighty issue put in your hands: is there evidence to show that Senator Winn killed his wife? As Ms. Stephenson presents evidence, evaluate it with that standard: does it have anything to do with proving whether Senator Winn killed his wife? When this case is completed, push all the other evidence to the side, except evidence proving that the Senator killed his wife. Look at the pile of evidence remaining. When you do, you will acquit the defendant of the crime charged." Wallace paced; reporters began to scurry, many thinking she was finished with her opening statement. Wallace walked from one end of the jury box to the other. The jurors where impressed with her candor and her belief in her client.

"Ladies and gentlemen, Andria Winn is dead; she has been brutally murdered. No one grieves her death more than her husband. The state will produce as much evidence as it can concerning the death, the blood, the gruesome circumstances surrounding the tragedy. This presentation will hurt no one more than Senator Winn who will have to relive again the horrible death of his wife. The defense does not contest her death; the Senator is the one who found her and reported her death, cooperating with and working with the police to find her killer. We would stipulate to the death, but the prosecution will not allow it. Ms. Stephenson wants you to see the horrible tragedy, hoping that you will feel some need to verify her death in this proceeding. But this trial is not about her death. You are not here to decide who killed her. That is a job for the police, one they have not yet completed. Your only job here is to determine whether Senator Ben Winn is the killer. This trial is not about Andria Winn. It is about her husband.

"In the final analysis, the prosecution will bring forth some circumstantial evidence that makes it no more likely that the Senator killed his wife than that you or I did it. Even much of that evidence will be called into question. But there will be no evidence to show beyond a reasonable doubt that the Senator is guilty as charged. Why? Because he is not, and when this trial is over the Senator will cry for justice, demanding that the police get on the now cold trail that leads to the killer.

"I am putting the Senator's life in your hands; I have confidence that he is in good hands." Wallace paused, standing in front of the jury. They were no longer focused on her; they were looking at the defendant. It was their job to protect him if he was not guilty. "Thank you."

Winn wrote a note on a legal pad at the table saying, "Nice, job counselor," and put in Wallace's view as she sat down. He knew it was an understatement. Stephenson was going to put her on trial as much as Winn. He knew that she was only here because he had insisted. Winn pulled his legal pad back. He would take notes throughout the trial and carry on a dialogue with his lawyer where appropriate. She wanted him to appear to be involved, interested, had warned him against staring off into space during the boring parts of the trial, knowing that the jurors would be sizing him up all the time, particularly when the evidence being presented was dull or uninteresting. She also wanted his input and would go over the case with Winn each evening after the trial.

Stephenson had done this many times before. The government got to go first. She liked that. While the defense had no obligation to present any evidence, Stephenson knew that a defendant who presented little evidence, and particularly one who did not testify, was viewed by the jury as having something to hide. She called her first witness, Byron Lane.

The crowd murmured and moved around as the Marshal in the rear opened the door to a witness room from which Lane appeared. He walked arrogantly up the isle through the gate into the area in front of the bench. He walked around the table on the prosecution's side, smiling at Stephenson, making clear his allegiance. The clerk asked Lane to raise his right hand and swore him in. He took the witness stand.

"Good morning, Mr. Lane. Would you state and spell your full name for the Court, please," said Stephenson.

Lane smiled as he spelled his name. Wallace hoped the jury picked up on his irreverence. A man's life was at stake; the jury would take that seriously—they would be offended by someone who did not, particularly if that individual was the lead investigator for the case, the man in charge with the Assistant

United States attorney of seeking what the jury thought was justice and truth. Lane did not care about justice and truth. He wanted to see Winn convicted of first-degree murder and sentenced to death.

Stephenson used Lane skillfully to paint a gruesome picture of the murder scene. After Wallace put her objection into the record, numerous photographs of the dead body were presented. Lane testified concerning his interview on the evening of the killing with Winn. Over an objection, he gave his opinion as to Winn's demeanor, describing him as "exceedingly calm and acting in a very calculated manner."

"Detective Lane, did you find a weapon at the crime scene?"

"Yes, I did; it was a Gold Cup Colt .45."

"Your honor, if I may have this marked as the Government's Exhibit 24," she said, holding up a clear evidence bag that contained the gun.

"Ms. Wallace?"

"No objection, your honor."

The clerk marked the gun and Stephenson handed it to Lane. "Does this look like the weapon you found?"

"Yes, it sure does. He killed her with that."

"Objection, Your Honor," said Wallace, jumping to her feet quickly.

"Sustained. The jury will disregard the last statement made by the witness. Detective Lane, you pull something like that again and I will hold you in contempt of Court." Maynard was not about to have a conviction in his court overturned because some "smart-ass" cop wanted to take a cheap shot.

"Your honor," said Stephenson, trying to move on quickly to draw attention away from the mistake of her witness. "If we could have this marked as the Government's Exhibit 25," said Stephenson as she handed the lab report on the gun to the clerk with a copy to Wallace.

"No objection, your honor."

"Detective Lane, are you familiar with this report?"

"Yes, it is a report from the crime lab done at my request

concerning the gun, you know, fingerprints, ballistics match, etc." Stephenson would later put on a lab expert to testify concerning how the tests were conducted. Wallace could prevent Lane from testifying concerning the report before such foundation testimony, but she wanted to let Lane be the one to talk about these issues. She thought it a strategic error by Stephenson. Lane was a loose cannon; the more Wallace could cross-examine him about the better. Stephenson walked Lane through the ballistics report to show that the gun was used to fire the bullet found lodged in the floor of the Winn home, and that the bullet was the one that killed Andria. She also used Lane to give his opinion that the gun was fired not more that a few feet from Andria to produce the type of wound she had and for the bullet to go completely through her body.

"Detective Lane, were there any fingerprints found on the gun?"

"No, it had been wiped clean," he answered smiling as he looked at Winn.

"And in your professional experience, what does that mean to you, Detective?"

"It means the killer wanted to wipe off any evidence of his fingerprints on the murder weapon."

"Objection."

"Sustained. The jury will disregard the last statement by the Witness. Detective Lane, you're pushing it."

"Detective, in your opinion why would someone wipe a gun clean like this?"

"To prevent us from finding any fingerprints on it."

"Your honor, if we could have this marked as the Government's Exhibit 26," said Stephenson holding up an evidence bag that contained a small green dish towel."

"Your honor, this is not something that has been previously shown to the defense," interjected Wallace as she came to her feet wondering what Stephenson was up to.

"Your honor, the Government did not have a lab report on this until a few days ago and did not know it was relevant to the case."

"Your honor, this was not on the list provided to us concerning evidence seized at the scene of the crime." Wallace was furious, but tried to keep from showing it. This was the very type Gestapo tactic that she would expect from these thugs, but she could not protest too much or the jury would read too much significance into it. It was unlikely that she could get the evidence suppressed, but more likely that she could only cause a delay in getting it introduced. All that would look bad to the jury, so she backed off. "Your honor, I simply want the record to reflect that the prosecution has not provided us with all of the information that we requested in discovery and that some of that withheld information is now being introduced at trial." Wallace continued to appear calm, to not upset the jury.

"Ms. Stephenson, does the government have any other evidence that has not been disclosed to the defense?" asked Judge Maynard, again angry. If they had a case, they could present it according to the rules. It was this very type of "trick" that resulted in guilty verdicts of guilty defendants being overturned.

Stephenson looked to Ball, who nodded her head that there was nothing. "No, your honor."

"The government is well aware of its duty to disclose to the defense all evidence that will be used in the trial," said Judge Maynard in a stern voice. It was clear to the jury that Stephenson was doing something inappropriate. "Ms. Stephenson, you have clearly violated that duty with this piece of evidence."

Stephenson said nothing. Maynard continued, "Ms. Wallace, would the defense like a recess to review the evidence?"

Wallace knew she was in a no-win situation. "No, your honor. We want to move this case along."

Maynard considered what to do. Judges hate to have to police these overzealous prosecutors to make sure they did not screw up their cases and get convictions reversed on appeal. "In light of the defense not wanting a recess, I am letting you proceed, Ms. Stephenson. Don't let it happen again."

"Thank you, your honor," said Stephenson, unaffected by

the event. She handed the bag to Lane to have him verify that he took it from the island in Winn's kitchen. She then introduced a lab report concerning the dishtowel.

"Detective Lane, what did you determine when you had the dish towel analyzed?"

"We determined that it was used to wipe off the gun, probably what was used to wipe off the fingerprints."

"And were there any fingerprints on the towel?"

The audience was in hushed anticipation. Lane smiled. "Yes."

"And whose fingerprints were on the towel?"

"There were portions of prints from three people on the towel: the Winn's maid; the victim; and the defendant, Ben Winn."

"There were no other identifiable prints on the towel?"

"No, there were not."

"No further questions, your honor."

"Ms. Wallace," said the Judge, turning the witness over to her for cross-examination.

"Mr. Lane ..."

"It's Detective Lane," he said arrogantly, smiling at the petite black woman walking toward him; he was sure he could handle this one.

"Excuse me, Detective. Detective Lane, I suspect you have put a lot of work into investigating Senator Winn."

"Yes, I have," he answered proudly.

"Has that investigation yielded a lot of paper?"

"A file about 18 inches thick," he said smiling.

"Do you have that file with you, Detective?"

"You bet," he said, picking up two large accordion files that he had lying on the floor and setting them on the railing to the witness box.

"All of this relates to the investigation of Senator Winn?"

"All of it," he answered with pride. He had buried him with paper if nothing else.

"Detective, did you run down all the other possible leads in this case?"

"Of course."

"I suspect that with the notoriety of Senator and Mrs. Winn, there were a lot of possibilities?"

"I investigated all of the normal suspects."

"Do you have files on those investigations?"

Lane looked at Stephenson. Maynard overruled her relevance objection.

"Detective, do you have files on all the other investigations that you conducted?"

"Sure."

"Do you have them with you?"

Lane again looked at Stephenson for help; she had none. Reluctantly he reached into a box that he had carried to the stand for a narrow folder that looked as though it could be empty.

"That's it?"

"That's all that I have kept."

"That's all you have for investigating all other possible leads and suspects in this case?"

"There was no reason to carry out a broad investigation after we discovered that the defendant killed her."

Wallace skipped the objection; she would play with this for a minute. "And, when did you know, Detective, that the Senator killed his wife?"

"The night she was murdered."

"And how did you know that the Senator was your man?"

Lane hesitated, then decided to go for it; he would not let some pretty lawyer push him around. He was a cop—a good one.

"I had a hunch," he said boldly.

"You had a hunch?" asked Wallace sarcastically as she looked to the jury.

"Yeah, you wouldn't understand. It's something police detectives understand."

Wallace smiled. "I'm pretty quick, Detective." She turned his arrogance into a sexist or racist statement; both worked certain members of the jury.

"Have you ever seen a defendant convicted on a policeman's hunch?" she asked as a few in the audience snickered.

"A hunch is the first step," said Lane, trying to approach this professionally. "After you get a hunch, you look for evidence to support it."

"So you did not look for evidence concerning who killed Andria Winn. You looked for evidence to support your hunch that her husband killed her."

"It was the same thing," said Lane weakly.

"Detective, did you ever consider any other suspects in this case?"

"No."

"Because you had a hunch it was her husband?"

Lane only answered after being instructed to do so by the Judge.

"So, Detective, since you had a hunch that Senator Winn killed his wife, you began to look for evidence that would support that idea, like whether they had any problems in their marriage, whether they ever argued ..."

"Objection, your honor," said Stephenson rising. "This is a speech, not a question."

"Overruled.'

"Detective, let me ask the question again. Is it correct that you immediately concluded from your 'hunch' that Senator Winn killed his wife, so your investigation was an effort to find evidence supporting that conclusion?"

"I knew he did it, so I got proof," said Lane, getting red in the face and showing his anger.

"You knew he did it because of your hunch?" Lane did not answer. Wallace went on.

"Did you interview the Winn's maid?"

"No, she was not there when the murder occurred."

"But weren't her fingerprints on the dishtowel you took from the kitchen?"

"Yeah, but she was the maid. It would be normal for her fingerprints to be on the towel."

"And you thought it would be normal for Mrs. Winn's fingerprints to be on the towel as well?"

"Yes."

"Because she lived there."

"Yes."

"Wouldn't it also be normal for Senator Winn's fingerprints to be on the towel since he lived there?"

"Somebody used the towel to wipe the fingerprints off the gun." Lane was coming off very defensively now.

"And you had a hunch that was the Senator, so you did not consider any significance to the maid's fingerprints being on the towel."

"No, I did not."

"Does the maid have a key to the Winn's residence?"

"I don't know."

"Did Mrs. Winn have a disagreement with her maid on the day she was murdered?"

"I don't know. I saw nothing that would lead me to believe that." Lane and Stephenson were beginning to wonder if there was something here they did not know about. The media was waiting for a Perry Mason presentation of the maid as the killer. Winn felt sorry for Julia, who he knew would be watching every second of the trial with her family.

"Detective, were there any other fingerprints on the towel?" Wallace had already looked at the report during direct examination.

"Not that could be identified."

"But there were other fingerprints on the towel."

"There were smudges and fragments that were too poor for the lab to make any conclusions about; they could have been fingerprints of the three people identified."

"But, they could have been fingerprints of somebody else, couldn't they?"

"It's not likely.'

"And how did you determine that, your hunch?" Lane did not answer; Wallace moved on from her rhetorical question.

"Isn't it possible that the fingerprints that you could not identify were left by a fourth person?"

"It's possible," he answered softly.

"I did not hear that," said the court reporter.

"Please repeat your answer," said the Judge.

"It's possible."

"So it's possible that there were fingerprints on the towel of someone you were not able to identify?"

"Yes."

"Detective, are your racially prejudiced?"

"Objection, your honor." A burst of noise erupted in the courtroom as Wallace went into this new direction. The black members of the jury perked up.

"Your honor, it is the prosecution that is putting evidence into this case concerning the Senator's alleged involvement with a black woman. I believe that evidence is a result of the witness' so-called investigation."

"Overruled. Ms. Wallace, I will let you go down this road, but be careful."

"Thank you, your honor. Detective, would you like me to repeat the question?"

"Of course I'm not a racist. The department is full of black policemen."

Wallace walked back to counsel's table and picked up a folder. She opened it and read from something as everyone waited.

"Detective, did you head up the investigation into the death of Ruppert Parker?"

"Yes, I did."

"And you testified as the government's lead witness into the investigation of that crime?"

"Yes."

"And you concluded that Mr. Ruppert was murdered by former mayor of the District of Columbia Washington Barkley?"

"The jury agreed."

Wallace resisted the temptation to get into that case; undoubtedly Lane was pursuing a hunch there, too.

"Detective, during that investigation, did you say: 'We should let all the niggers kill each other.'" There was pandemonium in the courtroom; each of the black jurors looked at Lane with scorn. They all knew cops like this guy. Maynard slammed the gavel repeatedly on the bench to restore order. Stephenson looked to be in shock. Her co-counsel, Tanya Ball, looked at Lane with contempt.

Lane considered his options. He had said it all right, but it was in the station with only other cops around. All of them were white cops. He could deny it; surely no cop would testify to impeach him, even if they hated him because of jealousy. Maybe, though, someone had taped his little tirade. Wallace would push the Judge to bind him over for perjury if she could prove he lied.

With some order restored, Wallace repeated the question.

"I may have said something like that," said Lane. "But you have taken it out of context."

"Can you give me your context, Detective, where you appropriately refer to black people as 'niggers?' " Lane did not respond.

"Your honor, I have no more use for this witness," said Wallace with contempt. Winn looked at his lawyer as she walked back to the table. In only a few minutes, she had turned half the jury and 80% of Washington, D.C. against the District police department. All this with a white defendant as a client. She had shown that while other suspects may have existed, the police department did not even look. Rather than try to find a killer, they tried to prove that the suspect at hand was the killer. All based on Lane's hunch. Lane would be humiliated in the media overnight. He would be ready to prove his case with more of a vengeance than ever.

THE "KITCHEN CABINET," as they referred to themselves, sat around the patio of Winn's house. It was easier for the rest to get around than for Winn, so their meetings were all here. The group consisted of Winn, Wallace, Savage, Bill Stevens, and Pete Smith. Winn and Wallace were drinking a glass of Chateau St. Jean Chardonnay. The rest were drinking Miller. The perimeter of the house continued to be staked out by private security people. The whole case was costing Winn a fortune, with security, lawyers, experts, investigators, and who knows who else. They often remarked that a poor person could not fight the government. Even though the poor get court-appointed attorneys, attorneys are only the quarterbacks. Wallace liked to say if you had $100 to spend on a lawyer, you got a $100 defense.

"You did good today, counselor," said Savage. After Stephenson's direct about the dishtowel, he was about to conclude that Winn had indeed killed his wife. "I have hated that prick Lane since the first time I met him."

"Yeah, and he has hated us since that time, too," added Wallace.

"It sounds like you beat the little bigot up pretty good," said Pete Smith, who had been given a rundown of the first day of trial. He had been returning from Phoenix; he was going back to Phoenix tomorrow.

"How's the nomination going?" asked Wallace in a feeble attempt to change the subject.

"If you get an acquittal in the next four weeks, we got it in the bag. Ben is the only guy with a significant number of committed delegates, but if this is pending, it would be a miracle to finish it off. The national committee is trying to trump up some play to put up a non-controversial compromise candidate and say that Ben can reclaim his place in four years when this has been disposed of. Then, of course, Randall Hardy wins and we get at least four more years of Democrats. And if you lose, we will probably not get the nomination on the first ballot." Wallace was the only one to smile at his humor over Winn being convicted. She turned to Smith.

"We need a killer and we are running out of time."

"Be patient, counselor. All good things come to those who wait, or some bullshit like that," said Smith, smiling.

"You seem pretty smug, Pete, what's up?" asked Winn.

"I'm playing out a lead. It could be nothing."

"After today, you still think we need a killer to win, Dot?" asked Winn.

"The jury thinks Lane is a son of a bitch, but that may not keep them from also thinking that you're a murderer. At the end of day one, it's a 50-50 shot. It's more like blackjack than roulette; we've got a chance. But so do they. And, I don't see it getting much better. If they're lucky, it can only get worse for us."

"You're quite the motivational type, Dot," said Winn sarcastically. No one else spoke until finally Savage changed the subject for some small talk, then decided he should leave and get back to the campaign office. Stevens and Smith followed. None of them spoke about it, but they knew that Winn and Wallace were sleeping together. They were pleased that Winn could find some pleasure in all this.

Twenty-two

The letter from Phoenix had reeked of credibility. Smith only had to figure out how to get some lead out of it. The envelope was, as expected, covered with prints from all the handling that occurred after its author had mailed it. The letter, however, contained fingerprints of only one person, but those prints were not contained in the FBI archives.

Gloria Speavy had seen a car, a driver waiting for Smith's primary suspect. If these were out-of-town boys, then perhaps it was a rental car. Smith managed to get the records of all the major rental companies at National and Dulles for people coming to D.C. from Phoenix between the Friday before the murder and the day of the murder who did not return their cars until after the murder. There were 14 people fitting the description. Smith sent four investigators to Phoenix to compile profiles on the suspects. Most were businessmen, traveling in Washington, D.C. on behalf of their companies. Two were families that had come to the nation's capital for vacation. One stood out. His name was Victor Keeting, aka Vince Keating, aka Joe McFarlane, a petty criminal who had been in and out of the Arizona penal system most of his life.

Smith had gone to Phoenix personally and tracked Keeting down; he was a part-time bartender at a yuppie bar, Camel Beach, on Camelback Road. It was not difficult work. Smith dropped enough money at the bar, indicating that he was looking for someone to carry out a job for him. He did not say what the job was, but indicated that someone needed to be quieted down. Keeting was a punk, never suspicious of Smith, eager to make a buck. He told Smith that he and a friend had a lot of experience at the kind of thing Smith was talking about. He said, "We're kind of like spies; we have even done work for the White House."

Smith arranged for Keeting to bring his friend and meet him at the Phoenician where he was staying. At 6 p.m. they knocked on the door.

"Mr. Smith, this is Johnny Do," said Keeting with a smile. Both were punks trying to pass as upper middle class rich kids. They wore Ralph Lauren pants and expensive loafers. Keeting had on a black button-up shirt and an off-white sports coat. "Johnny Do," aka John Albert, wore a patterned knit golf shirt.

"Come on in, boys. Anybody want a beer?" Both accepted. Smith took an envelope stuffed with $100 bills from a brief case and tossed it on the coffee table. When it landed, the crisp green C-notes feathered out of the envelope enough to make their mouths water.

"So I've got to know that you guys can get a job like this done. If anything goes wrong and this comes back on me, I could be ruined," said Smith, who had told them almost nothing about who he was or what he needed to have done.

"Don't worry about nothing, Mr. Smith. Whatever you've got, we've done bigger jobs," said Keeting proudly.

It took about three more beers apiece with the money remaining in plan view before they gave Smith enough information. He indicated that he needed a former partner shut up; he was causing IRS problems for Smith. Smith didn't care how they did it, but he wanted them to "get rid" of the guy. They eagerly agreed. Keeting indicated they had recently done a secret job for a very important guy in the government; they had "gotten rid" of somebody for him, too. They could be trusted to get the job done and keep quiet about it.

Keeting and Do were sitting comfortably in Smith's spacious luxury room when he pulled a Smith and Wesson automatic out from under the cushions on the couch.

"What's the deal, man? Are you some kind of cop or something? Is this a set-up?"

The door to the adjoining room opened, and three of Smith's men entered with guns drawn. They jerked the punks from their seats and threw them against the wall and frisked them. They had the session with Smith on videotape from two cameras hidden in the room. The cameras were still rolling.

After the frisking, Smith's subordinates held Do, as Smith took Keeting and shoved him against the wall.

"We got important connections, man. I want a lawyer. You guys are really fucking up," screamed Keeting.

"Who hired you to kill Andria Winn?" asked Smith.

"Who the fuck are you?"

Smith slammed his big fist into the stomach of the punk. He doubled over gasping for air; he felt like he was all mushed up inside.

"What the fuck do you want?" he asked, trying to regain his balance.

"Who hired you to kill Andria Winn?"

"Fuck you. I want a lawyer."

Smith hit him in the stomach again. This time, Keeting felt a trickle of blood run out of his mouth.

"There are no lawyers here, boy. You're going to tell me what I want to know, or we are going to do this until your guts and ribs are just one big bloody mess." It did not take much more. Keeting had a low threshold for pain and like most sociopaths was only thinking about pain at the present, not the pain he could experience for years to come. Keeting admitted they had been hired by a man named Robert who worked for somebody important in the government. He said he did not know Robert's last name or who he worked for. After a while, Smith believed him. He did know how to get in touch with Robert. He had a phone number. The phone number was written on a folded yellow note pad. It was a local Phoenix listing.

Keeting and Johnny Do were walked out a side entrance to the Phoenician at gun point and taken to a warehouse on the west side of Phoenix, where they would be held until needed again, or until it was time to turn them over. The phone number was unlisted. Smith called a friend in Washington who called back within minutes and gave him the information he wanted. The phone belonged to Robert L. Sparks. Sparks was a graduate of the Arizona State School of Law. He worked as the Administrative Assistant to Arizona Congressman Randall Hardy.

Twenty-three

"The United States calls Mr. Anthony Baroni." Stephenson turned to watch the Marshal open the door to the witness room and instructed Baroni to enter.

Baroni took the witness stand in an expensive gray double-breasted suit and a Nicole Miller tie with a design consisting of an assortment of license plates. Winn wondered if it was some subtle joke. His hair was slicked back. He was handsome, but did not look wholly trustworthy. He looked like a lobbyist.

Stephenson quickly got through the formalities with the witness. She tried to make him look as respectable as possible, making clear he was the partner in a successful law firm and naming some of the impressive corporate clients the firm represented.

"Mr. Baroni, did you know Andria Winn?"

"We were in love," he responded, feigning sorrow over the mention of her name. Wallace considered objecting to Baroni's assessment concerning Andria's feelings, but decided to let it pass.

"How long did you know Andria?" asked Stephenson, referring to the victim as if she was a long-time friend of the people's lawyers.

"We met about six months ago; it was love at first sight for us both."

"How often did you see Andria?"

"As often as possible. We both had very busy schedules. I would say three or four times a week."

Winn wrote a note to Wallace, saying: "How could this go on without me knowing." It was a statement more than a question.

"Did Andria have occasion to describe to you her relationship with her husband?" It came in under an exception to the hearsay rule as statements from a deceased victim. The rule only allows lies in under certain exceptions where the speaker cannot be cross-examined.

"She was afraid of her husband; he beat her and he subjected her to constant mental abuse." Reporters feverishly took notes, while courtroom artists sketched pictures of the boyfriend.

"Did you ever see any evidence that she had been beaten?"

"Oh, yeah," said Baroni sounding a little rehearsed. He and Stephenson had gone over his statements carefully. "He would never hit her where it could be seen in public. The bruises were usually on her stomach, arms, and thighs."

"What kind of mental abuse did her husband subject her to?"

"Objection."

"Sustained."

"What kind of mental abuse did Andria complain of?"

"He was always comparing her to his girlfriend, and Andria would always be told she came up short. He said he needed her for her money, but that she was like all white women in bed."

"And what did she think he meant by that?"

"He didn't like white women. He worshipped his black girl-friend and always let Andria know it."

"Who did Andria say the girlfriend was, Mr. Baroni?"

"Dorothy Wallace," he said, smiling as he looked at the gor-geous black woman at the table with Winn. He had seen her picture, but he was impressed that she looked even better in person.

"Did Andria ever express fear for her safety?"

"Yes, often. She was afraid he would kill her so he could keep her money and live with Ms. Wallace. She was sure he wanted her out of the way."

"When did you last see Andria?"

"The day she died. She spent the afternoon with me."

"Mr. Baroni, had Andria reached any decisions about her relationship with her husband on that day?"

"Yes, she was going to divorce him. We were going to get married."

Wallace looked at the faces of the jurors. They did not like him much, but they believed him. They could see Andria go-ing home to tell her husband that it was over, that she was ready to divorce him and take Daddy's money with her.

"No further questions, your honor."

Wallace stood as the Judge called her name.

"Good morning, Mr. Baroni."

"Good morning, Ms. Wallace," he said smiling.

"Have you been paid to tell the story you just testified to?"

Baroni looked at Stephenson. She objected, stressing that the government had paid Baroni nothing.

"Your honor, I did not limit my question to the government."

"Overruled. Answer the question, Mr. Baroni."

"Yes, but I have only told them the truth."

"Isn't it true, Mr. Baroni, that you were interviewed on the television show *Current Affair* about your relationship with Andria Winn and what she had told you about her husband, and her intention to divorce her husband and marry you."

"Yes, I agreed to talk to them."

"And how much did they pay you for 'agreeing to talk to them?' "

"$100,000, but I told them the truth."

"Did you appear on the syndicated television show *First Edition?*"

"Yes."

"And how much did they pay you for telling your story?"

"$60,000."

"Did you appear on the syndicated television show *Crime?*"

"Yes."

"How much did they pay you?"

"$45,000."

"Did you agree to an interview with the *National Enquirer* to talk about the Winns?"

"Yes."

"How much did they pay you?"

"$75,000."

"Did you agree to an interview with *Star Magazine?*"

"Yes."

"How much did they pay you?"

"$30,000."

Wallace went through a list of six more publications that had paid Baroni for his story. The jury was not pleased. Stephenson wanted to crawl under her chair. Why had Lane come up with such scum to support her case? Thank God they had Sally MacArthur to corroborate his testimony.

"Mr. Baroni, if your story had been that the Senator was very much in love with his wife, that he treated her with a good deal of respect and affection, that he never touched her in anger, and that he was faithful to her and did not know she was sneaking around to cheat on him—if this had been your story, do you think all of these news people would have paid you for your story?"

"Objection, your honor. The witness does not have any expertise to give this opinion."

"This is cross-examination, Ms. Stephenson. Overruled. Answer the question, Mr. Baroni."

"Would you like me to repeat the question?" asked Wallace.

"No. I don't know if they would have paid for the story or not."

Wallace paused, looking at the jury to show her disgust for the witness. She let him sit there and stew for a few minutes, as she walked to the defense table to kill time making the witness "freeze," then she returned to the witness box.

"Mr. Baroni, were you in love with Andria Winn?"

"Of course, I was," he said defiantly. His palms were beginning to sweat and he was wanting this to be over.

"Were you faithful to this woman you loved?"

Baroni paused suspiciously, then said he was.

"Mr. Baroni, do you know Ms. Laura Snyder?"

"Yes, I believe I do."

"During the last six months have you had a sexual relationship with Ms. Snyder?"

"No."

Wallace walked back to her desk and picked up a folder. She opened it as she returned to the witness box.

"Mr. Baroni, did you stay at the Mirage Hotel last January during which time you and Ms. Snyder stayed in the same room for four days?" Wallace had records where they had both charged items to the room.

"Yes," said Baroni hanging his head.

"Mr. Baroni, do you know Ms. Karen Walker?"

"Yes."

"During that last six months have you had a sexual relationship with Ms. Walker?"

"No." Wallace produced proof of trips to Aruba and San Francisco with Ms. Walker. She established travel with four other women during the last six months. She was prepared during her case to present five of the six women, each of whom would testify that they had a sexual relationship with Baroni. Three of the woman admitted that Baroni bragged about his sexual conquest of Winn's wife.

"Mr. Baroni, where were you on the evening Andria Winn was killed?"

"I was home."

"Doing what?"

"I was watching television about the time Andria was killed."

"Were you alone?"

"Yes," he responded, even though he had been with another woman, knowing that Andria would not be back for the night.

"So you have no alibi for the evening?"

Before he could answer, Wallace turned her back on him in disgust to return to her seat. "No further questions, your honor."

Twenty-four

S HE WENT HOME EVERY EVENING. The time she spent alone with Winn could be considered time spent on case preparation. The media vigil remained, but now only contained one television crew that alternated among the pool that agreed to share film if anything interesting developed. Little was reported about the time she spent with Winn now; there was concern by the general counsels of the media that they could open themselves up for a big lawsuit if they did anything that could be seen as infringing on Winn's sixth amendment right to counsel. Nevertheless, she and Winn concluded that the best judgment was for her to go home at some point each evening, even if it was late.

Wallace spent much of her time preparing for the case, reading material and preparing questions for her cross-examination of Stephenson's witnesses. Winn enjoyed watching her work and was usually involved in discussion of some strategy concerning how to approach a witness or an issue.

"Do you think Baroni was telling the truth about his affair with Andria?" She could see he was hurt; maybe he was not in love with her the way he should have been, but he did love her. He had blamed himself for the lack of romance in their relationship. Was he a fool all along?

"He lied about everything else."

"I'll take that as a yes," said Winn, knowing she would not give an evasive answer unless she wanted to spare him the answer she had.

"He's so fucking transparent. How could she fall for that?"

"Hey, he seems to do much better with women than he does with juries. I'm sure he charmed her with his best lobbying skills. From what he said to some of the other girls, he was quite proud to be involved with a Senator's wife, a future First Lady."

"What a piece of shit. Andria deserved better."

"You don't have to feel sorry for her. She could have destroyed your career by fucking around with this asshole. Let's keep her behavior in perspective."

"Are we doing any better than 50-50 after today?"

"Ben, it's rigged. The government wins 90% of the prosecutions it brings because it's the government. We all distrust the government. But yet, when you put us in a jury box and have the government's lawyers tell us a story, we believe. Juries understand why defendants lie. There is so much at stake that they never know whether to believe a defendant. Even if a defendant is guilty, the jury knows he'll lie and say he isn't. How many guilty people have you ever heard about in a prison?

"But juries cannot imagine why the government's people lie; they see them as impartial enforcers of the law who have nothing personal at stake in whether a defendant is guilty or not guilty. They do not come to the courtroom understanding that prosecutors, cops, and even judges are involved in some big ego game where every move is motivated by its effect on one's career and stature."

"So we're still 50-50?"

"Maybe 51-49?" she said with a smile, while closing a book and laying down her purple felt tip pen. "Now let's have sex so I can feel compensated for my day's labors."

THE GOVERNMENT'S CASE was moving quickly for such a publicized event. Stephenson had a simple plan. She went with Lane and Baroni first so that the jury knew what was important. Then she spent three days with experts and other witnesses, referring the jury back to the gory pictures of the murder and the murder weapon as often as possible. She would finish strong putting Sally MacArthur on the stand.

MacArthur walked into the courtroom, feeling fat, but looking almost sickly with her 97 pounds on a frame that was 5'6". She took the stand scared, yet exhilarated over getting to play a role in the drama she had been watching on television for a week.

"Ms. Stephenson, did you know Andria Winn?"

"Yes."

"And what was the nature of your relationship with her?"

"We were best friends."

"She confided in you about all aspects of her life?"

"Of course."

"Were you aware that she was involved with Mr. Anthony Baroni?"

"Yes, she was in love with Tony."

"Did she confide in Mr. Baroni as well?"

"Objection, your honor, calls for speculation."

"Sustained."

"What did Andria tell you about her relationship with Mr. Baroni?"

"She said she was in love with him; she could not talk to her husband, but Tony was always there to listen to her." MacArthur was visibly nervous. It was not uncommon for a witness, but it was the first such witness this jury had seen. Her voice trembled; her body was almost shaking as she squirmed back and forth in the witness chair.

"Mrs. MacArthur, how did Andria characterize her relationship with her husband?"

"It was not good."

"Take your time, Sally," said Stephenson to reassure her witness and try to calm her down. "Can you be more specific about what she said that led you to believe she had a bad relationship with her husband?"

"She was the classic case of a battered wife. Constantly subject to verbal and mental abuse; frequently subject to physical abuse—always living in fear of physical abuse. No one cared. No one but me and Tony. She was the wife of a very important man, a celebrity. No one would interfere—no one would believe her." Stephenson stepped back, letting MacArthur continue her role. She was in a zone, calming down. Repeating her own fantasies of spousal abuse, transferring her own frustration that no one believed her. Wallace sat patiently, letting the witness have the reins.

"Sally, did you ever see evidence of physical abuse on Andria?"

"Of course. He would hit her in places that did not bruise easily, and almost never hit her in the face or somewhere that the public could easily see."

"Did Andria ever tell you she was in fear for her physical safety with her husband?"

"Yes," eagerly responded MacArthur, followed by a story she made up about Andria calling in the middle of the night only a few weeks before her death. She was screaming, "He's going to kill me; he's going to kill me." MacArthur claimed she went to the Winn home and virtually pulled Andria from the raging Winn's hands. She told how Winn was yelling that she couldn't "fuck" worth a damn; he said he had to go to "his chocolate honey" for real sex.

"Why didn't Andria ever call the police?"

"She knew that they would not do anything because her husband was a U.S. Senator. She was afraid he would then beat her worse to punish her for calling the police." MacArthur and Stephenson had rehearsed this answer several times.

"No further questions, your honor," said Stephenson proudly. It was a case of circumstantial evidence, but in Stephenson's mind the women on the jury had to be convinced. They had to see that Winn was just another man who thought he could do anything to women and never be punished. She was going to stop that. Winn would be a lesson to them all; he would get the gas chamber.

"Good morning, Mrs. MacArthur." She nodded, but did not respond to Wallace. She was out of her zone, nervous again. No one had challenged her story yet. She had only been in the coddling hands of Stephenson and Lane who coaxed her and rewarded her for embellishing her story.

"Mrs. MacArthur, did you do an exclusive interview with *First Edition* concerning your relationship with Andria Winn?"

Her voice broke from nervousness, and no words came out the first time she tried to answer. Finally, a feeble "yes" came out.

"How much were you paid to tell this story?"

"I don't recall," she lied. Everyone in the courtroom knew what she had been paid.

Wallace picked up a contract between the television show and MacArthur from the defense table and approached the witness box. "Perhaps this will refresh you memory. Can you tell the jury what this is?"

"It's a contract with *First Edition*." Her head was hanging low; she was sick at her stomach.

"A contract between *First Edition* and you?" asked Wallace, leading the government's witness.

"Yes," she hesitantly admitted.

"Did you sign this agreement?"

"Yes."

"How much does this contract say *First Edition* will pay you for your story?" MacArthur did not answer. "Perhaps if you look at Paragraph 3 it will help you." MacArthur nervously shuffled through the pages.

"$500,000."

"They agreed to pay you half a million dollars to tell this story?"

"Yes."

"And, were you paid the half million dollars after doing the interview with *First Edition?*"

"Yes."

"In paragraph 21 of this contract, do you agree that you will not talk to any other representatives of the media until after any trial is completed?"

"Yes."

"And is it fair to say that you were paid such a large amount because you were giving them an exclusive story and exclusive access to you?" MacArthur did not answer. Wallace continued. "Mrs. MacArthur, if your story had been that the Senator was very much in love with his wife, that he treated her with a good deal of respect and affection, that he never touched her in anger, and that he was faithful to her and did not know she was sneaking around to cheat on him—if this had been your story, do you think *First Edition* would have paid you half a million dollars for your story?"

"I doubt it." Stephenson wished she had not answered the question. It was out of her mouth before she could think to stop.

"I doubt it, too, Mrs. MacArthur," said Wallace, pausing as she walked back to the defense table to let this first line of attack sink in. Jurors hated witnesses who benefited from telling a certain story. It was a historical problem with paid informants and witnesses who had cut deals to save their own hides from government prosecution. The advent of tabloid journalism had made the problem much more profound. For a juror looking to believe in a defendant, he or she could easily discount testimony that appeared designed to get the witness a huge financial profit.

"Mrs. MacArthur, why did you and Mr. MacArthur get a divorce?" Stephenson unsuccessfully objected to this line of testimony. The jury was beginning to sense that the government did not want them to know all of the facts about Sally MacArthur.

"I was a victim of spousal abuse."

"In fact, isn't it true that you reported to the police on several occasions stories similar to the ones you attributed to Andria Winn?"

"So?"

"Answer the question, please, Mrs. MacArthur?" pressed Wallace.

"Yes, my husband was a lot like Ben Winn."

"You reported to the police that your husband beat you?"

"Yes."

"Mrs. MacArthur do you recall the fight you had with your husband on September 23, two years ago."

MacArthur paused, then admitted that she could not recall that date specifically. Wallace handed her a copy of a police report filed after a 911 call.

"Yes, I remember, he beat me bad that night."

"Mrs. MacArthur would you read the second paragraph of the police report to the jury?"

Again, Stephenson jumped up strenuously objecting. She had not seen these reports, but knew this was not going to be good. Judge Maynard overruled the objection with a disapproving scorn for her continuous interruption of cross-examination. If Winn was convicted, this harassment would be another basis for appeal. She knew that in a murder trial he was going to give the defendant a lot of latitude in cross-examining the state's witnesses. If the state had a good case, then their witnesses should hold up.

"But the cops were men; they stick together; they would

never believe me," said MacArthur, now crying. Stephenson smiled. Damn right, she thought.

"Mrs. MacArthur, who signed this report as the officer making the report?" MacArthur fumbled to the last page of the three-page report. She was shocked, not wanting to answer. Judge Maynard instructed the witness to answer the questions asked.

"Who is the officer making this report, Mrs. MacArthur?"

"Sarah Williams," she whispered, only having to repeat the name when the judge asked her to speak louder.

"A woman?"

"I guess," said MacArthur, then adding in a stronger voice, "but she worked with a bunch of men."

"Mrs. MacArthur, will you please read the second paragraph of the report to the jury?" MacArthur was crying, crumbling on the stand. Wallace received permission from the Court to read the relevant paragraph from a copy of the report that she was holding.

"Mr. MacArthur was bleeding visibly from cuts on his hands, arms and one cut on the side of his face. He reported that Mrs. MacArthur had assaulted him with a knife. The wounds he had were consistent with a knife attack. There were no signs of physical abuse to Mrs. MacArthur, even though she had placed the 911 call and reported that her husband was trying to kill her. Mr. MacArthur denied treatment and said he did not want Mrs. MacArthur arrested. He indicated that she had a problem with substance abuse and was under a psychiatrist's care. He urged the police to leave so that he could take her to the Georgetown Psychiatric Hospital for treatment."

Wallace looked to the jury. The government had a decent theory, but their witnesses had big credibility problems. The jurors were beginning to feel the pressure. They had expected a slam dunk; why would the government indict someone, particularly someone this well known, unless they had him cold. The jurors wondered if there was something they did not know. Maybe the defense had successfully suppressed strong evidence of guilt.

"Mrs. MacArthur, have you ever been treated for substance abuse?"

"After so much mental abuse, I used it as a crutch."

"Have you ever been treated for substance abuse?"

"Yes."

"Have you ever been diagnosed as a chronic substance abuser?"

She answered only after Wallace turned to retrieve something from the defense table. Undoubtedly, proof of the diagnosis.

"Yes."

"Have you ever been diagnosed as having any other form of mental disease or illness?"

"Yes, I am anorexic."

"Is that the only additional diagnosis?"

"No, but that is the real problem."

Wallace then proceeded to document seven periods of hospitalization, ranging from a period of one week in a local private hospital to two months in the Mayo Clinic where MacArthur received psychiatric treatment. She also established that MacArthur was currently under out-patient care. MacArthur was broken, crying repeatedly on the stand, attempting to blame her illness on others. Wallace had no sympathy. MacArthur had put herself in this position; she had to pay the price. Her client's life was placed in jeopardy because of this pathetic woman's lies.

"I have no further use for this witness," said Wallace, dismissing the witness with the same disdain she had shown for Lane and Baroni.

Twenty-five

"**S**o where is your damn case?" Jake Butler screamed across his desk at Stephenson and Ball. "Air tight, huh? Your witnesses are shit. None of your reports had any of this crap. Did you know that these witnesses were crazies?"

Stephenson was in no mood for this abuse. Her day had been bad enough. That little "bitch" was a sell-out to the woman's cause. She was one of the "pretty" ones; they lived by different rules, always getting what they wanted because of how they looked. She was in no mood to be browbeat by Butler, even if he was technically her boss.

"Do you realize I've got the White House calling me. They

---

want to know what we have up our sleeve that we've not played yet. Stephenson, what the fuck are you going to do?" Butler knew his career was on the line. If they lost this case, he could kiss his future in politics good-bye. They had taken on one of the most popular political figures in the country, in the recent history of the country. A national hero. It did not matter if the Democrats somehow stayed in control, he would be axed in an effort to keep the blame from rising any higher. He had kept the Justice Department informed; they had talked to the White House. Everyone knew what his office was doing. But if it went south, he would be hung out, just another prosecutor out of control. They would take quick action and claim they could not have helped it; a prosecutor must have the independence to investigate where he believes a crime has been committed without political interference. They had to wait until it was over; now they could take action to ensure no such travesty ever happened again.

"My ass is on the line. Don't think just because you're a bureaucrat that you won't get to pay the price, too." Butler knew she would not, however. It was easier to assassinate the President of Russia than to fire a civil servant from the U.S. government.

"We'll win the case." said Stephenson, red in the face, tired of the abuse.

"And how do you figure that? Do you have a rabbit up your sleeve?"

"We'll win the case. There are nine women on that jury; they can see through this bullshit. They know Winn is scum and they will make him pay."

Butler pounded his desk twice, then threw a paperweight against the wall, causing one of his photographs with the President to fall in a loud crash with glass breaking. "Get the fuck out of here." She was absolutely crazy. How did he ever let this wacko have the Winn case? Why had he let it proceed so quickly? Butler continued to exchange calls with members of the Justice Department and the White House Office of Legal Counsel.

The political ramifications from a loss here were profound. He needed to do something. No one discussed, nor considered whether Winn was guilty or not. It was not a relevant concern. Careers were on the line.

"DOROTHY, IT'S BERT WALKER on line 4," announced Staci over the intercom. Stephenson had finished her case on Thursday, two weeks into the trial. The court recessed until Monday morning. Winn and Wallace were spending this Friday, as they would do Saturday and Sunday, in the office working.

"OK, Staci. I'll take it." Turning to Winn who was working on a redraft of his testimony, she added. "This should be interesting. I clerked with Bert at the Court; he's in the Office of Legal Policy at the Justice Department."

"Bert, what's up?" she asked. You would think it was just another day for Wallace, not a few days before the life of her lover would be put in the hands of a jury.

"Dorothy, you're making big headlines again. I knew you could not stay out of the limelight," said Walker, stating the obvious. He rambled, hesitant to get to the point.

"This case isn't good for anybody, Dorothy. Not your client, not us, not the country."

"Somebody should have thought of that before now, Bert." She hated these guys. They were so shallow, consumed with the public perception of themselves and their bosses. They stood for nothing.

"This is totally unofficial, Dorothy." He was nervous. He had been the one designated to make the contact because of his relationship with Wallace, but it had to be done with plausible deniability at the Department and the White House. He was cautioned that she might be taping him. "But I was just thinking—call this just my personal unofficial idea; I was thinking that if your client wanted to plead to something lesser like second degree or maybe even voluntary manslaughter, that the government might make that deal just to get this over with. You know, stop the bleeding on this thing. It's terrible for the country."

She smiled, too amused to be angry. No one was concerned about what the country was put through for the last six months. No one was concerned until it looked like their "asses" were in jeopardy.

"Did it ever occur to any of you guys, Bert, that Ben Winn is innocent and the killer is running around out there somewhere?"

"What do you mean?" asked Walker, not understanding how such a fact affected their offer. "You know that he will probably get convicted; juries know that the government doesn't bring cases against innocent people. Maybe Stephenson hasn't done the greatest job in getting her witnesses prepared, but your client is still looking at the gas chamber. I'm trying to do you a favor." He wanted to beg her to take the deal, but if he appeared to be on the run, she would never deal.

"Bert, you can take your unofficial off-the-record offer back to your people and tell them I said to get fucked."

"Dorothy, don't get personal, I'm just trying to help."

"You guys are like wet rats trying to jump ship. And you all stink. My client is innocent. You may be used to getting pleas out of innocent people." She knew they were. Defendants who could not continue to afford their defense, or were too scared of the possible consequences of not dealing with the government. "But you'll get no plea from Ben Winn. You guys make me sick."

"You have an obligation to present this offer to your client," said Walker, grasping for a way to pull this off.

"I thought this was unofficial, just your idea. Anyway, you let me worry about my ethical obligations. Take your offer and stick it up your lily-white ass." She slammed the phone down, letting her contempt reek out.

"Lily white ass," repeated Winn with a smile.

"You white people are all just a bunch of assholes."

"Thank you very much. Now could I please take your black ass home, pour you a glass of cold Chardonnay, and take advantage of you?"

She smiled, then began to fill up the two briefcases that she would take with her. They were feeling good about the case. She knew Winn would make a good witness. Few things beat a charismatic witness on the stand. The impact would be even greater in comparison to the key witnesses that the prosecutor had presented. They had no real defense, however. They were down to arguing that the government had not proved its case. It might be enough, but both she and Winn knew that juries had seen too much Perry Mason. They wanted the case resolved. They did not like to reach a verdict that left some unidentified cold-blooded killer walking the streets, their streets.

She raced the black Porsche out of the underground garage where camera crews were passing the time since there was nothing at the courthouse to cover today. They sped up Connecticut Avenue before the lazy crews could get into action. It was a hot, humid July afternoon. Washington, D.C. was one of the most beautiful cities in the world, but in July and August it was almost uninhabitable. Before air conditioning, anybody who was anybody left D.C. during these months for the cooler climate of Martha's Vineyard or elsewhere. The remnants of that tradition continued, with Congress and the Supreme Court both taking long summer recesses, only to return in September and October.

They did not talk as they went up Pennsylvania Avenue towards Georgetown. Winn was wondering if this could be the last weekend he would be able to drive down this street and see the city that he loved. He remembered coming to Washington almost two decades ago. He was young and ambitious. He acclimated to the world of politics quickly, often forgetting principle and acting out of political convenience in the decisions he made. He wondered how he would do it if he was given a second chance. There were so many things wrong with the system; maybe it was foolish to even think about trying to fix them. If he did not get the chance, he considered what he could do to influence others to hold onto their principles when they came to this enchanting, tempting city where the rewards of power were obvious and alluring. Maybe there would be time to write a book. He knew that people seemed to stay on death row forever.

TURNING WITHOUT REGARD to the positions they had staked out for months, the media trashed the prosecution throughout the weekend. The mainstream news shows were filled with lawyers criticizing the government's presentation of the case. Stephenson was ridiculed for being unprepared to rehabilitate her witnesses and for not having more credible witnesses available. Wallace was assessed as bright and skilled, with experienced defense lawyers marveling that she was doing this job without any prior criminal experience. All speculated she was being coached behind the scenes by more well-known defense lawyers, but they agreed she was doing a brilliant job all the same. Some argued that Winn would get acquitted on this evidence; others argued it depended on whether he took the stand and how he testified. Still others, particularly former prosecutors who were interviewed, believed that Winn would be convicted in spite of the credibility problems of the government's witnesses. They pointed out that in most cases the government's witnesses had similar problems, referring to drug cases where witnesses who were part of the crime were given deals to testify against their associates and cases where the primary evidence came from paid informants with long rap sheets. It was an ugly system that the American people were not used to looking at so closely. The prosecution would get a conviction in spite of the flaws in their case. There was little discussion about the actual guilt or innocence of Winn. No one discussed the issue of whether a killer was running free, knowing that the government had no intentions of trying to find him.

The trial almost obliterated coverage of the Democratic National convention in Seattle. CSPAN covered most of the convention live, but television time that historically was devoted to the convention was given to live coverage of the Winn trial and the never-ending analysis of every aspect of the trial. On Thursday evening during the second week of the trial, Randall Hardy had given an enthusiastic acceptance speech. Few people seemed to care, although most political commentators agreed that he would be the next President of the United States.

Twenty-six

ON MONDAY MORNING the courtroom was packed as it had been each day of the trial. There was a suspense building. No one expected the defense to put on much of a case. Wallace had called into question the credibility of the government's key witnesses on cross-examination, including the young arrogant cop. Some character witnesses were expected; it was anticipated that she would try to dazzle the jury with testimony from well-known celebrities concerning what a fine man Winn was. She would probably produce several witnesses concerning the relationship between the Winns, witnesses who would, of course, describe a relationship of marital bliss. An expert concerning the dishtowel and the wiping of the gun was considered to be a possibility. The core of the defense, however, was expected to be Winn's testimony. It was anticipated that Winn would take the stand and deny the crime. It was predicted that the jury could start deliberations before the end of the week or, at the latest, early next week.

"Ms. Wallace, is the defense ready to proceed?"

"We are, your honor," said Wallace as she stood up. She was dressed in the most stylish suit she had worn since the trial began. The suit was red, and cut to show her figure. She wore natural-colored stockings and black pumps. Her hair was tied back as it had been almost every day of the trial. She was lovely. One journalist had already joked that "scarlet" seemed to be an appropriate color.

"Your honor, the defense calls Robert L. Sparks to the stand."

"Objection, your honor," said Stephenson, jumping to her feet and knocking a file off the table as she rose. Papers scattered across the floor. Stephenson was visibly upset. "We did not get the name of this witness until Saturday night, your honor. We have not had time to prepare." Stephenson had figured out who Sparks was; Lane had done the research. He was the Administrative Assistant to the Congressman from Arizona, now the Democratic nominee for President. They had no idea why he was being called. There was no indication that he had ever worked for or with Winn, so he did not appear to be a character witness. Stephenson sensed she was being sandbagged.

"Ms. Wallace?" asked the Judge, waiting for her explanation.

"Your honor, we did not find out about this witness until Thursday of last week. As soon as we realized that he had information relevant to this case, we notified the prosecution."

"Your honor, this is obviously some grandstanding attempt by the defense. They have pushed for a speedy trial; they had ample time before the trial commenced to locate their witnesses and provide us with their names. The United States objects to any testimony from this or other secret witnesses now or at any time in this trial." Stephenson was nervous. She was not in control, a nightmare for a lawyer.

"Your honor, regardless of the prosecutor's view, the scales of justice engraved above the bench in this courtroom stand for something. They stand for the principle that this is a forum where the truth is sought. This is not about winning and carving another niche on some lawyer's six-gun. This is about the guilt or innocence of a man charged with a first-degree murder, a man who could face the death penalty. If the Court will indulge me, I am sure it will see how this witness has vital information concerning that search for the truth." Wallace was speaking formidably; no one watching expected her to be denied.

Judge Maynard took his half-eyes off, contemplating the issues, as he chewed on one end of the glasses. "Ms. Wallace, I will let you proceed. The objection is overruled."

"Thank you, your honor. The defense calls Robert L. Sparks to the stand."

All eyes were riveted on the door to the witness room as the mystery witness appeared. Stephenson's antics had captured everyone's attention. A man in his mid-thirties emerged through the door. In spite of his youth, he was balding. He looked ordinary in height and weight, dressed in a conservative blue business suit, with a white shirt and dark blue tie.

At the request of the Judge, Sparks faced the clerk of the court and took this oath. He then sat down in the witness chair. He was composed, but obviously stressed.

"Good morning, Mr. Sparks."

"Good morning."

"Would you please state and spell your full name for the record?"

"Robert L. Sparks, that's S-P-A-R-K-S."

"Mr. Sparks, what is your occupation?"

"I am the deputy campaign manager for Congressman Randall Hardy." The courtroom erupted. Maynard banged his gavel to attempt to restore order. A semblance of silence was returned after the Judge threatened to have the courtroom cleared. No one wanted to miss this.

"Mr. Sparks, how did you get this job?"

"I served as the Administrative Assistant to Congressman Hardy for eight years here in Washington, D.C. Last November, the Congressman asked me to leave my government duties to work on his presidential campaign."

"Mr. Sparks, do you know a man by the name of Victor Keeting?"

Sparks looked around the courtroom nervously, then gave the answer that Wallace was expecting. "I would like to exercise my rights under the Fifth Amendment to the Constitution and not answer that question on the ground that it may incriminate me."

"Objection," shouted Stephenson. "Your honor, I don't know what Ms. Wallace is up to, but she cannot put a witness on the stand who then refuses to testify."

"Ms. Wallace?"

"Your honor, we certainly have the right to subpoena any witness that has information relevant to the innocence of Senator Winn. If that witness refuses to testify on Fifth Amendment grounds, there is little I can do about it."

"Your honor, this is ridiculous. Ms. Wallace is trying to imply that this witness has some deep dark secret concerning the outcome of this case."

"Mr. Sparks," said the Judge turning to the witness, "have you consulted counsel on the action you have just taken?"

"Yes, your honor."

"And you have been advised that the penalties could be severe for improperly exercising your Fifth Amendment rights in response to a question asked in this courtroom?"

"Yes, sir. I cannot answer any questions concerning Mr. Keeting or the death of Mrs. Winn without being forced to incriminate myself."

There was a flurry of activity in the courtroom. Reporters scrambled to get this story out. Someone in Hardy's campaign seemed to be involved. Was Hardy involved? It was a twist too remarkable, for an already too remarkable case.

"Ms. Wallace, Ms. Stephenson, I would like to see you in my chambers. Would the Marshal please take Mr. Sparks into Witness Room No. 3. Court will be recessed. The Marshal will give you ten minutes' notice before the Court continues." Judge Maynard rose from the bench and left the courtroom. The lawyers followed.

RANDALL HARDY WAS TOLD BY AN AIDE that events were breaking in the Winn case that he would be interested in. They were doing a post-convention victory tour that had them in the Ritz Carlton in San Francisco. Hardy watched from his hotel room as Henry Rothstein filed his report.

"In a case that has already been more bizarre than fiction could ever be, an even more bizarre turn seems to be underway. Never before has a major political figure been charged with a capital crime. Now as the opening witness for the defense, they have called a high-level campaign official from Senator Winn's political rival, Randall Hardy." Rothstein continued to give his on-the-scene update from the front steps of the Federal Courts Building before the anchor in the CNN studios in Atlanta took over. He and his various experts, all hooked up live by satellite, had been ready to commentate on the trial.

The television screen was divided into four pictures with Rothstein in one slot and the anchor in the another. The other two windows contained individuals identified as lawyers, one a defense lawyer, the other a former federal prosecutor.

"Mr. Simms," said the anchor, addressing the former prosecutor, "what are we to make of this?" They had continued this play-by-play coverage of the Winn story for months now; they had been involved in marathon coverage since the trial began.

"It's too early to make anything of it. Ms. Stephenson does not seem to think that the witness has anything relevant to say. If it is a grandstanding play by the defense, the Judge will ferret it out."

"Mr. Ireland," said the anchor, shifting to the defense lawyer who was expected to give the contrary view. It would not be entertaining if everyone agreed.

"I strongly disagree. Ms. Wallace would not put this witness on the stand unless he has something to say concerning the death of Andria Winn."

"She has no experience," said Simms interrupting, "it may simply be a desperate attempt to manipulate the process."

"Ms. Wallace has shown that she is anything but inexperienced," responded Ireland.

"Henry, is there any speculation that Hardy may be involved somehow?" the anchor asked.

"It is being discussed around here, but it hardly seems likely that a man with so much to lose would be involved in something like this."

"Of course, the same thing could be said about Winn," replied the anchor.

"If I could," interrupted Ireland, "I'd like to point out that Congressman Hardy had everything to gain here. It was a foregone conclusion that he would be little more than token opposition for Senator Winn in the Presidential election. With Winn's demise, Hardy is now the likely next President of the United States."

"That is an insulting insinuation," replied Simms angrily. "No one could expect someone to risk so much just to win an election."

Hardy picked up the ashtray off the coffee table and threw it across the room into the television set, which exploded in sparks and smoke.

COURT DID NOT RETURN TO SESSION for the afternoon. The media frenzy was working at a high pitch. No one could get a worthwhile leak about what was going on. As far as anyone knew the Judge, the lawyers, the defendant, and the jury were all still in the courthouse. Ten hours later, at 7 p.m., the crowd was informed that the Court would reconvene in ten minutes.

Butler sat with Tanya Ball at the prosecution's table. He

looked worn out, slumping in the chair. Wallace sat with her client, expressionless. Maynard entered the courtroom.

"If the Marshall will return Mr. Sparks to the stand, Ms. Wallace can continue."

"Mr. Sparks, do you know Victor Keeting?"

"Yes."

"In what capacity do you know him?"

"After being instructed to do so, I hired Keeting to kill Senator Winn." It took five minutes to restore order to the courtroom. Only then did the audience quiet because it still was not sure how this fit in the case.

"What did you pay Mr. Keeting to do this job?"

"He was paid $25,000 when he accepted the job, another $25,000 when he left for Washington to do the job, and he was to get $50,000 when the job was completed."

"Where did you get these funds?"

"I keep an account for contributors who want to be anonymous."

"Contributors to the Hardy Presidential campaign?"

"Yes."

"Can you describe for us your last conversation with Mr. Keeting?"

"He wanted to be paid the $50,000 even though he had not killed the Senator. He had killed the Senator's wife by mistake." A hoard of reporters raced from the courtroom to get the story out; they left subordinates to get the remainder of the story. It took 15 minutes to restore order.

"Are you saying that Mr. Keeting came to Washington to kill Senator Winn, and on the evening of February 7 he shot and killed Andria Winn by mistake."

"Yes. He thought it was the Senator; she was wearing a man's bathrobe and had short hair. He called reporting that he had killed the Senator. Only when news reports came out the next morning did I learn otherwise."

"Mr. Sparks, who instructed you to have Senator Winn killed?"

There was a hushed anticipation. Everyone in the room on

was the edge of their seats.

"Congressman Randall Hardy."

"And do you have any evidence concerning those instructions?"

"Yes."

"What evidence is that?"

"I have a tape recording of a conversation with the Congressman made from my portable dictation unit."

Wallace returned to the defense table to pick up a cassette tape.

"Are you familiar with this, Mr. Sparks?"

"Yes. It is the tape I gave you this morning."

"Why did you make this tape, Mr. Sparks?"

"I was afraid. I knew that if I did not do what the Congressman wanted, someone else would. But I was afraid he would deny it, maybe even claim that I did it on my own."

"So you made this tape to protect yourself?" asked Wallace. It was difficult not to beat up on this witness. She thought he was scum, like moss that clings to a rock, trying to get somewhere by the weight of somebody else. Somebody who wanted to brag that they were important, because they worked for important people. It would not, however, serve her ends to chastise the witness.

"Your honor, if I may ask the bailiff to help me, I'd like to play this tape for the Court."

Maynard had already heard it, but it needed to go into the record. No one had noticed the large cassette tape player that had been brought into the room by the bailiff while the court was reconvening.

Winn watched in appreciative amazement as Wallace worked. The courtroom was completely silent as the bailiff pushed the play button on the recorder. The voices were distorted, but identifiable. One was the voice of the witness. The other, the unmistakable voice that millions of Americans could now identify as Randall Hardy.

"You said you could do it, so do it," said Hardy.

"Are you serious?" asked Sparks.

"I should be President. I have worked my whole life to earn the job. Now some punk GQ pretty boy comes out of nowhere and thinks he can run right over me. I have a right to do this. People are killed every day for the sake of their country. That is what is at stake here, the fate of this country. I want him dead. Do you hear me? I want him dead. I don't care what it costs. Use the money in the private fund. I want the son-of-a-bitch dead!"

After a Motion from Wallace, the bailiff stopped the tape. The audience was stunned. Even the reporters were slow to move.

"Are you testifying here after reaching a written agreement with the government?"

"Yes."

"Do you expect to be prosecuted for your involvement in the death of Andria Winn?"

"Yes."

"Your honor, based on the testimony of Mr. Sparks, and the evidence that he has turned over to the Court, I move that the Court direct a verdict in favor of the defendant, Senator Benjamin Winn."

"Mr. Butler?"

"We concur in the Motion, your honor."

"Very well, the Motion is granted. Senator, this Court extends its apology to you and its sympathy over the grief you have experienced over the death of your wife. You are free to go."

Twenty-seven

Sparks had been easy enough for Smith to locate. He decided not to play around. He confronted Sparks at his Phoenix apartment, and when Sparks refused to let him in, Smith began playing his interview with Keeting on a hand-held tape recorder. Sparks quickly ushered him inside, afraid that someone would overhear.

Sparks denied any knowledge of who Keeting was. Smith explained that his only way out was to make a deal. He was neither the trigger man nor the man who ordered to have the triggered pulled. He was a middle man; the crime could have occurred without him. The government would let him plead to something lesser, maybe aiding and abetting a felony, and Sparks had some chance of being back on the street before he was an old man. Sparks could give them Keeting and Hardy. Two murder one convictions would be plenty. Johnny Do would fit in somewhere, too; probably as an accessory to murder. He might deal his way out as well.

Smith did not use the rough tactics he had shown to Keeting. This was a worried young man, an educated man. He had made one terrible mistake at the instruction of one of the most respected and powerful men in the country. He would want to clear his slate of this.

Sparks produced a tape for Smith to listen to. It was an egotistical and angry Randall Hardy. Once before he had said something about having Winn killed, and Sparks boasted that he was sure he could arrange it. On the tape Hardy said he wanted it done. "Kill the son-of-a-bitch. He has no right to be President. I have worked my whole life to earn this job. It's mine. I want the son-of-a-bitch dead. You said you could do it, now do it." Hardy said to use the cash in the campaign slush fund, and make sure that he did not let the hired killers know who he was. Never mention Hardy's name — never, under any circumstances.

After the screw-up, Sparks agreed to pay Keeting another $25,000, not the full $50,000 that would have been due for killing Winn. Sparks tried to talk to Hardy about it, but he ignored the subject. He relegated Sparks into a position in the campaign where he would not have to work with him. Sparks said that Hardy "thought he owned me now." He did not think there was any trail to himself, but knew that if there was one it went right through Sparks. Sparks made the tape because he was afraid that he might get hung out by Hardy.

With the strong urging of Judge Maynard, Jake Butler had agreed to the plea that would subject Sparks to a maximum sentence of seven years; he could get out after serving half of that. Stephenson was outraged. She was fired on the spot and removed from the Judge's chambers by the Marshal. She would file suit against the Federal government for discrimination, but would end up leaving Washington, unable to get a job.

AMID A FLURRY OF QUESTIONS from the media, Hardy was whisked off to the San Francisco airport where he boarded a private jet with instructions to fly him to Phoenix. The court was in recess; Sparks had taken the Fifth Amendment. Even if Sparks cracked, he could deny it. It was his word against Sparks. He would take on damage from this, but he would be OK.

The perimeter of his estate in Phoenix was crawling with the media. It looked like pictures he had seen of the mob around Winn's home in Georgetown. The FBI had the place discreetly under surveillance. They were ready to make a move if events turned that way. They were surprised to see Hardy return here. Some thought that a sign that he was not involved.

Hardy sat alone in his den drinking bourbon when Henry Rothstein reported that a deal had been struck. Winn had been released. Sparks had agreed to testify against his boss, saying that the Democratic nominee for President, Randall Hardy, gave the order that resulted in the murder of Andria Winn. Sparks had a taped conversation.

"A tape," said Hardy to himself, leaning forward to hear more.

A transcript of the tape which had been submitted into the record of the Winn case was read on the air by Rothstein. It was expected that a warrant would soon be issued for his arrest for the murder of Andria Winn.

HARDY NEEDED TO HAVE HIS SIDE of the story heard. He went to the gates of his estate and told the reporters that he had a statement to give. They were hungry to hear what he had to say.

In his most dignified voice Hardy said, "I was supposed to be the next President of the United States. I have earned it. I have worked hard to get to where I am today." His voice was growing louder and angrier. His hands were beginning to tremble.

Hardy continued, "I will not be taken down by those who

are lesser Americans than I. Do you understand what it is that I am saying? I, Randall Hardy, am the next President of the United States. That office is mine and Winn does not deserve it. I had to have him killed. Don't you see?"

The reporters were getting nervous because Hardy was coming unglued. He was asking them to justify his actions.

"Are you admitting that you wanted Ben Winn killed?"

"I am telling you that it was the right thing to do. He will put the country in jeopardy. He won't be able to do the job properly. Look at what he has done. Nothing! I have done everything."

At that moment, Hardy pulled a .38 special from the waistband of his pants and aimed it at the reporters. Several dropped to the ground, but their cameras were still rolling.

"I did what I did for my country. I am a true patriot and would die for my country." With those final words, Congressman Randall Hardy put the gun to his head and pulled the trigger, his lifeless body falling to the ground in front of a live TV audience.

KEETING AND JOHNNY DO WERE TURNED OVER to the FBI in Phoenix by Smith's guys. They would complain loudly about the treatment they had received from Smith. No one cared. He was not the government. He was not bound by the Constitution. Both Keeting and Do were arrested for first-degree murder. Since their crime had been committed in the District of Columbia, extradition was not an issue. The FBI put them on a plane. They were booked on the second floor of the Federal Courts Building before the next morning. Do explained that he had only driven the car and did not know Keeting intended to kill anyone. Keeting had, however, confessed the whole thing to him and he could testify against his former comrade. Do explained that Keeting bought a gun off the street in Phoenix and smuggled it to D.C. in the luggage he checked. He was careful to use gloves from the time he bought the gun so that no fingerprints would be on it. Keeting bragged that the best thing to do with a murder weapon was just drop it at the scene;

it was untraceable. If you carried it off, it only increased the chance that you would get caught holding it or that someone would see you throw it away. Do explained that Keeting talked like he had done this before; he had not. They had gone to the Winn's home in the afternoon on February 7; the maid would not let them in, but while Do distracted her, Keeting managed to tape the lock on the door and the alarm magnet so that they could get back into the house. Keeting had said he was waiting for his victim when "he" came into the kitchen. He thought it was Winn; he shot her, threw down the gun and left, taking the tape off the door. They did not find out until the next day about the screw-up, that it was the wife Keeting shot.

Do said Keeting "got a real kick" out of the idea that they were going to "fry" Winn for the murder. Smith had found some residue left from the tape; the police had not looked. Smith would figure out that Andria was shot during the brief time that Winn was in the shower. Between the shower noise and the sounds you get used to blocking out in the city, he had not heard the gunfire.

A young homicide detective and Assistant U.S. Attorney took Do into a room for questioning. They were ecstatic. They knew that a case like this could make their careers. Everyone involved would be famous. The persons responsible for putting Hardy in jail could write their own tickets.

Twenty-eight

"Never doubted you for a minute, chief," said Savage grinning as he led Winn through the crowded corridor. "Well, at least not more than a couple of minutes."

"Thanks for the support," said Winn. "They almost had me convinced a time or two. But, they never rattled my lawyer," said Winn, smiling and sticking out his hand for his lawyer to give him five. One AP reporter got a good shot of the ritual, which would appear in newspapers throughout the country alongside a photo of the dead Randall Hardy.

THE PRIVATE SECURITY GUARDS and U.S. Marshals helped the Winn entourage get into one of the elevators. After a loud encounter with a reporter from the *Washington Post,* the elevator was cleared of all other people.

"LET'S GO TO THE LOBBY," said Winn. He was going to take them on now and get it over with. As the elevator doors opened to the ground floor, cameras began to flash and more reporters began to scream questions at Winn and Wallace. Winn looked to the platform that had been constructed for the announcement of his indictment. The government had continued to use it in its formal exchanges with the media about the case. Winn took Wallace's hand and walked up on the platform.

Winn held his hands up for silence. He looked like the same politician that Savage had seen in New Hampshire six months before.

"I'll make a brief statement if you guys will shut up," said Winn, smiling. The crowd began to silence itself; reporters who had been upstairs rushed out of the remaining elevators and toward Winn.

"Well, let me begin by thanking all of you for not losing faith in me," said Winn sarcastically, but smiling. The media people laughed, just as they always did in their give-and-take sessions with Winn.

"A bit more seriously, I'd like to thank the best lawyer in the world," said Winn, turning to Wallace. He put his arms around her and pulled her closely, gently kissing her for all of the cameras to see.

"Millions of Americans have anguished over this; they have shared their strength with me through cards and letters. I can never repay them for their trust and support. I am sincerely touched by their steadfastness."

"When are you going to Dallas?" yelled one of the WDCA reporters.

"People, I have had enough of this. I want to settle down and raise some kids," he said, turning to exchange smiles with

Wallace.

"Are you saying that you are withdrawing from the presidential race?"

Winn looked at Savage, then Wallace. He wanted so much more out of life than politics had given him. He wanted to give back to Wallace, who had laid her life on the line for him not once, but twice.

Wallace stepped up to the microphone. "And the White House would be a hell of a place to raise kids." She turned so that only Winn could hear her, saying, "You can have two loves, you know."

Winn turned to Savage, who nodded that he was ready for more. Winn looked at Dorothy, then turned to the reporters. "Well, let's see if the American people are ready to have a black woman as First Lady in the White House."